Puller's Runner

A Work of Historical Fiction about Lieutenant General Lewis B. "Chesty" Puller

Nick Ragland
Joe Rouse

Hamilton Books
A member of
The Rowman & Littlefield Publishing Group
Lanham • Boulder • New York • Toronto • Plymouth, UK

Hamilton Books
4501 Forbes Boulevard
Suite 200
Lanham, Maryland 20706
Hamilton Books Acquisitions Department (301) 459-3366

Estover Road
Plymouth PL6 7PY
United Kingdom

Library of Congress Control Number: 2009925328
ISBN: 978-0-7618-4606-2 (clothbound : alk. paper)
ISBN: 978-0-7618-4607-9 (paperback : alk. paper)
eISBN: 978-0-7618-4608-6

Cover photo: Chesty Puller on the right and his "Runner" on the left.
Official U.S. Marine Corps photo courtesy of U.S. Marine Corps.

To Marty and Nicole

Contents

List of Maps   vii

Acknowledgments   ix

Organization of the 1st Marine Division   xii

Introduction   xiii

Prologue, The New York Times   xv

1   Training   1

2   Guadalcanal   11

3   New Britain   51

4   Peleliu   71

5   The Korean War   93

6   Inchon and Seoul   104

7   Chosin Reservoir   122

8   After Korea   159

9   Ribbon Creek   166

Epilogue, The Death of a Marine Legend   175

About the Authors   177

Maps

The Pacific World War II xiv

Guadalcanal, September 1942 12

Battle for Henderson Field, October 24 – 25, 1942 32

New Britain 52

Cape Gloucester, Dec. 1943 – Feb. 1944 55

Peleliu, September 1944 70

Korea, 1950 95

Inchon, Yongdungpo, & Seoul, September 1950 103

Korea, Oct. 15 – Oct. 25, 1950 121

North Korea, Oct. – Dec. 1950 124

Koto-ri Permimeter, December 1950 132

Acknowledgments

This is a work of historical fiction about the Marine Corps' most famous Marine: Lieutenant General Lewis B. "Chesty" Puller. This story is told by a fictional character, Michael Abbo. John "Pop" Hayes is also a fictional character. All other named Marines are real historical figures.

The authors have utilized many sources in writing this book. The two primary sources are *Marine! The Life of Lt. Gen Lewis B. (Chesty) Puller, USMC (Ret.)*, by Burke Davis, and the masterfully written biography *Chesty*, by LtCol Jon T. Hoffman. We have also pulled much information from the following publications:

BOOKS

Alexander, Col Joseph H., USMC (Ret.). *The Battle History of the U.S. Marines: A Fellowship of Valor*. New York: HarperPerennial, 1997.

Brady, James. *The Marines of Autumn*. New York: St. Martin's Press Griffin, 2000.

Camp, Dick. *Leatherneck Legends: Conversations with the Marine Corps' Old Breed*. Osceola, WI: Zenith Press, 2006.

Cerasini, Marc. *Heroes: U.S. Marine Corps Medal of Honor Winners*. New York: Berkley Books, 2002.

Collier, Peter. *Medal of Honor: Portraits of Valor Beyond the Call of Duty*. New York:Artisan, 2003.

Davis, Burke. *Marine! The Life of Lt. Gen Lewis B. (Chesty) Puller USMC (Ret.)*. Boston: Little,Brown, 1962.

Davis, Gen Raymond G. *The Story of Ray Davis*. Fuquay Varnia, NC: Research Triangle Publishing, 1995.

Davis, Russell and Brent K. Ashabranner. *Marine at War.* New York: Scholastic Book Services, 1961.

Fehrenbach, T.R. *This Kind of War: The Classic Korean War History.* Washington, D.C.: Brassey's, 2000.

Griffith, Samuel B., II. *The Battle for Guadalcanal.* Champaign, IL: University of Illinois Press, 1963.

Halberstam, David. *The Coldest Winter: America and the Korean War.* New York: Hyperion, 2007.

Hallas, James H. *The Devil's Anvil: The Assault on Peleliu.* Westport, CT: Praeger, 1994.

Hammel, Eric M. *Chosin: Heroic Ordeal of the Korean War.* Novato, CA: Presidio Press, 1981.

———. *Guadalcanal: Starvation Island.* New York: Crown, 1987.

Hoffman, Lt Col Jon T. *Chesty: The Story of Lieutenant General Lewis B. Puller, USMC.* New York: Random House, 2001.

Hopkins, William B. *One Bugle, No Drums: The Marine at Chosin Reservoir.* New York: Avon, 1986.

Hunt, George P. *Coral Comes High.* New York: Signet Publishing, 1946.

Lawliss, Chuck. *The Marine Book: A Portrait of America's Military Elite.* New York: Thames and Hudson, 1988.

Leckie, Robert H. *Helmet For My Pillow.* New York: Random House, 1957.

Manchester, William. *Goodbye Darkness.* Boston: Little, Brown, 1979.

McMillian, George. *The Old Breed: A History of The First Marine Division In World War II.* Nashville: The Battery Press, 1949.

Miller, Donald L. *D-Days In The Pacific.* New York: Simon & Schuster, 2001.

Moskin, J. Robert. *The U.S. Marine Corps Story.* Boston: Little, Brown, 1992.

Nelson, Craig. *The First Heroes.* New York: Viking, 2002.

Owen, Joseph R. *Colder Than Hell: A Marine Rifle Company at Chosin Reservoir.* Annapolis: Naval Institute, 1996.

Ross, Bill D. *Peleliu: Tragic Triumph.* New York: Random House, 1991.

Russ, Martin. *Breakout: The Chosin Reservoir Campaign, Korea 1950.* New York: Fromm International, 1999.

Sledge, E.B. *With The Old Breed: At Peleliu and Okinawa.* New York: Oxford University Press, 1981.

Sloan, Bill. *Brotherhood of Heroes.* New York: Simon & Schuster, 2005.

Smith, S.E. *The United States Marine Corps in World War II.* New York: Random House, 1969.

Stevens, John C., III. *Court-Martial at Parris Island.* Annapolis: Naval Institute, 1999.

Twining, Gen Merrill B, USMC (Ret.). *No Bended Knee: The Battle For Guadalcanal.* Novato, CA: Presidio Press, 1996.

Uris, Leon. *Battle Cry.* New York: Putnam, 1953.

Warren, James A. *American Spartans-The U.S. Marines: A Combat History From Iwo Jima to Iraq.* New York: Free Press, 2005.

PERIODICALS

"Gen. Chesty Puller Dies: Most Decorated Marine." *The New York Times* 12 Oct 1971: 46.

Cannon, Jimmy. "The Best Marine of Them All." *The New York Post*, 1956, p.33.

Elliot, Frank. "Chesty's Driver." *Leatherneck*, Nov, 1982, p. 34.

Hoffman, LtCol Jon T. "Chesty Puller's Epic Stand." *World War II*, Nov, 2002, p.34.

——. "The Truth About Peleliu." *Proceedings*, Nov, 2002, p.50.

Maas, Peter. "Waste of an Old Warhorse." *Esquire*, Jan 1958.

Martin, Harold H. "Toughest Marine in the Corps." *Saturday Evening Post*, 22 Mar 1952.

PERSONAL PAPERS

Puller, Lewis B., Marine Corps Research Center, Boxes 1-8.

PAMPHLETS

Alexander, Col Joseph H.,USMC (Ret.). *Battle of the Barricades: U.S. Marines in the Recapture of Seoul.* Washington, D.C.: MCHC, 2000.

Gayle, BrigGen Gordon D., USMC (Ret.). *Bloody Beaches: The Marines at Peleliu.* Washington, D.C.: MCHC, 1996.

Nalty, Bernard C. *Cape Gloucester: The Green Inferno.* Washington, D.C.: MCHC, 1994.

Shaw, Henry I., Jr. *First Offensive: The Marine Campaign for Guadalcanal.* Washington, D.C.: MCHC, 1992.

Simmons, BrigGen Edwin H., USMC (Ret.). *Frozen Chosin: U.S. Marines at the Changjin Reservoir.* Washington, D.C.: MCHC, 2002.

——. *Over The Seawall: U.S. Marines at Inchon.* Washington, D.C.: MCHC, 2000.

We would like to thank the following individuals for their guidance and assistance in constructing this novel: Colonel Richard Camp, USMC (Retired), Deputy Director, Marine Historical Reference Branch; Mr. Danny Crawford, Branch Head, Reference Section; Mr. Mike Miller, Branch Head, Archives Branch; and Mr. Jim Ginther, Manuscript Curator, Archives Branch. Major Rick Spooner, USMC (Retired) was extremely helpful in providing valuable history and hospitality, and Mr. Jake Ruppert, author of *One of Us: Officers of Marines*, was kind enough to read the initial manuscript and grant helpful observations and insights.

We would also like to thank Kris Mullin and Mary Miller for their help in typing and editing the manuscript. In addition, we are grateful to Patty Hogan for her valuable comments and suggestions.

Organization of the 1ST Marine Division* (approximate figures)

Squad	12 Marines
Platoon	50 Marines
Company	200 Marines
Battalion	800 Marines
Regiment	3,000 Marines
Division	20,000 Marines

Infantry Regiments of the 1st Marine Division

1st Marine Regiment	(1st Marines)
5th Marine Regiment	(5th Marines)
7th Marine Regiment	(7th Marines)

Battalions of the 1st Marine Regiment

1st Battalion, 1st Marines	(1/1)
2nd Battalion, 1st Marines	(2/1)
3rd Battalion, 1st Marines	(3/1)

Battalions of the 5th Marine Regiment

1st Battalion, 5th Marines	(1/5)
2nd Battalion, 5th Marines	(2/5)
3rd Battalion, 5th Marines	(3/5)

Battalions of the 7th Marine Regiment

1st Battalion, 7th Marines	(1/7)
2nd Battalion, 7th Marines	(2/7)
3rd Battalion, 7th Marines	(3/7)

* Lewis B. "Chesty" Puller served with the 1st Marine Division both in World War II and Korea

Introduction

THE RUNNER

A runner is both an important and necessary part of a combat organization. During a battle, a runner's job is to deliver a message or to obtain information, usually at great risk to himself. When the phone lines are severed or the radio isn't working, the runner becomes the link between a commander and his men. He is often alone and on his own. It is a dangerous, demanding job. Frequently, the commanding officer would visit his men on the front lines. Usually, the runner would accompany him. In this capacity, he would serve as both a bodyguard and a runner. Even though the runner and his commanding officer would be separated by rank, it was not uncommon for a bond to form between these two men, shaped by their shared experiences.

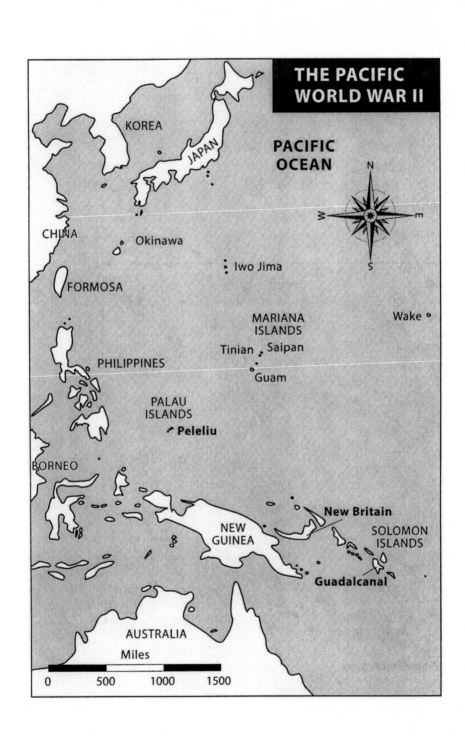

Prologue
The New York Times

I will not soon forget the date of October 11, 1971. The most famous Marine in the history of the Corps is dead. His name was Lewis B. "Chesty" Puller and it is doubtful that any Marine will equal his combat record. I was saddened yesterday when I read his obituary, and couldn't believe the *New York Times* got it wrong.

I was in New York for a conference and sat down in the lobby at 6:30 am with a cup of coffee and a copy of the *Times* to read before reviewing the agenda for my nine o'clock meeting. I came to the headline 'Gen. Chesty Puller Dies; Most Decorated Marine,' and noted the image of Puller in his dress blues; he looked older than I remember. They could have chosen a better photograph.

The article defined Puller as a cigar-chewing officer, but he mostly smoked a pipe. And it was Stonewall Jackson who he idolized, not Andrew. It also acknowledged Puller's four Navy Crosses; an award that recognizes extraordinary heroism at great personal risk in close combat against an enemy of the United States. Well, some Marines have two Navy Crosses, two Marines have three, and no Marine has four. Chesty didn't win four Navy Crosses, he won five. I ought to know this much about him, I was his runner and was with him when he won three of them.

That was the thing with Chesty Puller; the press never seemed to get it quite right.

The next day I flew back home to Chicago. On the plane, I read the obituary over and over. I kept finding it hard to believe that Chesty Puller was dead. He always seemed immortal to me. I sat in my uncomfortable seat, staring through the window at nothing in particular, thinking about Chesty's indelible strength and personality. His thundering voice was ringing in my ears.

The morning after I arrived home, I went to the office early. I pulled the obituary out of my briefcase and laid it on my desk. I then walked over to the small corner closet which usually held my coats during the winter months, but had become more of a storage bin as of late. I opened the closed door and grabbed a dusty, worn shoe box from the shelf. In the box were letters I had written to my mother and father. Two years ago, my mother had given me these and they had been on the shelf ever since. As I looked through the letters I realized that my mother had put them in chronological order. I had to smile. Mom was always very organized.

I sat at my desk and opened one of the earliest letters. It was from New River.

Chapter One

Training

This training is far more demanding than I ever imagined. You should see these gunnery sergeants. They are tough, profane, crusty men. Some have fought in France, many in Haiti and Nicaragua. If I was in a bar fight, I'd want these guys on my side. And then there is our battalion commander . . .

M. Abbo, letter to parents, 18 Feb 1942

NEW RIVER

My name is Michael Abbo. I was nineteen years old and I had been in the Marine Corps for fourteen weeks. After boot camp, then infantry training, I was sent to the tent city at New River, North Carolina, which would later become Camp Lejeune. I arrived in February 1942 on a cold, grey, rainy day and was assigned as a rifleman to B Company, First Battalion, Seventh Marines of the First Marine Division. I was one of the last men to join the battalion.

At that time, the new base was nothing more than a sea of tents on the edge of thousands of acres of coastal swampland. There were no barracks. Construction efforts were focused on roads, rifle ranges and a hospital. The Marines slept in canvas tents that were poorly heated and sparsely lit.

We were issued the utility uniform that we would wear throughout WWII. It was sage green, made of herringbone cotton twill. The two-piece uniform consisted of a jacket and trousers. Our boots were referred to as "Boon Dockers," and were ankle high, and were made of leather with the rough side out. Khaki canvas leggings were worn over the boots.

The battalion commander was a 43-year-old Major named Lewis B. Puller. Marines referred to him as "Chesty". The first time I saw Puller, we reported

1

to an open field where he called his battalion together, and I noticed him out front standing with a few of his officers, nodding as they spoke to him. He was shorter than I expected, with a rugged bull dog face, an out-thrust jaw and deep-set eyes that seemed to examine every man in that field. He had a booming voice that everyone could hear. As I listened to him speak, he sounded like my drill instructor at Parris Island.

Puller told us that we had come a long way, but there was still a lot of work to do. He said that we would continue to be trained even harder, to prepare us for war. Although it would be almost two months until the 7th Marines left New River for the Pacific, and almost eight months until we saw action, my training began immediately.

Most of the men in the battalion had been together since Puller took over in August. This would be my first hike with him and even though I was new, I was expected to keep up. That day we were going on a twelve-mile hike. He made everyone in the battalion hike: cooks, clerks, and corpsmen. There were no exceptions.

We started out early in the morning and Puller set a brutal pace. He turned out on the camp road and we went for a mile and then turned on to a trail that led into the woods. Even though it was cold I started sweating. The first mile is always the toughest. That's when you're out of breath and can feel the dead weight of your pack. And then the numbness sets in. It's around this time that the accordion effect takes over. The battalion starts to spread out and then everyone tries to catch up. When this happens you have to walk much faster or run, and the line contracts. Then it starts all over again. The men started cussing but this didn't last long. They soon realized they were just wasting energy.

Even though this was my first hike with Puller, I soon realized, I didn't like him. He was running us into the ground. After an hour the battalion stopped and we had a ten-minute break. We took our packs off and sat on them. I looked at the Marine next to me and asked, "What's he trying to do, kill us?"

He said, "It's like this all the time. Just wait, it's going to get worse, Puller's a ball buster."

After the break we started out again. I didn't think it was possible, but Puller went faster. Most of the Marines were young men, except for the sergeants. How could this forty-three year old man keep up this pace? As we were going through the woods, I kept tripping over tree roots and could feel it in my knees. I felt sorry for the people in the rear; they had to go twice as fast just to keep up.

Occasionally we would pass an exhausted Marine who couldn't make it. There was no way I was going to drop out. I hated this hike but I wasn't a quitter.

After four grueling hours of this we finished the hike. Several of the men didn't make it. I felt sorry for them but the sergeants didn't share my sympathy. Puller and his staff were pushing us far too hard.

Our feet blistered badly and many of us peeled off bloody socks after every hike. Puller constantly demanded that we push ourselves to the limit of physical exertion; and then push further. On a hike in March, he insisted we could not wear overcoats because exposing us to the cold weather was essential to effective training. After the hikes, we would eat before reporting to makeshift classrooms for lessons on combat tactics, which usually lasted most of the afternoon. When we weren't hiking or taking classes, we cleared out brush and trees to make room for rifle ranges, barracks, and other facilities. Eventually, we abandoned the tent city and slept in the field, camping in single tents or even in the open, exposed to the winter cold. The harder we worked and trained, the more Puller expected from us. It was a tough winter.

One day we were waiting in line to go into the mess tent and there was a big trash can standing two feet away from the tent. The company gunnery sergeant came walking along and told me to move it against the tent. I made the mistake of asking him "Why?"

The sergeant went berserk and began yelling at me. He was screaming so loudly that every man in the chow line heard him.

"Goddamnit, when I tell you to do something, do it. Who the hell do you think you are? Move it!" This man was so mad he scared me.

A few minutes later a lieutenant foolishly asked him, "What was that all about?"

The sergeant glared at the lieutenant and said, "Lieutenant, I've been in the Marine Corps for twenty years. I've been giving orders for eighteen of those years. That is the first time that anyone has ever asked me 'Why?'"

The lieutenant wisely replied, "Fair enough," and walked off.

I learned a valuable lesson that day: never question a Marine sergeant. Ever! My education in the Marine Corps was just beginning.

Spring came slowly, but eventually the weather improved. Puller continued to drive us with relentless training exercises and classes, instilling in our minds the importance of being prepared for war. In order to simulate the conditions of war, we trained under the live artillery shells of the 11th Marines, despite the possibility of an accident. Puller exposed us to the sound of large guns so when the time came, it would be as common as the sound of our rifles.

Our regiment, the 7th Marines, was ordered to Samoa. To bring our regiment up to fighting strength, the 7th Marines took with them some of the most experienced officers and non commissioned officers of the 1st Marine division.

In early April our battalion loaded onto the USS *Fuller*. This is the first time I'd ever been on a ship. As I walked aboard, I realized that I wasn't going to see my family for a long time. The thought made me terribly homesick. Also, I'd never been out of the country before. As I watched people waving from the dock I wondered how long it would be until I returned home. We sailed out of Hampton Roads and into the Atlantic. Troopships at their best are terrible. A blast of hot, foul air hit me as I entered the hatch and started down the ladder to go below. Canvas cots were stacked six high with very little space between them. I was assigned the third cot from the bottom. All my gear went on this cot. When we slept we had to lie flat on our backs or stomachs. If we tried to roll over, our shoulder would hit the cot above us. The lighting was poor and there was almost no ventilation. Space between the tiers of cots was so narrow we had to walk sideways.

That night as I lay in my cot with the boat rocking, I thought about the way my mother would greet me everyday after track practice. I'd lumber in through the kitchen door, she'd turn to me with a warm smile and say, "You are not eating in my kitchen all sweaty like that. Go take a shower." My fourteen year old sister would usually look up from her schoolwork only long enough to tease me, usually about a girlfriend. Some time between 6:00 and 6:15, my father would come home. He'd quickly settle into his chair and read the newspaper. We could all tell what kind of day he'd had by the way he held his paper. The more noise he made turning the pages, the worse the day was, and we knew to keep our distance. Promptly at 6:30, we sat down to eat. I never truly appreciated my mother's culinary skills until I'd had my first Marine Corps meal.

Soon enough, rough waters caused by storms made me violently ill. I was not alone. Many of the men and officers spent time crouched over the sides of the ship or in the toilets.

I found my sea legs by the time we crossed the Panama Canal and headed out into the Pacific.

We would grow filthier each day. The only showers were saltwater showers and there was no room to exercise. When it came time for chow we waited in line a long time. We ate standing at long folding tables. The sweating Navy mess men who served us wore undershirts and their arms were richly decorated with a wonderful mix of tattoos.

Eventually we would land in early May, to defend the island against an impending Japanese invasion. We thought we were going to be the first to fight, but the invasion never came.

SAMOA

The Samoan Islands of Upolu and Tutuila had good harbors and terrain where airfields could be built. In order to cut off major supply lines to Australia, these islands were likely targets of the Japanese. The 7th Marines were brought in to assist a small band of New Zealanders to protect the island from this threat.

After dropping a group of reinforcements from the 2nd Brigade on Tutuila, we pulled into Upolu's Apia Harbor in the middle of the afternoon. Upolu is an island about fifty miles long and thirteen wide, surrounded by a coral reef. The backdrop of the port at Apia looked more like a vacation spot than a base. Palms littered the foothills along the coast and the calm beaches made me believe, for a brief moment, that there could not possibly be a war happening near here. That first night in Samoa I slept more soundly than I had since leaving home.

The next day the work began. Unloading the ships was grueling in the heat, and Puller allowed us to sleep only a few hours a night until the boats were emptied. It seemed that unloading the supplies would never end. The lines of working Marines became more silent as the hours of each day wore on. Tempers flared if any Marine slowed or stepped back to rest, and even the officers looked beaten. When the ships were finally emptied, we started clearing trees and brush to build bunkers and firing ranges. We slept in small tents in the field and the rains brought horrendous bugs. We could only wash ourselves with what rainwater we collected. Puller was with us the entire time, digging holes and sleeping underneath a small tarp. He was a tireless worker, and spent his little free time playing cards with the officers and the battalion surgeon. In late May the word spread that he was promoted to lieutenant colonel, and by June the real training started.

Puller was a very competitive man and there was no doubt that his battalion was going to be the top of the 7th Marine Regiment. His battalion was going to be the best at hiking, shooting, patrolling – everything. We had to move from Apia to Faleolo on the northwest corner of the island to help defend the newly constructed airfield. It was twenty-five miles to Faleolo. We would get there by hiking. The sergeants woke us up early in the morning, and we were in formation by 6:00 am. We would carry a heavy load: field packs, rifles, ammo and rations.

We had grown soft from the trip from the States and now we were going to pay the price. We formed up into a column of twos and Puller took off. The early hour meant that we were getting a head start on the other battalions and I had a terrible feeling that we were going to get to Faleolo in record time.

Puller led the way over an asphalt highway. He was flying and some men behind him were running to catch up. I knew then that it was going to be a long, painful day.

By the time we stopped for chow we were doing all right. Only a few men had dropped out. But after lunch the sun and heat started working against us.

My mind went numb and all I could do was look at the man in front of me. The Marine next to me passed out and I stopped to help him, and bent down over him. A sergeant grabbed me by the arm and jerked me up and said, "Keep moving. A corpsman will take care of him."

Puller was pushing us to our peak of endurance. The sweat started pouring down my face. Puller moved so fast that the rear of the column had to run to keep the line from spreading. The pace was the fastest I had ever seen, especially for a hike of this length. With every break I'd take a couple of sips of water, and take my pack off, but only for a few minutes. Then it was full speed ahead.

My entire body began to hurt: my feet, knees, shoulders and neck. Men started falling out by the dozen, but Puller kept going. Every step became unbearable and the only thing that kept me going was cursing Puller.

Some time after three in the afternoon we arrived in Faleolo. Many of the Marines did not finish and we all dropped to the ground when Puller dismissed us. He walked up and down the line of collapsed Marines, congratulating us for making it to the end. Too exhausted to eat, I fell asleep without dinner.

Puller was highly concerned with the welfare of our feet, and before the next march, showed us an old trick he had learned in Haiti. He and the officers handed each soldier a small square of beef gristle, and told us to scrub our feet with it each morning. Barefoot, we followed along while he demonstrated. The next hike was eighteen miles over more rugged terrain, and though we suffered and some fell out of line, few were plagued by crippling blisters.

When we were in the field Puller had a policy that was strictly adhered to: the men would eat before the officers. I'm sure the officers did not like this but Puller was always at the end of the line, setting the example.

When we weren't hiking, we were participating in complex field problems that usually involved other units, some lasting two days. Puller was very serious about these, and his competitive spirit challenged us to excel over other battalions. He took great pride in our performance, which was a direct result of how hard we trained.

In mid August, the 7th Marines marched twenty-five miles back to Apia.

Before we started, Puller stood out front of the battalion and said, "I don't want nobody to fall out unless he passes out. If you can't hack this, I don't want you in my battalion."

That kind of talk made me dislike Puller even more. We had been over this asphalt highway before but we were in much better shape now. Even though Puller set a fast pace, most of us made it. I hated this type of training and thought there was far too much work with too little reward.

One afternoon after a short ten-mile hike, the company first sergeant pulled me aside as we were cleaning our equipment, "Abbo, you ran track in college?"

"Yes, I did First Sergeant."

"Well good, the Colonel needs a runner. I have volunteered you for the job and you better be damned good at it. Report to Colonel Puller at 1900," he said.

I was shocked, "Um, excuse me First Sergeant, but what is a, what exactly does a runner do?"

"You'll find out. Make sure you aren't late for the Colonel," he said as he walked off.

"Yes, First Sergeant."

I was very nervous to report to Puller, and found my way to his tent early. There was a table set up in front where he and three officers were playing cards. With a pipe dangling from his mouth, Puller was laughing and joking with the others, throwing the cards down playfully. He glanced up when I walked up to the table. Immediately, I walked up and said, "PFC Abbo reporting as ordered sir," in my best Marine form.

Puller stood, returned my salute and said, "At ease, Abbo, step into my tent here," which surprised me. He sat down behind a desk and then brought a match up to his pipe and asked, "So, do you know what the duties of a runner are, old man?"

"Not really, sir," I said.

Puller let out a grunt and took a long draw on his pipe, "Abbo, a runner is essential to field communications. When the phone lines are cut or the radio is down, it is you who becomes the link between me and my troops. When you carry a message in combat, the life of every man in the outfit may ride with you."

"Yes sir."

Puller had my service records out on his makeshift desk, and examined everything in the folder before he spoke again. "I see you're an expert shot, which will come in handy. I also see that you ran track at Notre Dame. I need someone who is fast and smart, which is why you were picked. It's a risky business, though. Are you up for it?"

"Yes, sir," I replied.

"You're from Chicago?" said Puller.

"Yes, sir."

He handed me my records and said, "Have your records transferred from B Company to Headquarter Company."

He looked at me for a few seconds and said, "Report to me at 0800 tomorrow. That's all."

"Yes sir," I said, and walked out of the tent.

I took my records over to battalion headquarters and the office was empty except for a buck sergeant pecking away at a typewriter. When he stopped typing I said, "Colonel Puller said to transfer my records to headquarters."

I handed the sergeant my records and he asked me what I was going to be doing.

I replied, "I'm going to be one of Colonel Puller's runners."

The sergeant looked up at me and said, "Let me give you some advice Abbo. He runs a tight ship. He expects you to perform and when you don't, there's hell to pay. When he was a first lieutenant I served with him on the *Augusta*, the flagship of the Asiatic fleet. He was in charge of the Marine guard on board ship. He's by far the most decorated man in the battalion. He won two Navy Crosses in Nicaragua. Chester Nimitz was the captain of the ship. You've heard of Nimitz, haven't' you? Well, Nimitz had relieved the two previous Marine officers because they couldn't get the job done."

"Sergeant, what year was this?" I asked.

"Let me think, Lieutenant Puller reported aboard in the fall of 1934. He got results immediately. After about a month, we pulled into Melbourne, Australia for a two-week stay. At the end of the stay our shooting team attended a rifle match with Lieutenant Puller. After the match we were crossing a river on a ferry. When the boat was about to dock a car ran off the slip and landed in the water. In a split second, Chesty ripped off his shoes and dove in the water. He pulled two women out of the car but the driver drowned.

"The next day his exploits were in all the Melbourne newspapers. When Nimitz read about it he called Chesty in and commended him for saving the lives of two women.

"I see from your records that you've been in this outfit long enough to know that he is a big believer in tough training. Just don't screw up, Abbo."

I was not the only runner in our outfit and the next day I learned that Puller was going to make sure we were well trained. He lined four of us up about a hundred yards apart. He gave a message to the first in line, who sprinted to pass the message along to the next. During the sequence Puller yelled, "Move it! Take it to the next in line!"

When the last runner had been reached, Puller asked for the message. He listened and then shouted the original message back to us, which differed slightly. He then folded his arms and told us to start the exercise again, "Listen up, we will do this until you get it right. The lives of your fellow Marines depend on you."

It was at this initial training session that I first met John Hayes. He was a tall lean Marine and the other two runners called him Pop. We introduced ourselves to each other, and they said to call him Pop, although he wasn't much older than me.

I asked, "Why do they call you Pop?"

He suddenly got a big grin on his face and said, "Hell, I'm 26 years old. Take a look around. Most of these Marines are kids: 18, 19, 20 years old. I'm old enough to be their father."

I liked Pop immediately which was a good thing because we would be sharing the same tent. He had a certain charm about him that made him appealing; an infectious smile always hung on his face, a friendly, easy-going manner, and a robust sense of humor.

After chow that night Pop and I sat on the ground in front of our tent. Pop was smoking a cigarette, just staring at the stars. He was a corporal. "How long have you been in the Marine Corps?," I asked.

"Two years," he said. "I joined a couple of weeks before Christmas, '39."

"Why did you join the Corps?"

"Had to," Pop said.

"What do you mean?"

"Well, it's pretty simple. The judge said one year in jail or you join the Marine Corps. I sure as hell wasn't going to jail," said Pop.

Before I could ask him what happened, Pop crushed his cigarette under his boot and said, "The cops caught me transporting moonshine back home in Kentucky and when I went before the judge the next day he gave me a choice. But it wasn't much of a choice."

He looked at me and said "How 'bout you? How did you end up in the Corps?"

"I ran track in high school, the quarter mile", I replied. "Notre Dame gave me a partial scholarship, and this coupled with the money I had earned during the summer, and my dad putting up some money helped me to go to Notre Dame. It wasn't easy for them. My dad is a tailor and couldn't afford the tuition. My first day in South Bend a priest gave the freshman class a speech on what was expected of us, and in the talk he said that sneaking off campus at night and drinking were forbidden and that if you got caught you would be expelled. Secondly, he said, if you do get expelled, don't think about coming to me saying 'what about my poor mother and father?' Boys, you are responsible for your actions. Remember that.

"My freshman year I behaved myself. But the second week of my sophomore year me and two other fellows snuck off campus one night and went into South Bend and had a few beers. We got caught climbing through a window in our dorm and the following morning we were expelled."

"What did your dad say, Mike?" Pop asked.

"He didn't say much. The hardest part was that I had disappointed him. I really regretted that. After that Dad said, 'get a job.' I was walking down the street in Chicago and passed a Marine recruiting office and I stopped. My father was a Marine in World War I, but he never talked about it. I thought if he could do it, then so could I. A few days later, after I passed all the tests I was sworn in. I went home and told my parents."

Pop looked at me and said, "Well, what did they say?"

"My father exploded. He said 'The Marines are nothing but goddamn cannon fodder.' My father rarely got mad and he never swore, but he sure did that day, Pop. That's how I got here."

"You know something Abbo? We both got here because of old demon rum."

I laughed and said, "I suppose we did."

"You're from Chicago?"

"Yep, how about you?"

"I'm from a little town in northern Kentucky. A place called South Shore. It's right across the river from Portsmouth, Ohio."

Pop stood up and said, "Mike, I don't know about you but I'm hitting the sack."

I followed him into the tent and went to sleep.

By August, Samoa had made us restless. We heard rumors of the Marines landing on Guadalcanal and wanted to be called into the fight. The second week of September, we finally got the word and sailed for Guadalcanal. We were ready.

Chapter Two

Guadalcanal

If we stop the Japs here, this could be the turning point in the Pacific and you know what – It's going to take time but I think we're going to do it. Last night we fought a tremendous battle . . .

M. Abbo, letter to parents, 25 Oct 1942

THE FIRST OFFENSIVE

After December 7, 1941, I watched, like much of the world, as the Japanese Army and Navy went on an empire building campaign that shocked the world. They had already taken much of eastern China. By violent force, over the next five months they proceeded to take Hong Kong, Korea, Indochina, the Philippine Islands, Malaya, Singapore, Borneo, the Celebes, the Dutch East Indies, most of New Guinea, Guam, Wake, and the Gilbert, Marshall, and Solomon Islands. Guadalcanal was the southernmost of the Solomon Islands. The price paid for these territories was overwhelming: over 300,000 killed, wounded or captured Allied soldiers.

The price the Japanese were paying was veiled by a ruthless arrogance. The vastness of the expansion made it more difficult to supply their soldiers. The conquered territories of Japan had begun to transform the empire from an aggressor to a defender. Both Napoleon and Hitler were ultimately defeated by reaching too far into Russia. The same thing was beginning to happen to the Japanese on Guadalcanal; in effect, it was one island too many.

Having been a veteran of this theatre of war, in later life I became an avid student of its history. During the intense heat of battle, no soldier understands

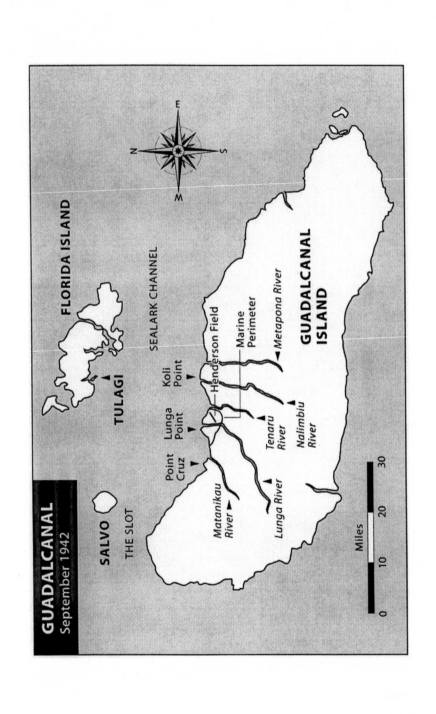

GUADALCANAL
September 1942

SALVO

THE SLOT

FLORIDA ISLAND

TULAGI

SEALARK CHANNEL

Point
Cruz

Lunga
Point

Koli
Point

Henderson Field

Marine
Perimeter

Metapona River

Matanikau
River

Lunga River

Tenaru
River

Nalimbiu
River

GUADALCANAL
ISLAND

Miles

0   10   20   30

how he got to a particular hill or why he has to defend it. Extensive readings and countless hours of talking to people who were in a particular place have helped me to piece together a better understanding of the hows and whys of the wars I survived.

Nineteen years old and camped out in the South Pacific, I had no idea of the military events that brought me to Guadalcanal. But later, after years of studying the history of this time, I learned about Martin Clemens, an Australian colonial, who arrived in the Solomon Islands in 1938. In February of 1942 the Japanese seized the Solomons. Instead of leaving with other Australians and Europeans, Clemens remained with a few others to serve as a coast watcher. At great risk to himself, he reported via wireless radio the actions of the Japanese.

But the Allies were not letting the Japanese conquests go unopposed. The Coral Sea battle in early May 1942 and the Midway battle a month later resulted in the loss of five Japanese carriers and two American. These battles gave the United States an opportunity to take the offensive.

On July 6, 1942 Clemens and his coast watchers reported that the Japanese were sending more troops, supplies, and earth-moving equipment to Guadalcanal. An airfield was to be built on the Lunga plain. Guadalcanal is a large island, of jungle rivers and rain forest over ninety miles in length and twenty-five miles wide. There are plains and foothills along the northern coast that rise up gradually to the backbone of a mountain that drops rapidly to the southern coast. Rainfall on the island is extremely heavy and the interior receives up to 200 inches a year. This rain, coupled with an average temperature in the high 80's results in a humid, unhealthy climate. Malaria, dengue and other fevers, as well as fungus infections afflict the local population. It would be even worse for the Marines.

For Japan, Guadalcanal had the only terrain in the area suitable for constructing a major air base. From this base the Japanese could cut off the sea-lanes between the United States and Australia, further restricting the flow of war materials being shipped to the South Pacific. To prevent this from happening, the United States decided to send in the 1st Marine Division.

The commander of the 1st Marine Division was Major General Alexander A. Vandegrift. In early April 1942 he was informed that the 7th Marines were to be dispatched first, sent to Samoa to defend against an attack. Meanwhile, the rest of the First Marine Division was sent to New Zealand for an additional six months of field training. After arriving in New Zealand in June, Vandergrift was stunned to hear that his undermanned division was to invade Guadalcanal on August 1, ready or not. That date would later be pushed back to August 7.

The command structure for the invasion of Guadalcanal was a complicated one:

Vice Admiral Robert Ghormley was the commander of the South Pacific area and he exercised strategic command over the invasion. Vice Admiral Frank Jack Fletcher was the senior task force commander. Rear Admiral Richmond Kelly Turner was the amphibious force commander. British Rear Admiral V.A.C. Crutchley was in command of the escort group, which protected the Amphibious Force. Major General Vandegrift would command the Marine forces on the ground.

On July 26, 1942 Major General Vandegrift attended a meeting on Vice Admiral Fletcher's flagship. Rear Admiral Turner was also present. Fletcher revealed that after the landing on Guadalcanal he would not expose his carriers to Japanese air attacks, and would be leaving on the morning of the third day, even though Turner indicated that he would need five days to unload the equipment and supplies. As a result, Turner had to face the consequence of Fletcher's decision: his supply ships, without carrier-based air cover, would also be leaving on the third morning with whatever supplies remained onboard.

Fletcher did not have confidence in this operation, and looked upon it as more of a raid than the permanent seizure of the island. Vandegrift came away from the meeting with the impression that Fletcher did not know or care much about the upcoming operation.

On Friday, August 7, 1942 the First Marine Division landed on Guadalcanal, Tulagi and the nearby islets of Gavutu and Tanambogo. This was the first major offensive operation of World War II. In addition, it was also the first time an American combat-loaded division had ever made an amphibious landing. Attached to the Division were Lieutenant Colonel Edson's 1st Raider Battalion, the 1st Parachute Battalion, and other Marine units. They attacked Tulagi and the nearby islets.

The 1st and 5th Marine Regiments landed on Guadalcanal with no opposition. The Japanese and the people working on the airfield fled into the jungle. The Marines landing on Tulagi and the islets, however, ran into a hornet's nest. After two days of fierce fighting, the Marines secured the islets and Tulagi. There were 1,500 Japanese killed while the Marines suffered 250 casualties.

The next night, Saturday, August 8, Major General Vandegrift was asked to join Rear Admiral Turner aboard his ship for an urgent meeting. Minutes earlier, Vice Admiral Fletcher advised Turner that he was pulling his carriers out of the operation because of the large number of enemy planes in the area. As a result, Turner told Vandegrift that he too would leave at dawn because his ships, without air cover, would be vulnerable to attack. Vandegrift was furious, but there was nothing he could do about it.

Later that evening, a little after 1:30 AM, a Japanese Naval Force cruised down the western side of the "slot" between Guadalcanal and Florida Islands. The Japanese slammed into Rear Admiral Crutchley's naval escort group and sunk four heavy cruisers, three American and one Australian. Approximately 1,300 sailors died that night and another 700 were wounded or badly burned. Japanese causalities numbered less than two hundred men. This battle would rank as one of the worst defeats suffered by the U.S. Navy.

As night fell on Sunday, Turner's Task Force departed and with it a vast amount of the Marine's equipment and supplies. Vandegrift knew he lacked both air and sea cover, and also was dangerously short of everything from food and ammo, to artillery and earth moving equipment. The official name for the Guadalcanal operation was Watchtower, but the Marines soon gave it a more appropriate name, "Operation Shoestring." The Marines learned to make due with what the Japanese left behind when they fled into the jungle: rice, dried fish, trucks, fuel, even cigarettes. The Marines were now stranded to fight alone.

HENDERSON FIELD

The survival of the Marines on Guadalcanal depended on the airstrip, Henderson Field. The field had been named for Major Lofton Henderson, a Marine pilot killed at Midway. Vandegrift's top priority was to defend it while finishing the construction. He spread his thin forces along the ridges and established a defense perimeter around Henderson Field that faced the sea.

Although the Japanese controlled the sea and air, the Marines held the ground. The Marine engineers worked night and day to prepare the 3600-foot dirt runway for airplane traffic. The first planes landed on Henderson Field on August 20, amid the roaring cheers of thankful Marines. The radio call sign for the island was "Cactus," and soon the pilots became known as the "Cactus Air Force."

On the night of August 18, the Japanese landed 1,000 soldiers twenty-two miles east of Henderson Field. The first big fight for Guadalcanal – the Battle of the Tenaru River – started in the early morning of August 21. The Japanese attacked the portion of the perimeter defended by the 2nd Battalion, 1st Marines at Alligator Creek. The Marines struck back with a deadly combination of rifles, machine guns and artillery. When the battle was over, there were almost 800 dead Japanese.

As the battle for Guadalcanal continued to intensify, Vandegrift strengthened his defense of Henderson Field by calling on Edson's Raiders, the parachutists and other Marine units who had returned from Tulagi on September 8.

The 1st Marines protected the perimeter to the east of the airfield, the 5th Marines to the west, and in between, facing south, were the 800 parachutists and Raiders. Lieutenant Colonel Merritt 'Red Mike' Edson was put in command of this combined force. These men had to defend a long, grass-covered ridge that ran south from Henderson Field because it offered the Japanese the best approach to the airfield. A force of 3,000 Japanese soldiers attacked on the evening of September 12, beginning the second major battle for Guadalcanal. For the next two nights, the Japanese unleashed everything they had, but the Marines held on, knowing that if they failed, Henderson Field would fall and with it, Guadalcanal. As with so many battles of this war, success relied on small groups of Marines fighting viciously to hold their positions. Waves of Japanese kept coming and the Marines continued to hold them back. Lieutenant Colonel Edson, the Marine commander, performed superbly, as did one of his company commanders, Major Ken Bailey. For their service, both were awarded the Medal of Honor, although Bailey's was awarded posthumously, as he was killed two weeks later. The ridge would always be referred to as "Bloody Ridge," or "Edson's Ridge." In the desperate fighting, the Japanese had lost over half their men.

In just five weeks on the island, the Marines too had lost a lot of men to combat, but disease, hunger and exhaustion were also beginning to take a toll. The Marines needed help, which came on September 18 as Chesty Puller and the 7th Marines came ashore.

THE 7TH MARINES LAND

Early in the morning, we climbed down the nets into the boats and headed toward the beaches of Guadalcanal. No one said much, and the silence confirmed our fear. As far as I could tell, Guadalcanal was a huge island of mountains with thick jungle on the bottom and grassy hills that rose up to the heights beyond. The 7th Marine Regiment landed with over 4,000 Marines and supplies of food, ammunition, and aviation gasoline. Pop and I rode in on Puller's boat and when we landed on the beach he told us to round up the company commanders. He told them he wanted men from each company to help unload the landing craft. Pop and I were assigned to this detail and we unloaded until late in the afternoon. Puller wanted everything clear of the beach. Captured Japanese trucks were used to take the supplies into the coconut groves that lay five hundred yards inland. At dusk we had not finished unloading the boats, which left in case of a Japanese naval attack. Puller told his commanders, "Get 'em dug in back there in the grove. The Japs may hit us tonight. I don't care how tired they are, make 'em dig in."

Puller carried with him a dirty, worn copy of Caesar's *Gallic Wars*, which he had for most of his years in the Marine Corps. Years later, when exposed to this book, I recognized that Puller always heeded Caesar's advice: When you make camp, fortify!

The coconut grove was a mess of splintered trees and stumps made by Japanese air and naval attacks. It was in this debris that we started to dig in. For the evening meal there was beef stew but many of the men were too tired to eat or to dig in, they just fell asleep where they were.

After darkness fell Japanese ships moved in and shelled the area. I was near Puller and heard his orders to get in the holes. "Get down and stay down."

The men who had not dug their holes now did so frantically. Every shell that came in shook the ground violently. This was my first experience with incoming naval gunfire. It terrified me. Pop and I had dug a three-foot deep hole and we hugged the bottom of it. No matter how deep the hole, it still wasn't deep enough. They shelled us for about an hour and during this time neither of us said a word. We were too scared to talk. When the shelling stopped, I spoke first.

"Jesus, that was awful."

"Mike, it's obvious what the Japs are doing. They don't want us to sleep, they want to wear us out," he said.

"I hope this doesn't happen every night," I said.

Even though we were exhausted, we were too frightened to get any sleep.

Three of our men had been killed and twelve were wounded.

Early the next morning, one of the battalion cooks came up to Puller and said, "Sir, we have a lot of Japanese rice but it's full of worms. What do you want me to do with it?"

"Hell, cook it and serve it," Puller replied.

The cook looked surprised and asked, "Are you serious, sir?"

Puller exploded, "You're goddamned right I'm serious." And then, perhaps realizing that he had been a little harsh, he said, "Look, we don't have enough food. We have to share our supplies with the rest of the division, so if we don't want to starve, we eat the rice. So boil it a couple of extra minutes and maybe the little buggers will shrivel up. Besides, a little protein will do the men good."

"Yes, sir!" the cook exclaimed.

Puller then left for division headquarters. When he returned he told his company commanders, "We're going out on patrol. We'll go down the west bank of the Lunga River. Our job is to find the Japs. Get your men ready. We move out at 1430."

Eight hundred men left the perimeter that afternoon and followed a trail into the steamy jungle. Puller was close to the front of the line with the radio operator. Pop and I were behind him. I had never been in a real jungle before. It was humid and putrid and so thick in many places that the sky was not visible. As we trudged on the sweat started pouring down my face.

Late in the day we came out of the jungle and started to pull our way up steep hills. When we reached a grassy knoll that seemed to be ideal for a campsite, we were ambushed. Startled from loud gunfire, I dove to the ground and saw Puller as he barked orders to bring up the machine gun squads. He spread out the battalion and told us to dig in. Pop and I dug in next to Puller's Command Post. The CP was just a hole in the ground. He shared it with his radio operator. When darkness arrived, Puller took Pop and they walked the perimeter. They were back in less than an hour.

Puller got back in his hole and Pop climbed into mine.

"What's going on?" I said.

"It's quiet but I'm sure the Japs are still out there. It's scary."

Puller came over to our hole.

"Get ready. I'm going to light my pipe and when they fire at me open up on their muzzle flashes."

Puller went over to the hole on the other side of him and told those men the same thing. Then he came back toward his hole and said, "Ok, here we go."

Out of the corner of my eye I could see the glow of his match and the Japs fired at him. Puller dove to the ground and we fired back.

I whispered to Pop, "After a stunt like that Puller is either the bravest guy in this outfit or the craziest."

Pop replied, "I don't know, but I bet the men sure liked it."

The rest of the night stayed quiet.

With the coming of daylight we resumed the patrol. The commanding officer of B Company, Captain Jack Stafford, was terribly wounded by a faulty rifle grenade. He had to be carried back on a stretcher over grueling terrain. Captain Chester Cockrell took over command of B Company. The battalion arrived back at the perimeter as it was getting dark and we dug in and took up a defensive position. When night came there was a lot of unnecessary shooting as the men were jumpy and inexperienced, firing at any noises they heard.

Puller finally lost his patience and picked up the phone, called his company commanders and told them, "Control your men and stop the firing. There is nothing out there." He could not reach B Company on the phone, so he told me, "Go down there and tell Captain Cockrell to stop the shooting."

"Yes, sir," I said, and took off.

In the tropics, when the sun goes down, the darkness comes quickly and completely. Its unknown can terrify you. The perimeter was a slight arc that extended toward the sea with the airfield behind us. It was pitch black.

Twenty yards from Puller's CP was a huge hole at least six feet deep and six feet across. I assumed it was the result of Japanese naval fire. I carefully walked around it. B Company's CP was about two hundred yards away. I walked along slowly, the foxholes were about ten yards apart and the Marines would ask, "Who is it?" to which I would answer, "Runner". I cautiously made my way behind the men.

It took about fifteen minutes to get to Captain Cockrell's CP. I gave him the message and then started back. Rather than follow the arc of the perimeter, I cut straight across thinking I would save time. It was a big mistake.

In the darkness I had wandered off course away from the line. I stopped when I heard something moving behind me. My heart started beating so hard and loud that I couldn't hear a thing. I wasn't sure if it was a Jap or an animal, and I started trembling. I got down on one knee, put my rifle to my shoulder and pointed it in the direction of the noise. I was afraid to fire, in fear of revealing my position. So I just waited. The darkness does strange things to a man and it makes your imagination run wild.

I soon realized that I had to gain control of myself or I would go crazy. I said over and over, "There is no one there. You are all right. Breathe slowly." After a couple minutes of this I finally calmed down and knew that all I had to do was listen for the sound of the surf and head in that direction, which would run me into our line. So I began to follow the sound of the ocean.

In a few minutes a voice said, "Who's there?" and I gratefully answered, "Runner". I now knew I was safe and could just follow the line to Puller's CP. I was moving from hole to hole when suddenly I went flying through the air. I let out a scream of a dying man and slammed into the ground with my rifle crashing down on top of me. I landed on my back and hit the ground so hard that it knocked the wind out of me.

I heard Puller's voice in the distance say, "What the hell is that? Find out!"

At first, I couldn't figure out what had happened. Then I realized I had been careless and fallen into the big hole by Puller's CP. I heard a voice nearby and it was Captain Beasley, Puller's operation officer.

At first I couldn't speak, but soon caught my breath and said, "It' Abbo, sir."

"Where are you?" Beasley asked in a whisper.

"Sir, I fell in the big hole," I said sheepishly.

"Are you alright?"

I answered, "Yes sir, but I can't get out. It's too deep. Can you give me a hand?"

I handed Captain Beasley my rifle and then he helped pull me out. We walked into the CP and Puller said, "What happened?"

"Abbo fell into the hole," Beasley said.

Puller turned to me, "Are you alright?"

"Yes, sir," I said.

Then he let me have it, "Jesus Christ, Abbo, these men are jumpy as hell and now you've spooked them all. You'd better start paying attention or you're going to be dead in a week."

Beasley got on the phone and passed the word, "Everything's okay. A runner fell in a hole."

It was not a proud moment; I was embarrassed and had disappointed Puller.

After I climbed into my hole Pop could not resist opening his big mouth.

"Abbo, you are amazing. You'll do anything to gain a little attention!"

"Pop do me a favor, will you?"

"What's that?"

"Kiss my ass."

The next morning Puller was talking to one of the corpsmen about the wounded men. We had been on the island now for five days and we hadn't washed or shaved. I smelled terrible.

After the report the corpsman said, "Sir, this is the dirtiest I've ever been in my whole life."

"Doc, I learned in Nicaragua that within a week you get used to being wet and dirty," Puller replied.

The corpsman looked a little surprised by Puller's reply and all he said was "Yes sir."

THE MATANIKAU RIVER

There was no doubt that Puller's fresh and well-trained battalion would become the main patrolling arm of the 1st Marine Division. The arrival of the 7th Marines gave the Division the opportunity to go on the offense, rather than stay in a static, defensive position. Puller's patrol would leave the perimeter and head southwest to the Matanikau River, while the First Raider Battalion would hike up the river from the sea, and the Second Battalion, Fifth Marines would wait at the mouth of the river, with hopes of trapping the Japanese.

On the morning of September 24, I was awakened by Puller's thundering voice, "Pop, Abbo, get the company commanders, we're going out on patrol." Puller only took his three infantry companies, which amounted to about 600 men. A Company took the lead, followed by Puller and his command group, including the radio operator and Pop and myself. B and C Companies followed us.

Again we had to navigate through the stinking jungle and climb the grass-covered ridges and back down again. It was exhausting work but didn't seem to bother Puller. He was often up front, which was rare for a battalion commander. It was obvious the men liked his aggressive spirit.

Late in the day, the point came upon two Japanese soldiers cooking rice. Both men were shot and Puller went to sample the rice as machine gun fire opened up on us. A Company was pinned down so Puller called for Captain Cockrell's B Company to assist. Puller stood and yelled, "Cockrell, bring 'em up." Terrified, I was watching men getting shot, but Puller completely ignored his own safety. He was out front, moving and yelling to rally the men. Puller couldn't tell how many Japanese he was up against, so when it started to get dark, we moved back to a long ridge and dug in for the night.

Puller tried to contact B Company on the radio but there was no answer. He said to me, "Abbo, I can't reach B Company, so get the hell over there and find out what's going on."

When I arrived I found that Captain Cockrell had been killed, the radio was knocked out, and B Company was spread all over the place. I ran back to Puller and told him what happened. He told Pop to find Captain Cox.

When Pop returned with Cox, Puller looked at him and said, "I guess you know that Cockrell's dead. You are taking over B Company. Now get down there and take charge."

Seven Marines had been killed and twenty-five wounded; eighteen of them stretcher-cases. By radio, Puller requested an airdrop consisting of stretchers and water. Puller made the rounds that night, encouraging the men. He was great at bucking us up and I was amazed at how secure it felt when he was around.

The Second Battalion, Fifth Marines (2/5) were sent out early the next morning to meet up with and support our battalion, and come under Puller's command. Major Otho L. "Buck" Rogers, Puller's Executive Officer, or his XO, was ordered to return to the perimeter with A and B Companies carrying the wounded and providing security.

Before we left, we buried the dead. There was no other way we could carry them back to the perimeter. Puller said a short prayer. I can't remember the words, but I do remember how I felt. It just seemed unfair that these Marines would be left alone on top of this ridge. A corpsman had collected their dog tags. I didn't like it, but the reality was, there was no other way to do it.

Puller headed out with his C Company and 2/5. We hiked all day along the trail and had no contact with the enemy, and I was glad that the day had passed and nothing happened. That evening we dug in again.

We ate our rations and it was not yet dark. I wanted to talk about something other than the war. I said, "Pop tell me about how you ended up running moonshine."

"Well," Pop said, "My uncle, my dad's brother, asked me after I graduated from high school if I wanted to work for him. He had made moonshine for years back in the hills. I had helped him occasionally but then he wanted me to deliver it and collect the money. He charged a dollar a quart, there was no credit, and he gave me a cut of the sales. I told him I'd do it. In return, he told me that if I got caught, I was on my own. The only people that could get you were those federal revenuers and they were never really around."

"What did your father say?" I asked.

"Nothing. Hell, it was good money," Pop said.

"How did you transport it?"

"He made it in fifty-gallon drums and from there it went into quart jars. It was 80 proof, powerful stuff. In the back of my truck I built a big drawer full of cubbyholes. Into each hole would go a jar of whiskey. On top of this was a big toolbox, so it looked like the whole thing was just a box of tools. The rear of the toolbox had a false back, which I could lift up and then slide out the drawer filled with whiskey. It was slick as hell."

"Would you deliver it during the day?" I said.

"No, never. Always at night. I was like a milkman. I would deliver the whiskey, get paid, and take back the empty jars. I was doing this for six years before I got caught."

I asked him, "So how'd you get caught?"

"One night after I made most of my rounds I came to a bend in the road and I saw a roadblock ahead. It was manned by federal agents. They must have known what they were looking for 'cause when they searched the truck it took them no time to find the drawer. Unfortunately, there were still about ten quarts of whiskey in it. The next thing I knew I was headed to Parris Island. I'm sure somebody ratted me out."

Then it started raining hard and we put ponchos over ourselves and stayed wet and cold for the rest of the night.

We moved out early the following morning and finally reached the Matanikau River. The Matanikau was more of a stream than a river and because it rained a lot on "The Canal" it was always a dirty brown. As usual, the going was slow and exhausting and the heat was draining us. We headed north to the beach, along the east side of the river. E Company of 2/5 started to cross the river at its mouth. As the men entered the water, the Japanese hit them with mortar and machine gun fire. The Marines pulled back with six men wounded. Puller ordered G Company to attack through E Company. After two attacks failed and twenty-five Marines had been killed or wounded, Puller pulled back G Company and called in the artillery to fire on the Japanese positions.

Late in the afternoon, Colonel Griffith's 1st Raiders arrived and it started raining hard. Division radioed Puller and told him that Colonel Edson, who now commanded the 5th Marines, would be in command of the combined operation. Puller would be the XO, or second in command, for this operation.

When dusk came, too late for more attacks, everyone dug in for the night. Later Pop and I could hear Puller and Edson discussing the plans for the next day: The 1st Raiders would move two thousand yards south and cross the river on the enemy's flank. C Company of 1/7 and 2/5 would attack straight across the river, and the third unit of the three-pronged attack was the landing of A and B Companies of 1/7, now back at the division perimeter and commanded by Major Rogers, at Point Cruz. They were to land in back of the Japanese and attack from the rear. Puller and Edson would remain at the mouth of the river.

The Marines would not fare well on Sunday, September 27th. The Raiders went south and ran into a company of Japanese that had crossed the river the previous night. The XO, Major Bailey, winner of the Medal of Honor on Bloody Ridge, was killed and Colonel Griffith, the CO, was wounded. Shortly before this, G Company of 2/5 attacked across the mouth of the river but came under heavy fire and had to pull back.

Major Rogers was told that morning that he was to take A and B Companies of 1/7 by boat and land to the west of Point Cruz in support of this operation. The four hundred men left in a hurry and unfortunately, Sergeant Robert Raysbrook, the radio operator, forgot to take his radio. The unit landed without opposition and moved through a coconut grove to a grassy ridge above. Then the Japanese hit them with mortar fire. Major Rogers was killed immediately and Captain Cox of B Company was seriously wounded. Captain Kelly took over command of the two companies, realizing the situation was grave, and that they were cut off from the sea. He quickly set up a defensive perimeter along the ridge. Without a radio, Kelly had no way to inform Puller or division of their dire circumstances.

Fortunately, a Marine pilot circled over and Captain Kelly had his men spell out HELP with their white t-shirts on the ridge. The pilot, Lieutenant Dale Leslie, dipped his wings to acknowledge and radioed Division who in turn passed it on to Edson and Puller.

With the top two Raiders down, Colonel Edson called off the attack. Puller was hot, "Christ, you can't do this! What's going to happen to my men? They're out there on their own."

Puller couldn't get Edson to change his mind so he stormed off. The radioman and I followed him to the beach. There Chesty found a signalman and in turn contacted the *Ballard,* a ship that was in the area. He requested that they send a boat to pick us up. We got on board late in the afternoon. Puller explained the situation to the skipper and he agreed to help. When the *Ballard* reached Point Cruz, Puller signaled the surrounded Marines to fight their way to the beach.

Puller could see the boundaries of his unit, and had the ship fire all around it. The guns fired to the beach and Puller had them walk the rounds up the hill to the ridge so a path could be cleared to the beach. Then he had the guns fire on the flanks of the men so they could withdraw safely to the beach. Meanwhile the captain of the ship had radioed Lunga Point for landing craft to evacuate the men, and the boats were on the way.

Through binoculars Puller saw Captain Kelly starting to move his men downhill, toward the beach. When they reached it, they set up a small defensive perimeter on the beach while the Japanese kept firing at them. B Company arrived first and started getting into the boats, which had grounded thirty yards from the shore. The Marines carried the wounded out to the boats and came back for more.

At the same time, Puller, the radio operator and I quickly got into one of the small boats and went toward the beach. He was yelling orders and we stayed until all the men were evacuated.

I soon realized Puller's quick thinking and aggressive action had saved both companies from being slaughtered. The only positive thing to come from this operation was that the Marines knew there was a large concentration of Japanese on the island. Since arriving on Guadalcanal, our battalion had suffered ninety-one casualties, including our executive officer and three company commanders.

The next day, our battalion was back in its defensive perimeter. Because of the casualties, morale was low. Puller called together his officers. "Gentlemen, you have to learn from this experience. More importantly, you are more than just commanders. You are leaders. I expect you to lead from the front, not simply give the orders to attack. Since my childhood I have been taught that in the Confederate Army, an officer was judged by stark courage alone, and this made it possible for the Confederacy to survive for four years, against incredible odds. There are many qualities in the make-up of a man, but stark courage is absolutely necessary in the make-up of an infantry officer. Good night, gentlemen."

While we were in a defensive position, Pop and I shared a small tent next to Puller's CP. In front of our tent was our hole. Before it got dark, we started talking.

"Have you always lived in Kentucky?" I asked.

"My whole life, except for my time in the Corps.

"You don't seem to mind the Corps."

"It's ok. I'm pretty much used to the outdoors. Since I was a little kid my Pappy would take me hunting and we'd camp out for days in the woods. Hell, we lived on whatever we got. We shot it all. So I don't mind the shooting part, it's those damn sons of bitches shooting at me that I have trouble with."

As we both laughed, I asked him his impressions of the Colonel.

"He's just like my old man," Pop said. "Tough but fair. I remember when I was sixteen and I was a little bit of a wise ass. One day I came home from school in my old Ford pickup and when I parked, I blocked the driveway. Not on purpose, I just blocked it. Pappy came home after work and walked into the house and told me to move the truck. So I threw him the keys and said, 'here you go.' He grabbed me and threw me against the wall. My reaction at the time was to clench my fists like I was ready to fight. Pappy looked at me and said, 'Son, I respect your courage but your judgment is just piss poor.'"

I said to Pop, "What did you do?"

"What do you think I did? I moved that truck as quick as I could. There was no messing around with my old man. He was the head sawyer at a lumber mill north of Portsmouth. He was rough as hell and I usually did what he told me to do. Puller's just like him. He's a hard man, but he's ok. As far as I know he's the only guy in this battalion that has any real combat experience. I know he served in Haiti and Nicaragua. I heard he's one of the most decorated men in the division. I'll tell you what Abbo, I'm not getting in Puller's way."

"What's your old man like?" said Pop.

"He came over from Italy when he was ten years old. Worked like a dog. His father was a tailor and so he learned the trade from him. When my grandfather died he took over the business. He always worked six days a week and sometimes seven. I didn't get to spend too much time with him because he was always working. I have a lot of respect for my father. I was the first one in my family to go to college, but then I screwed that one up."

"Did your father ever take you hunting?" Pop asked.

"No, my father wasn't a hunter and the first time I fired a rifle was in the Corps. Amazingly, I was really good at it. My dad likes to fish though. Every summer since I was a little kid, he would drive the whole family up to Northern Wisconsin where we'd stay for a week. We rented a small cabin on a lake and a little fishing boat. After breakfast we'd take the boat out on the lake and fish for walleye. When the fishing got slow, we'd start talking. I learned a lot from him about his father and how hard he had it when he came over from Italy. My grandfather didn't get married until he was 42. He couldn't afford to. My grandmother was 30. They're both dead now, but they were wonderful people. In some respects, I learned more on that little boat than I did in all my years of school. It really was the best time for us to talk."

BACK TO THE PERIMETER

In late September, our battalion got the word that we were replacing 2/7 on the perimeter. We would be positioned south of the airfield, in the jungle flats. Puller immediately put us to work improving and fortifying the perimeter. The first thing we did was cut away the undergrowth and put up barbed wire. Then we dug deep fighting holes. Puller's command post was a bunker made of coconut logs and sandbags.

As time passed, we were beginning to adjust to the climate, terrain, bugs, and the lack of food and water. We were always hungry and only ate two meals a day. In order to drink, we had to carry water from the nearest river, several hundred yards away. We never slept much because of the nighttime bombings and biting mosquitoes. Also, about this time, the 7th Marines began to look like the Leathernecks that had been here since August 7: thin, hollow-eyed, with yellow complexions brought on from taking attrabrine, which prevents malaria. In short, we were exhausted and undernourished.

At the end of September, Admiral Chester Nimitz, the U.S. Pacific Theater Commander-in-Chief landed at Henderson Field to get a clear picture of how the Marines were doing on Guadalcanal. On his way he stopped in Naumea to meet with Vice Admiral Robert Ghormley, Commander of the South Pacific Area. Nimitz thought Ghormley looked burned out, and was surprised to learn that numerous combat aircraft were in the area, but were being held back. He also wanted to know why Army soldiers had not been sent to Guadalcanal. Nimitz was disappointed by the lack of aggressive naval patrolling, which allowed Japanese forces to land on Guadalcanal at night with no resistance. Nimitz spoke at length with Vandegrift to discuss these points. It took time but Nimitz would make the changes.

While he was on the island, Nimitz looked up Puller and for a few minutes Pop and I heard the former shipmates talking about their time on the *Augusta* and about the situation on Guadalcanal. Then the Admiral had to leave. We heard Puller tell Captain Kelly that he knew Nimitz would shake things up.

In the beginning of October it became obvious that the Japanese were making night landings with large amounts of troops west of the Matanikau River. Intelligence indicated that the Japanese were getting ready to attack. We had to respond.

Vandegrift decided to hit them first, prevent them from coming to the river, and keep their artillery from hitting the airfield.

RETURN TO THE MATANIKAU

The Matanikau operation was well planned, taking on a hammer and anvil formation. Edson's 5th Marines were to head to the mouth of the river. They would be the anvil.

Next, the Whaling group, under the command of Colonel Bill Whaling, would cross the river 2,000 yards south of the coast and then push north to attack the Japanese. Next, Lieutenant Colonel Hanneken's 2/7 was to follow Whaling across the river and head to the first line of ridges and then turn north and attack the Japanese from the rear. Finally, Lieutenant Colonel Puller's 1/7 would follow 2/7, head west to the second line of ridges and steer north to cut off the Japanese line of retreat. These three forces would hammer the Japanese against the anvil: Edson's 5th Marines at the river.

We moved out early in the morning of October 7 and hiked most of the day. Although we heard rifle fire, there was no contact with the enemy. We arrived at the river shortly before dusk, set up our perimeter, and dug in. We had a quiet night, and during the next morning it started raining hard. We headed out at first light and it was exhausting and slow going. The trail was a deep, muddy mess because we had been following the forces of Whaling and Hanneken. Led by Puller, the Marines of C Company crossed the river at dusk and the remainder of the battalion made it across at several hours later. We had cold rations for dinner, dug in, and tried to sleep.

The next morning was clear and surprisingly cool. The attack started off with a short artillery barrage. An hour later Hanneken's E Company was pinned down by heavy machine gun fire. Hanneken radioed Puller for help, and he ordered Captain Moore of C Company to assist him. At the same time, Division called and ordered Hanneken to break off the fight and head to the mouth of the Matanikau. Puller then threw A Company and B Company into the fight. At the peak of the battle, someone from regiment called Puller. "Be prepared to withdraw. Take your battalion to the mouth of the river and join up with 2/7."

Puller exploded, "We're in the middle of a big fight. How in the hell are we going to withdraw? Why don't you come up here and see what's going on?" He slammed down the field phone. He was especially mad since Colonel Sims was on the other side of the river and had no idea what was happening to us. He got his company commanders on the phone and told them to report immediately. They arrived a few minutes later and his instructions were crystal clear, "Gentlemen," pointing straight ahead, "the Japs are down in those ravines. Don't let 'em get away!"

Puller knew he had the advantage and he ruthlessly exploited it. First, he called in artillery. Then he ordered his mortar men to start firing into the ravine. To avoid the deadly fire, the Japanese charged up the hill at us. Our machine gunners cut them down. Those that were left quickly withdrew to the bottom of the ravine where they suffered more losses. Now realizing they were trapped, the Japanese climbed up the opposite hill and our machine guns finished them off.

Puller had destroyed most of a battalion. The slaughter went on for more than an hour, and the enemy unit was finished as a fighting force. When the battle was over, Puller was called by regimental headquarters and told to return to the perimeter. He looked at Pop and me and said, "Round up some men and search the bodies, but be damned careful. Some of them might be playing possum. If you have any doubts, shoot them. I want maps, papers and anything else that may help us. This is not a souvenir hunt. Get going."

We got forty men together and ten of us searched the bodies while the rest covered us. It was not a pretty sight. The ground was littered with Japanese bodies and if they moved or moaned they were greeted with a rifle shot. We had learned the hard way-we weren't taking any chances. Many of the Japanese had been blown apart and I had never seen anything like it. It made me nauseous and I couldn't help it but I threw up. I hated this ghoulish job, but I didn't have a choice. In searching their packs, we came across letters and pictures of their wives and children. The pictures tormented me. A lot of the papers and maps we found were covered with blood and gore. We did find some documents that looked official in pouches. They were all written in Japanese so I had no idea how important anything was.

The gruesome task took about an hour. We returned to the CP and gave the papers to Puller. He asked, "How many bodies?"

"Sir, over six hundred. There were a lot of them."

He shook his head slowly, "We had six killed and twenty wounded. 2/7 lost seventeen and twenty-six wounded. It's a tough business, men."

"Yes, sir."

We left a few minutes later, heading for the beach, carrying the wounded. We reached the mouth of the Matanikau in the afternoon. There was a boat that picked up the wounded and we climbed into a few trucks that drove us back to the airfield, which took a long time because only twenty men could fit on a truck. From the airport we hiked back to the perimeter where we had a late meal.

Pop and I got into the chow line. This was our first hot meal in several days and the cooks spooned something on our plates that looked like beef stew. We sat on the ground and started eating.

When I tasted it, I looked at Pop and said, "What kind of meat do you think this is?"

"It's horse meat," he replied.

"No really, what do you think it is?" I asked.

Pop said, "It don't taste like anything I've eaten before."

I finished my supper but, hungry as I was, it didn't go down too well.

The next day we found out that the three day operation had been the largest ever run by Marines; and a costly one: 65 dead and 125 wounded but the Marines had killed over 700 Japanese and another 70 had been killed at the mouth of the Matanikau River.

The documents we found revealed that the Japanese were building up for a major attack on the airfield and that they were planning to move artillery east of the Matanikau so their guns could reach the airfield. When I heard this, I felt a little bit better about having participated in the task of searching the bodies of the enemy.

In mid October, the Army's 164th Infantry Regiment landed on Guadalcanal. With more men ashore, Vandergrift could afford to put more men along the Matanikau. He also shifted 3/7 to the west, 2/7 was to take over the entire 7th Marine sector and our battalion (1/7) went into reserve near the main airstrip.

That night two Japanese battle ships hit the main airfield and the recently opened fighter strips with almost a thousand 14-inch shells. The shelling was horrifying and we were close to the center of the target. If we listened closely, we could hear the short, low booms of the rounds leaving the ships perhaps miles off the coast. The shells would then come screaming in on top of us. My insides felt like a giant hand had squeezed them. My entire body was locked in fear as I struggled to catch my breath. Buildings, huts, tents, and planes were ripped apart. Gasoline exploded, rising in enormous waves of flames. Every shell violently shook the ground and Pop and I put our hands over our ears as one explosion after another jostled us around in our hole. Our ears started ringing. It was the worst shelling we would encounter on the island. It was the most terrifying hour of my life.

When it was finally over, Pop said, "I wonder if there is anything left?"

"I don't see how," I said.

Early the next morning, Puller went over to regimental headquarters and when he returned he got his company commanders together and gave them the report:

"Gentlemen, we got hammered last night. The airfield is a disaster; most of our planes are damaged or destroyed. As far as we know all the aviation gas has blown up. Forty-one men killed including, as you know, two lieutenants from this outfit."

For the next two nights the Japanese Navy came back and gave us more of the same. The Marines wanted to know where in the hell was the U.S. Navy.

Nimitz started to make changes. On October 16th he relieved Ghormley as the commander of the South Pacific area and put in his place the more aggressive, Vice Admiral William "Bull" Halsey.

ALONE

General Vandergrift expected the Japanese attack to occur along the Matanikau, so in anticipation he started to reposition his forces on October 20th. Our battalion was moved back to "Bloody Ridge", south of the airfield, where Colonel Edson had fought the Japanese earlier. 1/7 took the left half of the perimeter and 2/7 took the right half.

The following day Colonel Sims told Puller to put a platoon sized listening post about 1500 yards out on the left side of the line. Puller knew if there was an attack these men wouldn't have a chance so he angrily told Sims, "It's crazy to sacrifice that platoon."

Sims replied "Put them out!"

Puller told Captain Fuller to put out a platoon and he chose Sergeant Ralph Briggs' unit. They were out of sight but had contact with battalion by telephone. Puller then told Pop, "Get the battalion armor and some men, and then pull those 50-caliber machine guns from the damaged planes at Henderson Field. Have the mechanics down there help you. Then bring them back in a truck. Abbo, you stay here."

Pop returned later that day with eight guns. Puller said, "Give two guns to each company. I want barbed wire strung along the front with cans of pebbles hanging from it. If the Japs are coming, I want to hear 'em."

On the 23rd, Puller got word that 2/7 would be moving out the following morning, heading to the western side of the perimeter to help defend against an attack from the Matanikau. Our battalion was now left alone. It was up to us to defend the entire 2500 yard sector with our under strength battalion. Puller called his company commanders together and laid out his plan: "Gentlemen, 2/7 is pulling out and heading to the Matanikau. Division thinks that is where the Japs are going to hit. Maybe so. I think there's a chance they will hit us right here and I want to be ready for them. There is no way we can cover the whole damn front, so here's what we're going to do:

"Captain Kelly, you take a platoon from each of the companies and cover the ground that 2/7 is leaving. Occupy the forward slope of "Bloody Ridge". I'm also sending most of my headquarter personnel to help you out. So, Captain Kelly is taking the right side of our line. Next to him, will be Captain Haggerty's B Company, then Captain Moore's C Company, and finally Captain Fuller's A Company on the far left. 2/7 will pull out early tomorrow morning."

Puller kept speaking to the silent group, "As soon as it gets light, feed your men and get them going. We have this whole sector to defend and a hell of a lot of work to do. I want at least fifty yards of brush cleared in front of you, a hundred yards would be ideal. I want the fighting holes dug deep. Also, if we get hit, we will be using a lot of ammo, so bring up as much as you can. If you can get yours hands on any barbed wire, get it.

We can't afford to have any weapons jam up on us so make sure they are cleaned and oiled. I will be around first thing in the morning. Good night, gentlemen."

When we went back to our hole I said, "I don't like this Pop."

"What do you mean?" he asked.

"Two battalions used to cover this whole front and now it's just us. And we don't even have a full battalion. With all the killed, wounded and sick we are down to about six hundred men. We're spread pretty thin. And there is no reserve to back us up."

"What choice do we have?" said Pop.

"None, but at least Regiment could give us a few extra men."

"Ain't gonna happen Mike."

It stayed quiet and we were able to get a little sleep. Before daylight, we were awakened by Puller's voice, "Pop! Abbo!"

"Yes, sir."

"Get something to eat, then we're going to make the rounds," he said.

"Yes, sir."

After breakfast, we reported to Puller.

We started out with Captain Fuller's A Company on the left front and then worked our way right. Nothing escaped his eye. He would tell the men to dig deeper, clear more brush, hang more cans on the wire, or pile the sandbags higher.

He often asked the men: "Where's your field of fire?" or "Do you have enough ammo?"

He wanted all the field phones opened so that all his companies and platoons could hear his orders. When we got back to Puller's command post, he picked up the phone and called General Pedro Del Valle, the commanding officer of the 11th Marines, which was the artillery regiment of the 1st Marine Division. Puller said, "If we get hit, can I count on you for support?"

Del Valle said, "I'll give you all I can."

Before dark that night, the artillery batteries that reached Puller's perimeter were registered out in front of his lines. At dusk Puller took Pop and me and two other runners on a tour of the line. When we started he said, "I want you to know where the company commanders are located. Make damn sure you remember because this whole battalion may have to count on you." He was very intense. When we arrived back at his command post, he asked us, "Can you all find the CPs in the dark?"

Everyone answered, "Yes, sir."

"Good. Now go get some chow." he said.

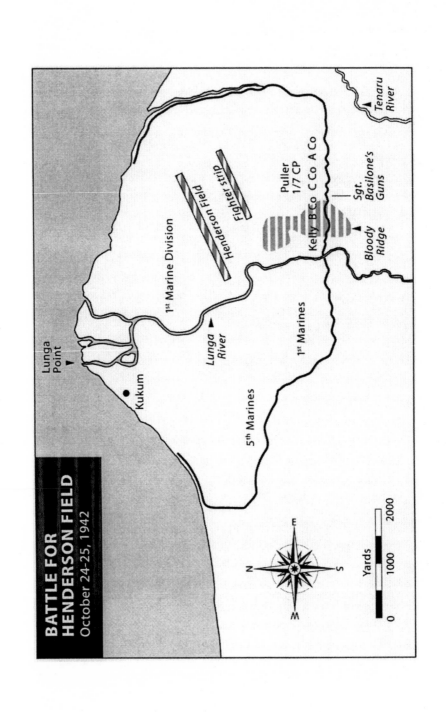

BATTLE FOR
HENDERSON FIELD
October 24-25, 1942

Lunga
Point

Kukum

5th Marines

Lunga
River

1st Marine Division

Henderson Field

Fighter strip

1st Marines

Puller
1/7 CP

Kelly B Co C Co A Co

Sgt.
Basilone's
Guns

Bloody
Ridge

Tenaru
River

N E S W

Yards

0   1000   2000

THE BATTLE FOR HENDERSON FIELD

After eating we arrived back at the CP. In it was Puller, Captain Beasley, the operations officer, Sergeant Major Frank Sheppard, who was the senior enlisted man in the battalion, the radioman, Pop and me. Puller passed the word that there would be a 50% alert; half the men awake in the holes and the other half could sleep. The moon was hidden by thick clouds and it began to rain, a perfect night for an attack.

The phone rang around 9:00 PM. Puller answered and held the receiver off his ear. We could hear the entire conversation. It was Sergeant Briggs, and he was almost whispering, "Colonel, there are about three thousand Japs heading your way."

Puller's eyes widened, "Are you sure?"

"Yes sir."

Puller answered, "All right Briggs, get out of there, and be careful. Pass through the lines at A Company. I'll tell 'em you're coming. We'll hold our fire as long as we can."

"Yes sir."

Puller called the unit on the left and informed them that Briggs was heading that way. Then he called all his company commanders, "They're coming. Get your men up on the line, now!"

The phone rang again, it was Fuller of A Company, "The Japs are cutting the wire on our front."

Puller then spoke to all his commanders on the battalion circuit:

"Listen up. Hold your fire until you get an order from me, we need to be sure that the outpost is clear before we open fire. If the bastards break through use your bayonets. Keep someone at every phone. Wait."

In a matter of minutes, the Japanese tore into the line between A and C Companies. Puller then growled with his tidewater drawl over the battalion net, "Commence firing."

The Marines opened up with rifle and machine gun fire, and then the battalion's mortars came crashing down on the Japanese.

The 7th Marines' ranks were packed with a high number of old salts when they shipped out to Samoa the previous spring. Puller's 1/7 had their share of the Marine Corps' best mortar men and machine gunners; these men took a deadly toll on the Japanese. Among these men was machine gunner Sergeant "Manila" John Basilone. His group of machine guns was in the middle of C Company and the concentrated fire was so deadly that a hill of bodies accumulated in front of his position. After the first attack faded, Basilone ordered some of his men to flatten out the mound of bodies that was blocking his field of fire.

The first phase of the battle seemed to last fifteen to twenty minutes. Then the Japanese pulled back when they realized they could not hold on to their meager gains. Puller got on the phone to Brigadier General Del Valle, "Pour it on – this is a major attack."

Del Valle assured him, "Lewie, it's on its way."

Puller looked at Beasley and told him he was going down to C Company and would be right back. He then said to me, "Come on, Abbo."

We didn't have far to go since C Company was in front of us, and there was a little firing to deal with, but not much. In a few minutes we reached Captain Moore's CP. I think the Captain was a little surprised to see Puller and his presence helped reassure him.

Puller asked, "How's it going, Captain?"

Moore answered wearily, "They punched through the center of our line, but we pushed them back. We're holding, Colonel."

"Keep it up, Captain; it's going to be a long night, old man."

"Yes, sir."

As he turned to leave, Puller said, "I'll be back in my CP. Keep me informed."

"Yes, sir."

We then left and returned to the CP, which was fifty yards to the rear.

The second major assault started an hour later and again the Japanese stormed out of the muddy, bloody jungle flats and poured into the barbed wire while the rifles and machine guns of the Marines ripped them apart, and the mortars and artillery did their murderous work.

Puller got on the phone and talked to the regimental executive officer, Lieutenant Colonel Bull Frisbie. "They're hitting us across our whole front. We need help and we need it now!"

Around midnight Colonel Jerry Thomas, the Chief of Staff of the 1st Marine Division, called Puller:

"I've only got one battalion left in reserve. The Matanikau battle looks like a diversion so I'm sending the Army's 3/164, commanded by Lieutenant Colonel Bob Hall. Father Keough, the 7th Marines Catholic chaplain, has volunteered to guide the battalion to your CP. They are on the way. They should be there by 0200."

Puller asked, "Does Father Keough know where to find us?"

"Yes."

"Okay, we'll be waiting for him."

Shortly before 2:00 AM Puller looked at me and said, "Let's go meet 'em."

"Pop you stay here."

We left the CP and went down to a jeep road about a hundred yards behind the CP. Puller knew exactly where he was going and at this time the moon had come out from behind the clouds; we didn't need a flashlight. Ten minutes later we heard the men coming up the road but couldn't see them yet. They came around the bend and we saw Father Keough leading the way. He said, "Here we are, Colonel."

Puller shook his hand vigorously, "Father, Thank God you got here."

He then turned and greeted Lieutenant Colonel Hall, and as usual, he wasted no words, "Colonel, you don't know how glad I am to see you. We can't worry about rank right now. I don't know who outranks whom and I don't give a damn. It makes sense that I'll be in command until daylight at least, because I know what's going on here and you don't."

The Army Colonel wasn't surprised, "That's ok with me. I'll follow you."

Puller gave a quick nod, "I want you to make it clear to your soldiers that my Marines, will be in command in those holes when your officers and men arrive."

Hall agreed, "All right, let's go."

Puller led the way with Father Keough, Hall, and me following him. A group of runners had been sent to the jeep road and told to wait for us. When Puller got to the first runner, he asked him what unit he was with and then peeled off a platoon of men and told them to follow the runner. By the time we got to the end of the line all of Lieutenant Colonel Hall's men had been fed into position.

We went back to the CP with Father Keough and Hall. By this time, there had been at least six Japanese assaults on our lines. The ammo was running low from the continuous fighting, and the weapons were wearing out, but the Marines were holding on. Captain Fuller of A Company called in, "Colonel, I'm getting short of ammo."

Puller grunted loudly into the phone, "You've got bayonets haven't you, Fuller?"

A silent moment passed before Fuller answered, "yes sir."

"Alright then. Hold on."

Puller turned to Pop, "You and Abbo get a couple of men and run some ammo down to Captain Fuller."

We jumped quickly, "Yes, sir."

We went outside and found two men and told them to help us get some ammo down to A Company, which was off to our left front. We grabbed all we could carry from the ammo dump and headed down. It started to rain again suddenly, and it was hard going, the mud was deep and slippery. The fighting intensified and the closer we got to A Company, the more careful we had to be. Bullets were whizzing by us and the sound of the guns was deafening. We crawled the last twenty-five yards though the mud, dragging the ammo. It was too dangerous to stand up. We finally dropped the ammo outside Captain Fuller's CP and I went inside. He was on the phone and looked worn out. When he hung up I said, "The colonel sent you some ammo."

He gave me a slight nod and said, "Thanks."

We left and we made our way back to our CP. When we arrived, I could see Puller outside the bunker, talking to another Marine. It was Sergeant Manila John Basilone.

Puller asked, "How are the guns holding up?"

Basilone answered, "We're using a lot of ammo and it's boiling away the water in the cooling jackets of the guns, so I told the men to piss into them. We have no water."

Puller glanced down at Basilone's feet to find that the Sergeant wasn't wearing boots or socks. "Where the hell are your boots?"

Basilone cleared his throat, "They've rotted sir, so I took them off."

Puller shook his head, "Jesus Christ, Basilone, get some boots when this fighting is over, or you're going to end up going lame."

"Yes, sir."

Then Basilone was gone. He headed back to C Company loaded like a packhorse. He had all the ammo and spare parts he could carry. He was a one-man band and was about to become one of the first enlisted Marines to win the Medal of Honor. Tragically, I later learned he was killed on Iwo Jima.

Puller then went back into the bunker, picked up the phone and called his company commanders, "All right, it is getting close to dawn and you know damn well they're going to try it one more time. Get out there and steady your men. Be ready."

Soon after, they hit us one more time but were beaten back by the Marines and soldiers, fighting side by side.

When the sun came up on the morning of October 25 the battle for Henderson Field was largely over. Because of the great defense that our battalion put up, the battle was mostly one-sided. The Marines, and, later in the night, the soldiers had torn the Japanese apart.

When it was daylight Puller called Captain Fuller and asked if he had heard from Sergeant Briggs. Fuller said no and Puller asked to be kept informed.

Puller then took Sergeant Major Sheppard, Pop and me to walk the lines. It was obvious that a great battle had been fought here, and who had won it. There were hundreds of Japanese bodies and in many places they were stacked two and three high. The ground was littered with spent shell casings, ammunition containers, busted weapons, and the air was still heavy with the smell of burnt powder and the stench of death. It was a sickening sight.

When we returned, Puller talked to Lieutenant Colonel Hall. "Let's reorganize this damn front. You take your men and string them out along the left half of this sector and I'll take the right half. And one other thing Colonel, your men did an outstanding job last night. I don't think we could have held on without you."

"Thank you Colonel Puller. I'll pass that on to the men."

"Well, let's get ready. I'll bet those bastards are coming back." And with that Puller walked back to his CP.

We ran into some of the intelligence people from division and Puller gave them a couple of platoons of men to provide security while they did the gruesome job of searching the dead. Thank God we didn't have to do this.

Later that morning Sergeant Briggs and his men started returning to the perimeter. He immediately reported to Puller, "Colonel, we got out of there as soon as you told us. We split up and headed towards A Company. The Japs were all around us. We could hear them talking and they walked right by us. It was a long night."

All of Briggs' men made it back except four.

Nineteen of Puller's men had been killed; thirty wounded, and there were twelve missing. It was estimated that the Japanese had lost over 2,500 men. Two Japanese regiments had been torn apart.

The Japanese were not finished, however. That night they attacked again but were pushed back by the Marines and soldiers. The attack was weak by comparison to the hellish battle of the night before.

After the battle was over, Puller was recommended for the Medal of Honor by Lieutenant Colonel Merrill Twining, the 1st Marine Division's Operations Officer and Colonel Frisbie, the Executive Officer of the 7th Marines. Colonel Sims, the Commanding Officer of the 7th Marine Regiment approved it, but Puller never got it. Instead, he received his third Navy Cross. He spent the next few days taking care of his men. He made sure we went to the river to bathe. We were filthy and for most of us, our socks and underwear had rotted.

The battalion area was a mess, but Puller made no effort to clean it up. One day a young officer, new to the battalion, rounded up some men and went about cleaning up the debris. Puller was sitting in a chair outside his tent and when he stood up, I knew the lieutenant was in trouble.

"Hold on there, Lieutenant. These men are worn out from fever and fighting. Leave 'em alone! If you want this place squared away, you do it."

The lieutenant quickly disappeared. I started to realize that even though Puller was a hard man, it was obvious that he had a sincere interest in the well being of his men. I also realized that both his prior combat experience and his brutal training had saved a lot of our lives. I was forced to admit, however reluctantly, that I admired this tough man. I still did not like him, but I stood in awe of him.

THE CLOSING DAYS OF GUADACANAL

With the battle of Henderson Field over, it was apparent that the U.S. was going to win the larger battle of Guadalcanal. The Americal Division had arrived on the island and Halsey had sent more fighter planes to Henderson Field. The United States was now on the offensive.

In early November Hanneken's 2/7 Battalion patrolled across the Metapona River. He was almost cut off and forced to withdraw back across the river to Koli Point. Colonel Puller's 1/7 and two other battalions were sent out to help him.

When Puller received word to move out he issued orders for rations and extra ammo. He wasted no time in preparation and we hiked at a fast pace to Lunga Point, arriving late in the day. We boarded landing craft and headed toward Koli Point. There was a lot of confusion in the dark and we had a difficult time finding it. The last of the boats unloaded at midnight, and we slept on the beach. Early in the morning we set up a defensive position on the west side of the Nalimbiu River. We stayed there for a few days. We then moved east toward the Metapona River. We were inland and 2/7 was on our left flank moving along the coast. We made it to the west bank of the river in the afternoon, where we dug in for the night. I wish I had a nickel for every hole I dug on that hellish island. I bet it would have funded the rest of my education.

The next morning we crossed the river and walked along the coast while 2/7 was inland, on our right flank. The coast was mostly jungle and swamp with very little beach, so moving was slow and difficult.

Puller was three hundred yards behind the point of his column, with his command group, the radioman, and the Marines who were stringing out the heavy reels of telephone wire. We were moving at a stop and go pace. I was five or six men behind Puller with Pop in back of me. We stopped and I turned around to talk to Pop. He said, "This ground is rougher than a cob." Then the lights went out. I had no idea what happened. The first thing I remember is the smell of burnt powder. I won't forget that smell. Then my eyes began to focus on the smoke. I still couldn't figure out what was going on when I heard someone yell out, "Jesus Christ, we took a direct hit!" It was then that I realized that I was on the ground, and must have been knocked unconscious from the blast. I saw a lot of Marines down, and a few of the corpsmen were working on them. My mind was working in slow motion.

I was lying on my side and crawled over to the Marine in front of me. He was on his back and his shirt was full of blood. I ripped it open and found a terrible chest wound. When his heart pumped, blood flowed out of the wound. I had bandages in my pocket, which I applied to his chest. I pushed down with both hands to try to stop the bleeding. As I kept pushing, I started looking for a corpsman.

A minute later a corpsman came up to me and said, "Forget it. The back of his head is blown off."

I looked around. There were many men on the ground. And then I saw Puller lying there. His legs were covered in blood. After twenty-three years in the Marine Corps his luck had run out. Pop appeared to be in good shape and was working on a wounded Marine behind me.

Puller told the Marine with the field telephone to bring him the phone.

"The wire has been cut, sir," he replied.

Puller crawled over to the line and spliced it together. Among the casualties was the artillery forward observer and many of the communications people. Puller grabbed the phone to call in the artillery, but they were out of range. He then called headquarters to tell them that he was wounded but still in command.

A corpsman came over to patch up his wounds. Puller waved him off, "Take care of the men first."

When the battalion surgeon and the corpsmen had finished treating the wounded they started working on Puller. He was still lying on the ground. He was hit once in the arm and several times in his left leg and foot. There was a good-sized wound in his thigh. The corpsman cut the leg of his trousers and started patching him up. All the while, Puller was on the phone as if nothing was wrong. When the doctor was finished, he told Puller that he would have to be evacuated.

Puller barked, "Like hell! I'm not going anywhere."

It started to get dark and 1/7 dug in for the evening. A couple Marines dug a large hole and helped Puller into it. As the night wore on, however, he realized that he could no longer walk and called Regimental Headquarters, "I am unable to lead my troops. You better send someone to take over."

Colonel Sims called after midnight, "Major Weber, a company commander from 3/7 will be taking over. He will be there first thing in the morning."

Puller replied, "We'll be ready for him."

Weber arrived a little before dawn and assumed command of the battalion.

Landing craft arrived on the coast at daylight to remove the five dead Marines and the twenty-six wounded. Puller wouldn't move until the last man was put on the boat. After everyone was loaded, he looked at Pop and me and said, "Give me a hand."

We pulled him up out of the hole and he put his right arm around my shoulder and his left around Pop as we slowly walked him to the boat.

I could tell he was in a lot of pain but he didn't say a word. We walked about twenty yards and he said, "Hold it."

He turned around. A lot of men were watching him, and he growled, "I'll be back."

The loud cheering of the men continued as we placed him on the boat that would take him down the shore to Kukum inside the perimeter.

Puller was taken to the division hospital where he was operated on. He had seven holes in his arm and leg and the doctor took out all of the shrapnel except for the big piece that was lodged in his thigh. To remove this piece they would have to evacuate Puller from the island. Chesty told them to leave it in.

While Puller was in the hospital, our battalion remained in the Metapona position, but malaria was attacking the men in the 1st Marine Division at an alarming rate: it was doing what the Japanese couldn't do. There were 2,000 cases in October and 3,000 in November. Two of Puller's Company Commanders, Captain Fuller and Captain Moore were so sick that they had to be evacuated from the island.

After almost two weeks, Puller was released from the hospital and took over command of our battalion once again. He came back with a noticeable limp, but as determined as ever. Three days later we moved back to Bloody Ridge and for the first time since mid-October the entire regiment was together. Two hundred new men joined the battalion, which brought us up to full strength.

The first thing Puller did when he returned was visit his men. He had received several bottles of whiskey from his friends in the rear.

"Abbo," he yelled out.

"Yes, sir," I replied.

"Get in here."

"Yes, sir."

"Grab a couple of these whiskey bottles and let's see how the men are doing."

He would give the bottles to the troops and always say the same thing, "Take a little nip and then pass it around."

On Thanksgiving Day there was a feast and we ate the best meal we had on the island. Pop, as always, was in a talkative mood. We were sitting down on a log eating our dinner and Pop said, "I can tell you what my family is doing today. My mother is the oldest of ten children and we always have dinner with her brothers and sisters. We usually eat at our house. It's a real tradition. We eat in three shifts: the children eat first, then the men and the women eat last. There are just too many people to eat all at once. In the morning all the men go hunting and we get back about three o'clock. My mom and my aunts have been cooking for most of the day. This is the second Thanksgiving in a row I've missed."

"Well, Pop, you aren't alone. You have lots of company."

"Yeah, I guess I do. Mike, what's your Thanksgiving like?" asked Pop.

"Pretty much like yours. My mom and aunts do the cooking and we all eat together. It takes us two hours to eat because there is lots of conversation and great food and I miss it as much as you do."

There is something about not being home on a holiday that makes you appreciate the absence of family and friends.

"Mike, how long do you think this damn war is going to last?"

"I don't know any more than you do, Pop. It's a long way to Japan and I think the Japs are going to fight us every inch of the way."

Later that night, Pop and I were cleaning our rifles outside of the tent. It seemed as if we were always cleaning our rifles. There was something ironic about a filth encrusted man cleaning his weapon, but you saw it all the time. While we were at this task, a Marine came up to us and said, "Guess what I found?"

I looked up at him and said, "Well? What?"

"A case of sake."

Pop jumped up, "Where is it?" he asked.

"It's gonna cost you," the Marine said with a smirk.

"How much?" I asked.

"Five bucks a bottle."

"That's ridiculous," I said, "we'll give you five for two bottles."

The Marine thought for a second and then said, "Okay."

"Let's go get it," Pop said eagerly.

"Nothin' doin'," the Marine said, "just give me the money. I don't want you bastards to know where the stash is."

"You show up here with the bottles, pal, and we'll give you the cash," I said.

"I'll be back," he said.

About half an hour later, the Marine returned with two bottles of sake. It was almost dark. Pop took five dollars out of his moldy wallet and handed it to the Marine, who in turn handed him two dirty, unopened bottles of sake.

Pop turned to me and said, "This one's on me."

We went over to our tent, sat on the ground and opened the bottles. I looked at Pop and asked, "Have you ever tried this stuff before?"

"Nope."

"Neither have I," I said, "and here's to ya."

We raised our bottles and took a big gulp at the same time. When it hit my throat, it burned like hell.

"Jesus Christ, this stuff is awful," I said.

Pop's facial expression said it all, but he remained ever optimistic, "I've had worse," he said.

The second and third swigs went down a little easier. With each gulp the bitter taste and burn grew more tolerable. Pop and I leaned back against a log and stretched our legs.

Pop broke the silence first, "So, Abbo, when was the last time you got laid?" he asked.

I would have been more surprised at the question, but this was Pop, after all.

"Well, let's see," I answered, taking a drink from the bottle, "it's been so long, I can't remember back that far."

"Well, the last time for me," he said, "was in Portsmouth, Ohio. I used to frequent a whorehouse there quite a bit. It's called Mabel's – it's a real dive but I used to run booze there so they treated me alright."

Once again, I was intrigued with one of Pop's tales.

He took a couple more sips from the bottle and continued, "So I was home on leave last year and decided to stop by. I was upstairs having a grand time with a real beauty. We had just finished and were smoking a cigarette when we heard a racquet going on downstairs."

"I just thought it was another brawl, being Saturday night at all, but then suddenly someone started pounding on the door yelling, 'This is the police! Open up!'"

"Well, I couldn't have any more run-ins with the law after my moonshine incident, so I quickly pulled on my clothes, grabbed my shoes and socks, and opened the window, which got stuck and only went up halfway."

"A second later, a big, fat cop breaks the door open and runs toward me. I started to squeeze through the half-open window. Before I could get onto the fire escape, the cop grabbed a hold of a leg of my pants. I squirmed out of them, grabbed my keys and wallet, climbed down the fire escape and soon realized the cop was too fat to get through the window. I ran down the alley in my underwear, hopped in my truck and drove away."

A huge grin appeared on Pop's face and he said, "That cop got my pants, but at least I kept my honor."

"Well, some guys have all the luck," I replied.

We had a good laugh and drank more of the sake.

"Let's see, it was New Year's Eve of my freshman year. I'd been dating this girl from Chicago for a few months. Things had been progressing quite nicely.

"At about two in the morning, I took her back to her house. We'd had quite a bit to drink and our judgment wasn't the best. It was snowing like hell that night. I parked on the street and walked her to the house.

"We ended up in her bedroom, and before I could even get my coat off, I heard someone coming down the hall. She whispered, 'Quick, get in the closet.' Then I heard the bedroom door open, the light went on and her father said, 'What the hell is going on here?'

"She immediately answered, 'Nothing.'

"It was quiet for a few seconds, and then the closet door flew open. Her father was a big man and he grabbed me by the coat collar, almost lifting me off the ground. He jerked me out of the closet, dragged me through the hallway and down the stairs. He opened the front door and gave me such a hard kick in the ass, it sent me flying head first into the snow.

"Then he yelled, 'Don't you ever come back here, you little bastard!' When I got up I heard the door slam behind me."

Pop was howling with laughter, holding his sides, trying to catch his breath.

I started laughing too. I looked up at him and said, "You know what? That night I kept my pants, but I'm not so sure about my honor."

When Pop stopped laughing he asked, "How did he know you were in the closet?"

"The melting snow from my shoes led him right to me," I said.

I don't know when we went to sleep that night, but the sake was all gone.

The next thing I remembered someone was kicking my boots. Hard. So hard I felt it in my head. Then a roaring voice increased my pain, "Abbo! Hayes! Get your asses up!"

It took a while to register, but I soon realized that it was Puller. Pop and I gingerly crawled backwards out of our shelter half tent. We must have looked like hell. We tried the best we could to stand at attention.

Puller was sucking on his pipe, and he pulled out two letters.

"Here, take these letters to headquarters to be mailed," he barked, handing a letter to each of us, "and make it quick!"

"Yes, sir."

As I tried to clear the cobwebs, I began to worry about the situation. "Pop, do you think he knows we were drinking?" I asked.

"Well hell yes he does, genius. Didn't you see the bottles on the ground in front of the tent?" Pop said.

"Ah, hell," I replied, "well why do we both have to take these letters?"

"Isn't it obvious, Mikey?" Pop answered, "He's mad. His runners are screw offs."

We avoided Puller all day and didn't see him again until right before chow. It had been a long day trying to recover from our hangovers. As we were walking from our tent to the chow line, Puller approached us.

"Well, you boys look a little better than you did this morning. I was afraid you might be coming down with the malaria or something," he said.

"No sir, we're fine," Pop said quickly.

I just nodded my head and fell into line behind Pop, hoping Puller wouldn't say anything more.

For the first time since joining the battalion in February, I noticed that Puller was much more at ease. The tough training and savage fighting were over, for now. Puller was now focused on taking care of his men. More supplies were coming onto the island and so the food improved and we were given new clothing because ours had rotted. Many of the men were sick and had to be evacuated.

Puller's leadership style was different from most of the other officers. Although he was tough, he was not a bully. When in the field he never used the privileges of his rank that he was entitled to. He liked working with and talking with his men. He was always approachable but no one got too close. There was warmth to him that I hadn't seen before and I was finding it hard not to like him.

One day I was bathing and washing my clothes in the river with a lot of other Marines and Puller appeared. He stripped down, walked into the river and started washing his clothes like the rest of us. It was easy to see his wounds. I also noticed the eagle, globe and anchor tattooed on his arm. At times like this I felt like he was more like an NCO than an officer. It wasn't hard to understand why the men liked him: he had the common touch.

Around this time Puller promoted Sergeant Major Frank Sheppard to lieutenant. I wondered how it felt to go from the top of the enlisted ranks to the bottom of the officer ranks. I was promoted to the rank of corporal and Pop to sergeant.

The day before Christmas the 7th Marines were relieved by the Army. Our days on the island were almost over. On New Year's Eve Puller told Pop and me that he was ordered back to the States by General George Marshall, the Army Chief of Staff. He wanted Puller and several other combat leaders to visit Army bases in the States and tell the soldiers about Guadalcanal and the Japanese. He thanked us and said he'd be back in three to four months. Puller flew out the next morning. Our battalion had lost eighty-nine killed, 156 wounded and four men missing in action.

Somehow, Puller affected me in the way I thought about battles. The casualties, the blood and gore, the incoming fire, and the noise and horror were all reduced to numbers. The Marines lost a total of 1,152 men killed and 2,799 wounded.

AUSTRALIA

On January 5, 1943 the entire regiment boarded the same ships that had brought us to Guadalcanal in September. Getting on board was no easy task because we had to climb the cargo nets to the decks of the ships. The Marines and corpsmen were weak from disease, fighting and malnutrition and many needed help climbing the nets. Although life on the crowded transports was never pleasant, this time was an exception. After three and a half months on the island, the ship was like a slice of heaven.

Our destination was Melbourne, Australia. Melbourne was located around a large harbor with many protected areas and beaches that would be suitable for amphibious training. After Guadalcanal I thought that Melbourne was the most beautiful city I'd ever seen. We cruised into the harbor on a warm, sunny morning.

There was a brand new hospital staffed by an American unit from Cleveland, Ohio. They had everything except patients, but the 1st Marine Division would soon take care of that problem.

When we unloaded from the ships, many of the men needed help disembarking. With the heavy weight of the packs and equipment we were unable to decelerate as we came down the steep, slanted gangway. We were sicker than we looked. Although we didn't realize it at the time, Melbourne would be the only pleasant experience in a very long war for the Marines of the 1st Marine Division. Our regiment was sent to Balcombe, a beautiful suburban area on the bay.

The leaders of the division wanted to get us well again so they could put us back into the fight. We were taken off the routine dose of Atabrine and malaria recurred in increasing numbers. Two weeks after we landed in Melbourne I was walking down a street with Pop. I had been feeling terrible for the past few days and suddenly got dizzy and passed out. I woke up in the hospital operated by the Cleveland Medical unit.

For the first two weeks I was very sick and slept a lot and don't remember much. Everything seemed to be just a blur of conversation and doctors and nurses going back and forth. I was in a ward with about twenty other Marines and next to me was a crusty old Marine whom I knew must be a gunnery sergeant because I heard someone call him "Gunny."

At the start of the third week he looked over at me and said, "Hey kid, you don't say much. What unit are you with?"

"I'm with the 1/7, Gunny. How about you?"

"I'm with 1/5."

"How do you like Melbourne?" I asked.

"Haven't seen much of it. When I got here I came down with malaria."

At the end of the week I was feeling better and several members of our ward were given liberty but we had to report back by eight o'clock that night.

The gunny and I put on our uniforms and left the hospital, jumped into a cab and he yelled "Flinders Street."

The cab dropped us off and we walked into a bar. It was ten o'clock in the morning and the bar was empty except for the bartender.

The bartender came up and said, "What can I get you fellows?"

The gunny said, "Bring us a couple of beers."

When the beers arrived he picked up his beer, looked at me and said, "Cheers. So you with Chesty Puller's outfit?"

"Yep," I said.

"What company?"

"I'm with Headquarters. I'm one of Chesty's runners," I said.

"Well, kid you must have seen a lot of action."

"Gunny, you know Chesty Puller?"

"I was with him down in the banana country."

"What's the banana country?" I asked.

The gunny laughed and said "Nicaragua! I arrived in the country in February of '30. I was a corporal then and Chesty was a lieutenant. We served with the Guardia National."

"What's that?"

"The Guardia was led by Marine officers and NCOs. The bulk of the Guardia came from the local population. I was assigned to Company M, which was commanded by Chesty. The second in command was Gunny Bill Lee. We worked out of a town called Jinotego. Our responsibility was to track down the guerrilla bandits led by Augusto Sandino. Most of our time was spent in the field chasing them. We always moved on foot with our supplies loaded on pack mules. Between February and August we were involved in a bunch of fights and frequently ambushed. We lived off the land and followed the bandits wherever they went. We didn't carry radios so there was no communication and if we got into trouble we were pretty much on our own. Chesty and Lee were tough and aggressive as hell. Puller was awarded his first Navy Cross for his leadership in five fights against the bandits. Lee also got a Navy Cross.

"In June of 1931 Chesty was ordered to Army Infantry School. He left with the Nicaraguan Presidential Medal of Merit, the country's highest decoration. And that ain't all. The local people gave him the nickname El Tigre or the Tiger of the Mountains."

The gunny downed the rest of his beer, turned to the bartender and said, "How about two more?"

"Was that the only time you served with Chesty?" I asked.

"Nope. After infantry school, the situation in Nicaragua got worse, and Chesty was sent back there in July of '32. He was a first lieutenant by then."

The bartender put the beers on the table and the gunny took a big drink before he continued.

"In September, Chesty, Bill Lee and forty of us headed north to pursue Sandino. We had the mules loaded with thirty days of rations. A couple days out someone took a shot at us. This put us on alert, and we crossed a stream and moved uphill. We had walked into an ambush. A machine gun opened up on the front of the column. I saw Gunny Lee go down. I thought he was dead.

"The bandits were hitting us with dynamite bombs, rifle grenades and automatic weapons. The fight had been going on for fifteen minutes when Lee regained consciousness. He ripped the Lewis machine gun off the pack mule, set it up and opened fire on those bastards. Now we had the momentum. Chesty jumped up and charged uphill toward the bandits, with us following. When we got to the top of the hill they scattered. They had ten men killed and I'm sure we wounded a boatload of them. We had four men wounded and one killed. We carried the wounded and headed back to Jinotego. Bill Lee, while not in great shape, because of a head wound and a bullet in the arm, walked.

"Four days later we were ambushed again and Bill Lee opened up with his Lewis gun and the bandits took off. Company M pulled into Jinotego in early October. In his report Chesty called Gunny Lee an "Iron Man." "The name stuck and Lee would forever be known as 'Iron Man Lee.' Puller and Lee each got another Navy Cross. Chesty's second and Lee's third.

"Right before Christmas, Company M had another mission. The Nicaraguan President wanted to dedicate the new railroad between Leon and El Sauce and he was afraid that Sandino was going to cause trouble. Puller was told to take his men to El Sauce to protect the area until after the celebration. Chesty, Lee and sixty of us boarded a train in Managua and headed for El Sauce. A couple miles from El Sauce about 250 bandits attacked us. We jumped off the train and started shooting. The fight lasted over an hour. We killed thirty-one of them, and we lost three. It was one of the biggest fights of the war. The President of Nicaragua was so pleased with Chesty that he promoted him on the spot to the rank of Major in the Guardia. On January 2nd 1933, all the Marines left Nicaragua for good.

"But when Chesty left Nicaragua he was not only known as one of the Corp's top jungle fighters but also one of the best patrol leaders in the Corps. And it was here in Nicaragua that I first heard people refer to him as Chesty."

The stories and the beer kept flowing. I do remember eating something for lunch. What time I left the bar or how I got back to the hospital is a mystery. But when I woke up in my bed in the hospital the next morning, I was still wearing my uniform and I had the worst headache of my life. The Gunny's voice only made it worse.

"You don't drink much, do you kid?"

I didn't answer.

I was shocked to learn that the hospital was so full of malaria cases that they had to spread the Marines out all over the city. It was later reported that the admission rate for malaria went as high as seventy-five percent of the 1st Marine Division.

At the beginning of the fourth week I was released from the hospital. I never saw the gunny again.

When I returned to our camp on the outskirts of Melbourne, the first person I ran in to was Pop.

He greeted me in typical fashion, "Well, well, look who's back. You were gone so long we thought you went home."

"I wish," I mumbled.

"Come on now, Mikey, this sure beats the hell out of a bug-infested jungle where we get shelled by the Jap Navy every night. Plus, I met a peach of an Aussie girl who just might have a friend or two who is desperate enough to go out with you."

"Okay, lover boy, count me in," I answered.

Pop smiled, very pleased with himself.

The Marines were warmly received by the Australians and we marveled at how similar they were to us. It was summer when we arrived and although Australia was a foreign land, it soon became a familiar one. We were welcomed in the pubs with the pungent smells of beer and tobacco. Friendly accents greeted us at every turn. Melbourne was a bustling city with quaint Victorian buildings and beautiful gardens. I was happy in Australia although so many miles from home; just being in a city again made me homesick. We soon adopted the Australian folk song "Waltzing Mathilda" as the division's unofficial theme song. For now, I had escaped the war.

It was at this time that Pop introduced me to Maggie. She was a beautiful red-headed girl, with deep blue-green eyes, fair skin and a smile that was hard to resist. After the introduction was made, Pop said that he and his girlfriend Mary, an acquaintance of Maggie's, were off to the movies. We were on our own.

I looked at Maggie, "What would you like to do tonight?" I asked, trying to hide my awkwardness, "After all, this is your city."

"Actually, I'm from Brisbane," she said. "With all the men in the war, I have a temporary government job down here. But I know a charming pub nearby where we could have a few pints and a nice dinner."

I hadn't been out with a woman in over a year, and I had an incredible time with Maggie. Just before midnight, she told me that it was getting late, and she should be getting home.

We walked about three blocks until we arrived at Maggie's door.

"Well Maggie, I had a wonderful time tonight, and I hope I get to see you again," I said.

I was surprised when she leaned in and kissed me, and shocked when she grabbed my hand with both of hers, pulled me close and said, "Come on in, Yank. I'm as lonely as you are."

From that night on, every opportunity I had was spent with Maggie. Over the next six weeks we went to the movies, took long walks through pristine parks, went to dances, and dined in local restaurants. I was having a marvelous time.

One night I showed up at Maggie's apartment. She answered the door crying.

"What's wrong?" I asked.

"I have to go home to Brisbane," she answered.

"What? Why?" I asked.

"My husband's been wounded. He's in a hospital there."

I was stunned. I slowly turned and walked off the porch. As I headed down the street I thought to myself, life is full of surprises!

When Puller arrived in Australia at the beginning of April 1943, he discovered that he was no longer commander of his battalion but now the regimental operations officer. A week later he was hit with malaria and ended up spending several weeks in the hospital.

When he was released, he found himself promoted to the executive officer of the 7th Marines. In June and July the leadership of the 1st Marine Division changed. General Rupertus took over command of the division and General Vandegrift left and would soon become Commandant of the Marine Corps. Julian "Bull" Frisbie became the new CO of the 7th Marines.

One afternoon, Pop and I were waiting in line to go into the PX, the Post Exchange. There was a long line and Chesty showed up and spotted a second lieutenant near the front. He walked up to him and said in his usually gruff voice, "Lieutenant, end of the line!" Chesty had wrongly assumed that this lieutenant had pulled rank on everyone and that is how he ended up at the front. But the lieutenant had started at the back and worked his way to the head of the line.

I said to Pop later, "No one told Puller that he had made a mistake."

Pop said, "Of course not. Who in their right mind is going to correct a Marine colonel, especially Chesty Puller?"

Our wonderful time in Australia was coming to an end. The malaria was under control and the men had gained back the weight they had lost and finally the division was healthy again. We were scheduled to attack the western end of the large of island of New Britain in December 1943.

As the day for the invasion approached, Pop and I once again became Puller's runners, and spent the remaining days with him. A few days before we left, Puller was approached by Major Ray Davis, a Puller student from the Basic School in the 1930's, who was now in command of the 1st Special Weapons Battalion.

"Sir," said Davis, "my batteries are being doled out to the regiments and I'm supposed to remain behind. I would like to go with you."

Puller looked at him and said, "I'll tell you old man, it's a hell of a note when a man wants to go to war and no one will let him. We'll put you on the roster!"

We would land on December 26, 1943 on the western end of New Britain at a place called Cape Gloucester.

The purpose of the New Britain landing was to isolate Rabaul, a large Japanese base on the eastern end of the island. The goal was not to occupy it but to destroy it by massive amounts of bombing. This would save both lives and material.

The 1st Marine Division's main objective would be the capture of two Japanese airfields at Cape Gloucester, on the western end of New Britain.

Before we sailed, Frisbie, Puller and the command group reviewed the plans for the landing: The 7th Marines would land at Yellow Beach, the 1st Marines would follow Frisbie's 7th Marines ashore and lead the assault against the airfields. The 5th Marines would serve as division reserve. The 1st and 3rd Battalions of the 7th Marines would land first and the 2nd Battalion would stay in reserve.

One hundred thousand Japanese soldiers were waiting for us to invade Rabaul, but we weren't going there.

Chapter Three

New Britain

This is a heck of a way to start the New Year. We landed on this island five days ago. It hasn't stopped raining. We're starting to call this place 'The Green Inferno'. There is mold everywhere. My boots, socks and clothing are starting to rot. The mud is so deep, we can hardly walk through it. The jungle is teeming with snakes and bugs. The officers are as miserable as we are.

M. Abbo, letter to parents, 31 Dec 1943

A PERFECT LANDING

We finished packing the transport ships at Cape Sudest, New Guinea, on Christmas Eve, 1943. It felt like it had taken weeks to load the ships, which seemed to be busting at the seams. Puller, Pop and I and most of the regimental command were aboard LST 67.

We sailed from New Guinea before dawn on Christmas morning. Some of the men began to sing traditional carols but given the discomfort of the overly loaded ships, the unbearable heat and knowing we were heading into harm's way, it was hard to be jovial. It was not how I wanted to spend my Christmas morning.

It was a short trip to Cape Gloucester and I was sitting up on deck cleaning my rifle and getting my gear ready. Most of the Marines onboard were doing the same.

A Marine sitting next to me said, "I sure miss home, especially on this day."

Pop put his rifle down and said, "I've been waiting all morning – what I want to know is when you cheap bastards are going to give me a present?"

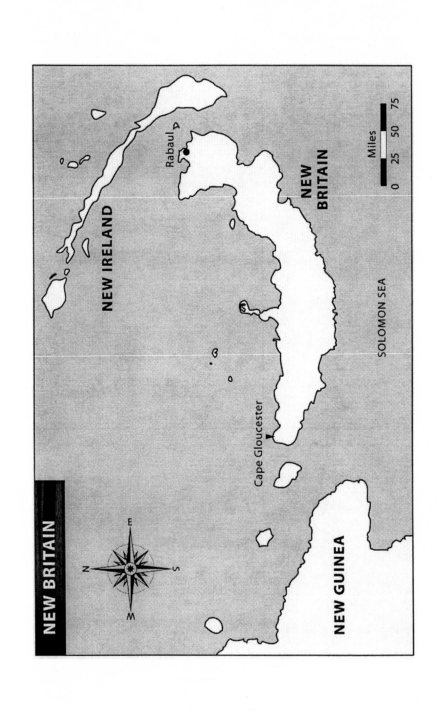

NEW BRITAIN

I reached into my pack, pulled out a pair of dirty socks and held them up to him and said, "Pop, how about a pair of socks?"

"If they was clean, Abbo, I sure would take 'em."

Then Pop said, "This is the third Christmas in a row that I haven't been home. You'd sure as hell think the Marine Corps would let us spend Christmas in some nice place instead of this stinking ship."

I said, "Pop, the Marine Corps wants to keep you lean and mean. If they sent you some place nice for the holidays, I think they'd be afraid that you'd come back fat and happy."

Army pilots had been blasting the island for weeks. It was decided we would come ashore at Silimati Point, now called Yellow Beach, which lay about seven miles southeast of the airfields. I spent Christmas night mostly thinking about my family, and trying to fight the inescapable heat.

Cape Gloucester came into view early on the morning of December 26th. As the sun was rising on another clear, hot day, the Cape was blanketed by the thick smoke of aerial bombs and naval gunfire. At 7:45 am the 1st and 3rd Battalions of the 7th Marines stormed ashore and met little opposition. The Marines soon figured out why. Beyond the narrow beach was a swamp that was six feet deep in many places. The few defenders quickly disappeared into the jungle.

The Marines slowly worked their way through the swamp. Some fell into deep water holes created by the aerial attacks. Many trees had been toppled in the blasts, and were easily knocked over if you leaned on them. An hour later the 2nd Battalion had landed and taken over the center of the regimental zone. Frisbie, Puller, Pop and I and the command group landed at this time. 1/7 moved slowly east, and fought the Japanese on their flanks, destroying a small force and two field guns. Before the morning was over, the battalion captured Target Hill, which was the highest point in the region.

To the west 3/7 met little resistance. Approximately eleven thousand Marines landed at Cape Gloucester that day. The division had executed the most nearly perfect amphibious assault of World War II.

That night, the Japanese attacked the center of the perimeter and hit 2/7. It started raining hard and the night turned into total blackness. Frisbie told Puller to get reinforcements and ammo up to 2/7. Puller rounded up some people from headquarters, and men from other units and he lead us across that awful swamp. It was deep, and sometimes the water would go up above your shoulders. You could not see the man in front of you, but you could hear him. It took us about a half an hour to cross. I don't know what kind of creatures swam by us and I don't ever want to know. We finally reached dry ground and delivered the ammo. After sunrise the Japanese pulled away leaving behind their dead.

Over the next two days the Japanese attacked a few times but they were just small probes. Colonel Frisbie gave Puller a lot of responsibility because he was always up front.

During the first seventy-two hours the 7th Marines lost eighteen killed, fifty-eight wounded and three missing.

On December 29th the 5th Marines landed and supported the 1st Marines. The next morning the Marines had control of both landing strips.

Early that evening, Pop and I were waiting outside the regimental command post when the Japanese started shelling us. The CP took a direct hit. Four Marines were killed and seven wounded. Puller walked out without a scratch.

The division was now in two different locations. The 1st Marines and the 5th Marines minus 3/5 were located by the airstrips and the 7th Marines and 3/5 were near Target Hill. Because the division was split up, General Rupertus gave the Assistant Division Commander (ADC) General Lem Shepherd command of the combined forces of the 7th Marines and 3/5.

SUICIDE CREEK

On New Year's Day 1944, General Shepherd sent his troops southeast toward Borgen Bay. The following day 3/7 ran into a broad, shallow jungle stream which blocked their advance. It was twenty feet wide with high banks on each side. The jungle was so thick you couldn't see ahead more than ten feet. 3/5 joined them on their right. The Japanese were dug in on the other side. As the Marines of 3/7 tried to cross they were shot down.

General Shepherd needed more firepower to break the stalemate, but his tanks could not move through the thick, stinking mud. Shepherd ordered his engineers to build "a corduroy road" out of logs through the swamp so the tanks could move forward. But now the Marines had to cross the creek.

3/5 crossed the creek upstream in the afternoon and made contact with the enemy. The CO of K Company 3/7 called in to report that he was tied in with 3/5 but Lieutenant Colonel McDougal said there was no one on his left flank. A gap opened between the two battalions.

I was standing outside the command post when Frisbie and Puller came out. Frisbie looked at Puller and said, "Lewie, get some more firepower down at that creek and then go on down there and find out what's going on."

"Yes, sir," replied Puller.

Frisbie went back into the CP and Puller got in a jeep and signaled for Pop and me to get in. We drove over to the regimental weapons company, which was commanded by a mustang Captain, Joe Buckley. A mustang in the Corps is an ex-enlisted man.

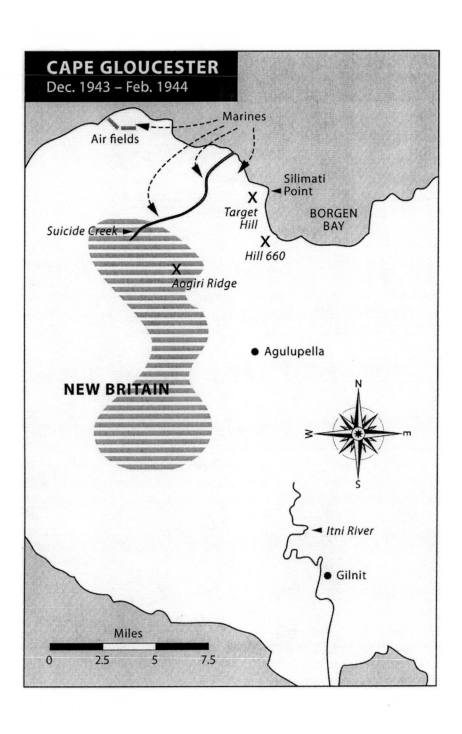

CAPE GLOUCESTER
Dec. 1943 – Feb. 1944

Air fields

Marines

Silimati
Point

Target
Hill

BORGEN
BAY

X

X
Hill 660

Suicide Creek

X
Aogiri Ridge

● Agulupella

NEW BRITAIN

N
W   E
S

◄ Itni River

● Gilnit

Miles

0   2.5   5   7.5

We pulled up and Buckley saw Puller and said, "Afternoon, Colonel."

Puller wasted no time, "Joe we need halftracks. We're having trouble crossing that damned creek."

"How many do you need, Colonel?" Buckley asked.

"Send us four of them if you can. I'll be down there waiting."

"Aye, aye, sir," Buckley answered.

We jumped back into the jeep and drove down the bumpy corduroy road. It was a very unpleasant ride. When we got within 100 yards of the creek Puller yelled out "Hold it."

He jumped out and we followed him. He talked to the CO of K Company. The halftracks arrived a few minutes later but could not cross the creek. Their 75 mm guns had no effect on the Japanese.

The attack was stalled and Puller got into the jeep and we drove back to the Regimental CP. Puller was back there ten minutes when Frisbie gave him the order to continue the attack immediately. We drove back to the creek and Puller relieved the K Company Commander, for both his inaccurate reporting and his failure to advance. Puller appointed a new commander and before it got dark part of K Company had crossed but most of 3/7 remained on the west side of the creek.

Later that night, Puller spoke to the CO of 3/7, Lieutenant Colonel Williams. Puller said, "How many men did you lose?"

"Colonel," replied Williams, "we lost eighty-eight men trying to cross that damned creek. My men are all calling that deathtrap, 'Suicide Creek.'"

The next day, 3/7 advanced slowly and only half of the battalion had crossed the creek. Puller was back in the CP and Frisbie was unhappy with the progress, so he told Puller to go to K Company and get them moving.

When Puller, Pop and I arrived at the creek, he spoke to Williams and the CO of K Company. After he looked over the terrain Puller told the two commanders, "I think we can cross this damn creek right here but the banks are too steep. Get me a bulldozer and we'll cut the banks down. There is a dozer back there working on the road."

A few minutes later the bulldozer arrived. The driver jumped off and Puller told him to follow him. They moved cautiously toward the creek and took cover behind a tree.

Puller put his hand on the man's shoulder and said, "We can't get the tanks and halftracks across this creek until we cut these banks down. It's a dangerous job but we gotta get across. There's no other way to do it."

"Yes, sir," the driver nodded.

They both walked back to the dozer and the driver climbed on.

Puller looked at Williams and said, "Tell your Marines to pour it on and keep him covered."

The Marines started firing into the jungle across the creek and the dozer started to cut down the bank. A minute later the driver was shot by a sniper. Several Marines rushed out and pulled him off the dozer. Another engineer took over. He jumped on and soon he was shot.

Another Marine engineer showed up. The Marine engineers had no shortage of courage or imagination. Puller said, "Hold up."

The engineer looked at Puller. He had a shovel and an axe handle in his hands and said, "Sir, I think I can move the controls with these handles and at the same time protect myself."

Puller gave this Marine a strange look. I am sure Puller thought he had seen everything after twenty-five years in the Marine Corps, but obviously this was something new. He finally said, "All right, Marine, give it a try."

The engineer ran over to the dozer, which was still running, and crouched down, staying out of the line of fire. He started to move the controls with the shovel and axe handle, and began to slowly cut down the bank.

A few minutes later, Puller said to himself, "That is the damnedest thing I have ever seen." It was raining and Puller had his pipe in his mouth and he turned it upside down to keep the tobacco dry. He reached in his back pocket and pulled out a pouch of tobacco. He got a disgusted look on his face as he squeezed the pouch and water ran out of it. He threw it on the ground, but he still kept the pipe clenched between his teeth.

All the while the Japanese were firing at the driver, and you could hear the rounds hitting the dozer. In thirty minutes or so he had the near bank cut down and crossed the creek and began cutting into the far bank. Slowly and carefully he took down the bank, and in another thirty minutes both banks were cut down.

He backed the dozer up to the near bank where Puller was and got it out of the way so the tanks and halftracks could get by. By this time, darkness had set in and Puller put the Marines into the defense. Afterward, he walked up to the driver, who was standing by the bulldozer and asked, "Where in the hell did you learn that trick?"

"Back home, sir," he answered.

"Well, great work, old man," Puller replied.

Puller then walked over to the two wounded Marines who were lying on the ground and were being treated by a corpsman. He bent over and said "You are two gutsy Marines" and then he looked at the corpsman and said, "Doc, take good care of these men."

That night Puller called his people together and gave them their orders. The three Sherman tanks and halftracks would cross the creek in the morning. Puller looked at Captain Buckley and said, "When you cross that creek tomorrow, blast the hell out of them. Go in between 3/7 and 3/5. K Company 3/7 will mass behind you when you cross."

The 7th Marines had lost eighty-seven men that day and 3/5 had lost fifty-eight.

The next morning the tanks and half-tracks roared across the creek and blew away three bunkers. After that, the Japanese withdrew and the Marines advanced rapidly.

THE TRIFECTA

While Lieutenant Colonel Williams waited for 3/5 to catch up with his battalion, Colonel Frisbie told him he was relieved and that Puller would temporarily replace him. Frisbie didn't think he was aggressive enough.

When Puller got the word late that afternoon from Frisbie that he was in command of 3/7, we drove up to where 3/7 was located. Puller called the company commanders in and as usual he got right to the point.

"I'm taking over. The Colonel has been relieved. You can bet on one thing; I have no intention of being relieved. With the tanks we have the fire power and we're going to attack in the morning. I want you to blow your way through those bastards. Make their lives hell!"

It rained hard that night. It had not stopped raining since we landed on the island. Pop and I dug a hole and then Pop made a lean-to out of some big sticks and then he put his poncho over it. Then we both climbed in the hole and wrapped my poncho around us. Even thought we were in the tropics, our wet clothes made us cold.

I said, "Pop, I just can't get warm. I'm shivering like crazy."

"I'll tell you what Mike; I'll bet them Japs are hurting more than we are."

On January 5th, Colonel Frisbie told Puller that the regimental intelligence section had captured a Japanese document that ordered Aogiri Ridge to be held at all costs and there was a rough sketch of the hill. The only problem was no one knew where it was. So, naturally, Puller went looking for it.

The next two days we made little progress and it rained hard both days. We were miserable. My whole body was waterlogged. Late in the afternoon of the second day 3/5 ran into trouble and a dozen men were wounded, half of them officers, including Lieutenant Colonel McDougal and his XO. Shortly before dark, Frisbie gave Puller command of 3/5 until the arrival of a replacement. Puller was now wearing three hats: The XO of the 7th Marines, and the CO of both 3/7 and 3/5. He had won the Marine Corps trifecta.

We followed Puller over to 3/5 but when we got there all the phone lines were down. By this time it was dark and Puller told me I'd have to report back to regiment.

He said, "Tell Colonel Frisbie that 3/5's phones are out and we will stay put until we get further orders. Pop, you stay here with me. And Abbo see it you can get me some tobacco."

I left immediately and knew that regimental headquarters was located somewhere to our rear. It took a while to find the command post in the dark. I walked along the corduroy road and finally got there after about forty-five minutes. I had to be careful of Japanese who might have gotten behind our lines and also the men in the rear who might mistake me for a Jap.

I reported to Colonel Frisbie. When I entered the command post and gave him Puller's message he said, "This is Lieutenant Colonel Walt. He is taking over 3/5 tomorrow. I want you to guide him to Colonel Puller's position first thing in the morning so he can take over. It's too late tonight. We'll wait till daylight."

"Yes, sir," I said. "Sir, Colonel Puller wanted to know if it was possible if he could get some tobacco."

"I'll see what I can do," Frisbie replied.

"Thank you, sir," I said, and left the tent.

Early the next morning, I met Lieutenant Colonel Walt outside of Colonel Frisbie's CP. We were waiting for the jeep to drive us up to Puller.

I said, "Good morning, sir."

Walt replied, "Morning. How long have you been Colonel Puller's runner?"

"Since Guadalcanal, sir."

"Well you're in good company, Corporal. He taught me in Basic School."

"Yes, sir."

Just then, Colonel Frisbie walked out of the tent and handed me two pouches of tobacco.

"Make sure Colonel Puller gets his tobacco," he said with a slight smile, "and tell him I'm not the damn PX."

"Yes, sir, thank you, sir," I replied.

The jeep drove up and Walt sat in the front while I climbed in the back. I was to soon find out Lewis Walt was cut from the same cloth as Puller. The two of them would remain lifelong friends.

When we drove to the CP of 3/5 Puller was outside talking to some of the men. When he saw us drive up he walked over to the jeep and greeted Walt.

"Welcome to 3/5, Lew," he said.

"Thank you, Colonel," said Walt. "Can you fill me in on what is going on?"

Puller said, "Follow me."

They walked as far forward as they could without getting shot and crouched behind a large tree.

Puller told him, "We're in a tough position Lew. They got snipers up in the trees and the ground is loaded with machine guns."

They finished the conversation and began to walk back to the CP. I then walked up to Puller and handed him the tobacco.

"Thank you, Abbo," he said.

"Sir, there's a message from Colonel Frisbie."

"What's that?" he asked.

"Sir, he said to tell you he's not the damn PX."

Puller just smiled and began reloading his pipe.

Walt took over 3/5 and Puller went back to 3/7.

AOGIRI RIDGE

The Marines went looking for Aogiri Ridge, hidden somewhere in the thick jungle where intelligence knew the Japanese were waiting. 3/5 was advancing slowly through the dense jungle when the ground started to rise upward. They had found the base of Aogiri Ridge, and the rain continued.

Puller's 3/7 moved around the left of the hill and met no resistance. Walt's Marines lost fifteen killed and 161 wounded as the Japanese beat back attack after attack. Late in the day, due to heavy losses, Frisbie attached two of Puller's companies to Walt.

On January 9th, Lieutenant Colonel Henry Buse, Jr. took command of 3/7 from Puller. Now Chesty was again the full time XO of the 7th Marines.

That afternoon 3/5 was running out of steam but had a 37mm anti-tank gun that had been brought forward. Walt yelled for Marines to push the gun up the steep hill. No one moved. Walt had just taken over; they were exhausted, and maneuvering the gun up the hill would be a sure way to die. There were no volunteers so Walt and his runner put their shoulders to the wheels and started shoving the gun up the hill. They would stop every few feet to fire. When the Marines of 3/5 saw the tremendous courage of their new CO they rushed to help push the gun up the hill. As men were shot, they were replaced by others and the big gun slowly moved up the hill, until they reached the top. It was then dark.

Walt's men held the top of the ridge. He ordered his men to dig in and get ready for an attack. The Japanese were only yards away. That night, with the help of supporting artillery, Walt beat back five vicious bayonet attacks through a driving rain. When morning came the fighting was over, with more than 200 Japanese bodies littering the ground. General Shepherd renamed the ridge

'Walt's Ridge,' and that morning Lew Walt was added to the list of Marine legends. He was also awarded the Navy Cross for his aggressive leadership.

The final Marine objective was Hill 660. Lieutenant Colonel Buse's 3/7 took two days to seize the hill and by the 16th the battle for Cape Gloucester was almost over.

The next day, General Rupertus moved the 7th Marines to the airfield and replaced them with the 5th Marines. A few days later the weather changed and we had ten days of dry weather.

It was during this time that Frisbie recommended Puller for his fourth Navy Cross for taking command of the two stalled infantry battalions and moving them forward. No other Marine had ever won four Navy crosses. Life around the airfield was much better now with the dry weather, and while the Japanese would shell us, at least we were out of the jungle.

One night after chow, I asked Pop about his life back home, "So you spent your nights running moonshine for your uncle? What did you do during the day?"

"My uncle also had a stable of fighting cocks and I took care of them: trained and fought them," Pop answered nonchalantly.

"Pop, are you serious or what?" I asked incredulously.

"Yes," he said. "I trained and fought all kinds of birds. Red Quills, Irish Grays, and Round Heads, but we only fought the males, obviously."

"Was this legal in Kentucky?" I asked.

"Hell, no, and it wasn't legal in Ohio either, and that's where we held the fights. There is a little town southwest of Portsmouth, and we had a lot of the fights there. They usually were on the weekends and we fought the birds in the winter because they molt in the summertime.

"There was a big barn and the guys who ran the operation built bleachers for spectators and in the center, a ring of hay bales was formed and inside this the birds would fight. There was usually a pretty big crowd, maybe two hundred people, and of course, there was a lot of betting going on."

I looked at Pop and asked, "What about the cops?"

He smiled. "I'm sure there were some payments made to keep the authorities away, or at least tolerant. As far as I can remember, the place never got raided."

"Are these birds natural fighters?" I asked.

"For the most part, yes, but I spent a lot of time conditioning them. The cocks are usually about one-and-half to two years old before they can fight. Roosters have a natural spur on the backs of their legs and you cut these off and leave a stump. Over the stump you put a gaff, which is one-and-a-quarter to two-and-an-eighth inches long. This gaff that goes over the stump is hollow and tied on to the leg with a piece of leather.

"The gaff has a sharp point on it and the cock jumps in the air and slashes down with the back of his leg. This action is what kills or hurts his opponent."

I thought Pop was pulling my leg, but through the tone of his voice and the sincerity of his eyes, realized that he was serious. Cockfighting was actually one of Pop's unconventional passions. So I asked him "Do you have to train these birds?"

"Sure, I'll usually put a piece of carpet on a board and run the bird back and forth on the board between my outstretched hands. This builds endurance. The next thing I do is throw the bird up in the air and try to get him to land on his feet. This creates balance. There is a helluva lot of work involved in conditioning these birds."

As usual, Pop's story began to intrigue me. "How do you know if you have a good fighter?" I asked.

Pop smiled, "Breeding is important, of course, but the ultimate test is the first fight. You do not want a bird that'll get hurt and run. You want one who will fight to the death."

"Pop," I said, "all this training and fighting sounds a lot like the Marine Corps."

"You've got that right, Mike," Pop answered. "Fighting cocks, that's what we are."

STONEWALL JACKSON

Puller's quarters, near the airfield, was a shack a few feet off the ground with a wood floor and roofed with big leaves. It was a primitive looking affair, more like a native hut, but it kept him dry. During the next few days the men rested and Puller spent much of his time walking around and talking to them. One day after we had returned from one of his tours, Puller sent Pop to regimental headquarters to mail a few letters. He was in a very relaxed mood and it was obvious that he wanted to talk. He had a soft side that few of the men got to see. We were standing outside and he said, "Abbo, when was the last time you wrote your mother and father?"

I said, "Sir, yesterday. I try to write them at least once a week, but sometimes it doesn't work out that way."

Puller looked at me and said, "Those letters from you are very important to your folks. In many ways this damn war is harder on them than on you."

"Yes sir," I answered dubiously.

"Sir, do you know where I can get my hands on a decent book? I haven't read anything since we left Australia," I said.

Puller walked into his shack and said, "Come on in here."

I followed him in and on the floor there was a box full of books, maybe ten or twelve of them in there. He picked up the box and put it on the top of a crude table that served as a desk.

"Pick one out and take it," he said.

I slowly looked through the box and chose a biography of Stonewall Jackson, written by Henderson.

Puller said, "That's a good choice. That book is one of the best books ever written. In a way, it's my professional bible. Take good care of it and return it when you're finished."

The book had been read many times. It was dog-eared and reminded me of a used textbook I had bought in school. I wrapped it in a poncho when I wasn't reading it. I read the book in a week. Several passages were underlined but the one I will always remember was this:

> With the officers he was exceedingly strict. He demanded,
> too . . . that the rank and file should be treated with tact and
> consideration . . . His men loved him . . . because he was one
> of themselves, He was among the first to recognize the worth
> of the rank and file.

It all made sense now, why Puller went out of his way to care for his men, and why he was so tough on his officers. He was trying to emulate Stonewall Jackson. It was that simple.

On January 28th when I stood up after a terrible night's sleep I felt dizzy and I knew I had a temperature. I was sure my malaria was coming back. I went over to Puller's shack to return his book and I must have looked as bad as I felt. As soon as I walked into his quarters he said, "Abbo, you look awful. Get over to sick bay."

"I'll be alright, sir," I said.

"Get over there. Now!" Puller growled at me.

I put the book on his desk and left the shack. I walked over to sickbay and when I walked in the chief corpsman took my temperature and said, "Lie down Corporal, you aren't going anywhere. Your temperature is 103. You have malaria."

For the next few days I remember very little. A corpsman said, "Colonel Puller had stopped in to see you but you were sleeping. I heard General Rupertus had put the Colonel in charge of a combined force of over 1,000 men and his job was to pursue the retreating Japanese through the jungle."

I asked, "Where are the Japanese going?"

"I don't know," he said.

"When did Colonel Puller leave?" I asked.

"On the morning of January 30th," he answered.

For the next couple of weeks I slept a lot and no one knew anything about Puller chasing the Japanese. During this time I slowly recovered and began feeling much better. On February 16th, I was released from sick bay and although I felt a little weak I was glad to get out of there.

Puller and his men returned to the perimeter at Borgen Bay two days later, where trucks picked them up and drove them to the airfield. They had captured a few prisoners and some important documents but the Japanese Army had retreated faster than the Marines could pursue them.

Later that afternoon I was lying on my cot and Pop walked into the tent. He was dirty and unshaven.

I sat up and said, "Have you been on vacation again?"

"Hell no," he said with a grin, "but it sure looks like you have. How you feeling, Mike?"

"I'm okay, Pop. What happened on the patrol?"

Pop sat down on his cot and put his pack on the ground, laid his rifle on top of it and said, "We left the day after you got sick. General Rupertus wanted someone to go after the Japanese as they retreated to the south. He knew it would be a long patrol, maybe out there for a month on your own. I guess Chesty was the logical choice for patrol leader."

"How many men went?" I asked.

"We started out with a few men and were sent to Agulupella and Chesty picked up four infantry companies as he went, plus the 1st Battalion, Fifth Marines. He had about 1,300 men and I think they came from about every unit in the division. Before the patrol set out, however, intelligence discovered that the Japs were retreating to the northeast."

"Then what happened?" I asked.

"Because of this Rupertus detached 1/5 to go after them. Chesty, and the four hundred of us who were left, headed south through the jungle to Gilnit. We had 150 natives carrying supplies, but we soon ran out and needed to be re-stocked by air. Piper Cubs flew over and dropped rations along the way. One day they dropped hundreds of bottles of insect repellent. Well the men started bitching and saying 'What in the hell is this stuff for?' When Chesty heard this he said, 'Boys it's not for the mosquitoes, it's to start a fire with.' Mike, we were always wet and that was the greatest stuff to get a fire going that you ever saw.

"The rain and mud made it a damn lousy patrol. Honest to god, I think the only happy man was Chesty. He is a hiking fool."

"Did you get any of the Japs?" I asked.

"We killed about seventy-five Japs and captured some supplies and equipment which we destroyed. We also found some important documents that we brought back with us. We stayed around Gilnit for a few days and then hiked back to Agulupella. That's about it. You know something Mike, hiking through that rainy, muddy jungle was a pain in the ass."

I looked at Pop and said, "Well, it looks like you're gonna be Chesty's permanent hiking buddy."

"Yea, and it looks like that malaria has rotted your brain" Pop replied.

At the end of February Puller was promoted to Colonel and was put in command of the 1st Marine Regiment. Soon thereafter Pop and I were transferred to the 1st Marines.

Our remaining time on the island was spent on training. When we weren't in the field fighting or training, life on Cape Gloucester had improved. The perimeter now had good roads, dry tents and a PX or post exchange. The food was better, there were movies, and the division band even gave a few concerts.

On April 23rd the Army relieved us and the next day the 1st Marines boarded ships. We were leaving Cape Gloucester. The 1st Marine Division had taken a good portion of the island of New Britain away from the Japanese. 438 Marines had died and 815 had been wounded.

PAVUVU

We left New Britain and sailed for an unknown destination. It was rumored that we were returning to Melbourne, however, it was not to be.

The 1st Marine Division was sent to Pavuvu, an island twenty-five miles northwest of Guadalcanal. We were sent there to rehabilitate.

A group of Army staff officers who flew over the island thought it would be a wonderful place for the division to rehab. After all, from the air, it appeared to be a pleasant, picturesque place, with gentle surf, beautiful white beaches, a long shoreline and many neatly spaced groves of coconut palms. Had these officers landed on the island, they would have quickly changed their minds.

We landed on April 29, 1944. There were no buildings. It was almost like a bad joke. The plantation had been abandoned for years and the ground was littered with stinking, rotting coconuts. As we came ashore there was a steady rain falling and it rained all day.

I was assigned to a working party whose job it was to erect the tents. We started digging holes in the mud for the tent poles and trying to sew up the rips in the canvas. Both the tents and cots were in very poor condition. This went on late into the night and by this time, everyone's gear was soaking wet. It was a terrible way to start out, and everyone was mad, from Puller, all the way down the line.

Cape Gloucester was the wettest campaign in World War II and because of this we were in poor physical condition. Many of the Marines were covered with jungle rot. Pavuvu's hot, humid climate would not help the healing process.

It took us a few days to get the tents set up. Rain and poor drainage turned the tented areas into a sea of mud that never dried up. Drinking water was in short supply and fresh food was a rarity. And at night the rats and land crabs came out. There were no showers, mess halls or any of the basic amenities that were supposed to be at a rehabilitation area. After the tents were set up we spent weeks picking up the rotting coconuts to be dumped into the swamp or burned. We would load the stinking coconuts onto trucks to be hauled away. If they split apart while we were lifting them, the coconuts would spill foul milk all over us. It was a lousy job. Even today, I hate the smell of a coconut.

While this was going on Pop and many other Marines were hauling tons of crushed coral to pave roads, company streets and bivouac areas. It also took weeks to get the mess halls built and working. Until they were completed we lined up for chow out in the rain and mud.

The Marines slowly transformed Pavuvu into a little bit of civilization. Mess halls, a small PX and other semi-permanent structures had been built. Bivouac areas were drying up now that the rains were less frequent and the men and vehicles could move around the island without getting stuck.

As bad as this was Puller set the example: he waited in line like any other Marine and he lived in a small tent with a dirt floor. It was obvious to all his troops that they came first.

In June, Puller flew over to Guadalcanal for three days to visit his brother Sam, who was the XO of the 4th Marine Regiment. When Puller returned you could tell he had enjoyed his time with his brother: if it was possible he seemed more relaxed.

At the end of July, the first sergeant approached Pop and me in the morning, "Give the Colonel plenty of space. He just got word that his brother Sam has been killed."

"What happened?" Pop asked.

"He was shot by a sniper after he landed on Guam," replied the first sergeant.

When I saw Puller later that day I told him, "Sir, I was very sorry to hear about the loss of your brother."

Puller looked at me with a great sadness in his eyes that I had never seen before. He just shook his head slightly and walked on.

I never had a brother and I wondered, with most American men serving in both Europe and the Pacific, how many of these men would lose their brothers. It was a depressing thought.

Most of July and August was spent on landing exercises on the inlets and beaches. The exercises placed heavy emphasis on landing from amtracks or amphibian tractors. This was something the division had never done in combat.

As July came to an end, a change came over the division. The last of the rotten coconuts had finally been cleaned up, and the mud was mostly gone. There were less complaints about the mud, the food, the rats and the crabs. The men were more focused on cleaning their weapons, checking their gear and other routine chores of preparing for combat.

The high point of our time on Pavuvu was when Bob Hope put on a show. All the Marines crowded into a big open field. He brought with him Jerry Colonna, Frances Langlord, Patti Thomas and his USO troupe. They put on a great show on a little stage by the pier. I have never laughed so hard in my life. I don't think any American did more to boost the morale of the servicemen than Bob Hope. I will always be grateful to him for giving up the time with his family to entertain us. It really lifted our spirits and for a couple hours it made us forget what a terrible place Pavuvu was. Which is funny because for the rest of my life, every time I'd see Bob Hope on TV or in the movies, I'd think of Pavuvu.

During the summer Puller received three lieutenant colonels to take over his battalions. Major Ray Davis was given the job of XO of 1/1.

Shortly before the regiment left for Peleliu, the CO of 1/1 asked Puller for permission to go over to the island of Banika, where most of the supplies were stored. There was also a Navy hospital over there, too, with lots of nurses. I think this man had a serious drinking problem. He did not return for two days.

Puller came up to me then and said, "Abbo, find Major Davis."

Ten minutes later I returned with Major Davis and Puller was furious.

"Where in the hell is your commander?" he growled.

"He went over to Banika two days ago and I haven't seen or heard from him since," replied Davis.

"Wherever he is, he is no longer commander of the 1st Battalion, 1st Marines. You are! When he returns, tell him to report to me immediately," barked Puller.

"Yes, sir," said Davis.

Later that afternoon, the hung-over commander showed up at Puller's tent. Puller relieved him on the spot. You could hear Puller's angry outbursts all over the area, "I don't give a damn where you go, just get the hell out of my regiment! Now, get out of here!"

In addition to the newly appointed Major Ray Davis of 1/1, Lieutenant Colonel Russell Honsowetz would be in command of 2/1 and Lieutenant Colonel

Stephen Sabol, 3/1. These battalions would now be well led. The XO of the 1st
Marines would be Lieutenant Colonel Richard Ross.

Later in the day Colonel Puller asked me to find Colonel Honsowetz. When
I came back with Colonel Honsowetz, Colonel Puller was gone. He had been
told to report to General Rupertus. Colonel Honsowetz said he would wait.
Honsowetz sat down in the chair outside Puller's tent. He had a file with him
that he was reading. As he looked over the file he took a pen out of his pocket
and made some notes. Then he looked up at me and said, "Any idea when
Colonel Puller will be back?"

I said, "No sir, Colonel." Then I asked, "Have you served with Colonel
Puller before?"

Honsowetz looked at me and said "Yes I have. He taught me at The Basic
School in Philadelphia. He also taught Colonel Sabol and Major Davis."

"Sir, what course did he teach?" I asked.

Honsowetz answered, "Colonel Puller, he was a captain then, taught the
small wars package. After his experience in Haiti and Nicaragua he was a
natural for this. And his three rows of combat ribbons did not go unnoticed
by all the new second lieutenants. I thought it was one of the best courses in
the Basic School. He taught there from 1936 to 39."

Honsowetz reached in his pocket, pulled out a cigarette and lit it. He continued, "The next time I saw him, I was in China, 1941. Major Puller was
serving as XO of the 2nd Battalion, 4th Marines in Shanghai. By this time,
the Japanese had attacked and taken over much of the Northeastern portion of
China including Shanghai and many of the other major ports. It was a tense
situation because the U.S. had small forces in the international sections of
both Peiping and Shanghai.

"In early March, I was serving as officer of the day when a report came
in that the Jap Army had violated the neutrality of the International Zone,
marched into the American Sector of Shanghai, and arrested dozens of Chinese on the streets. I alerted Major Puller and with a platoon of Marines we
went to the scene. Major Puller pulled a gun on the Japanese Commander and
gave him five minutes to free the Chinese prisoners and withdraw from the
American sector. When the Japanese realized that he was not going to back
down they released the prisoners and left."

"Sir what would have happened if the Japs didn't back down?" I asked.

"I've thought about that a lot," Honsowetz answered, "A fight would have
started for sure. Would we have been killed or captured? Could the U.S. entry
into the Pacific War have started early? I just don't know."

Honsowetz looked around and then he said, "Abbo, I'll tell you something
else about the Colonel. I know he also served in Peiping in the early 1930's.
He commanded the Horse Marines there."

"Sir, what's that?"

"These men were hand picked from the Marine Legation Guard in Peiping and even though they were called the Horse Marines they rode Mongolian ponies. I never saw this outfit but I understand it was a great honor to be a part of it."

"Colonel Puller sure gets around doesn't he, sir?"

"Yes. He sure does," Honsowetz replied.

Colonel Puller returned a few minutes later. Honsowetz stood up and Puller said, "Good afternoon Russ, come on in."

Under the so-called twenty-four month rule, nearly a third of the regiment's officers and enlisted men were to be rotated back to the States. Word filtered down from Corps headquarters that the rule was being set aside. Only a small number of the Marines would be sent home because, without them, there weren't enough Marines to make the assault on Peleliu. Unfortunately I was not one of the Marines that got sent home. Neither was Pop.

There were rehearsals on Guadalcanal on the 27th and 29th of August, and the landing maneuvers went well. We were ready.

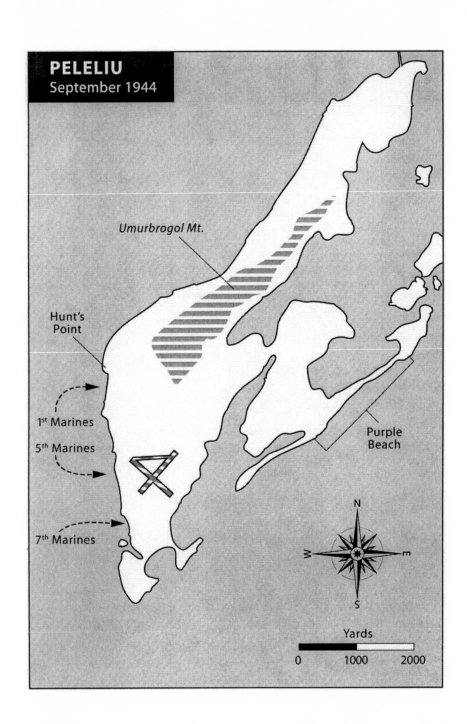

PELELIU
September 1944

Umurbrogol Mt.

Hunt's
Point

1st Marines

5th Marines

7th Marines

Purple
Beach

N
W   E
S

Yards
0   1000   2000

Chapter Four

Peleliu

I'm all right. I'm onboard ship now. The nightmare is over for us. After nine days of vicious fighting they relieved our regiment. We lost over half our men. We paid a terrible price for this island and I wonder if it was worth it. The extraordinary courage and fighting spirit of these men will stay with me forever . . .

M. Abbo, letter to parents, 4 Oct 1944

THE FORTRESS

The logic behind taking Peleliu was simple: protect MacArthur's eastern flank as he approached the southern Philippines. Peleliu was to be seized for its airfield. Admiral Halsey was against it. He felt the airfield would not be worth the casualties it would take to secure the island. Peleliu is shaped like a lobster claw, with a long upper pincher and a shorter lower one separated from the main body of the island by swampland. At the pincher's hinge was the airfield. The island is six miles long by two miles wide.

The south end of the island was flat but the central and northern parts consisted of cliffs, crevices, caves, and steep gorges all mixed together. In the center it rises 556 feet to the Umubrogol Mountain. It was a fortress of underground, mutually supporting strong points, the entire mass filled with over 600 caves, bunkers and pillboxes. It was here that the Japanese had most of their mortars and artillery.

The Japanese had also changed their tactics from an all out defense of the beaches to a defense in depth. Let the Marines get ashore and then bleed them. With the latter tactic the battles had been longer and American casualties had been much higher. There would be no more wasteful banzai attacks. The Japanese soldiers were prepared to fight to the death.

UNDERWAY

We left Pavuvu on September 3, 1944 for the 1,500-mile voyage to Peleliu. Thirty LST's carried the assault troops. We could see the destroyers on the fringes protecting against submarine attacks. On the way to Peleliu, weapons were field stripped and cleaned. Ammo, K-rations and salt tablets were issued.

One afternoon while cleaning my rifle I said to Pop, "I'm worried about Peleliu. Guadalcanal and New Britain were long, drawn out battles, but we surprised the Japs. Both landings were unopposed, but when the 2nd Marine Division invaded Tarawa last November, the Japs were waiting for them. The Marines had over 3,400 casualties in only three days of fighting."

"I'm sure we learned a lot from that battle," Pop said.

"Maybe, but then a few months ago we attacked Saipan, Tinian and Guam. You know the Jap artillery on Saipan literally tore the Marines and soldiers apart. Yeah, we took the island, but at what cost? Sixteen thousand casualties; seventy-five percent of them were Marines. On Tinian, 2,300 more casualties. And then Guam: the Marines and soldiers suffered 8,000 more casualties, including Puller's brother. So I ask you this, Pop, what's going to happen to us on Peleliu?"

Pop stared off beyond me, "I don't know, Mike, but it seems like every time we land on an island, we start losing men faster than hell. It don't look too good, does it?"

I didn't, or couldn't, answer him.

Before we landed, the Navy shelled Peleliu for three days and stripped the island of most of its foliage, turning it into a vast wasteland. It then became apparent that the ground was much rougher than it had first appeared.

The night before the landing Puller brought his battalion commanders and regimental staff into the small ward room on his ship. Puller was always spartan in his speech and it was a blunt appraisal of what might lie ahead.

"Gentlemen, here's the order of battle: The 1st Marines will land on the left flank and take the Point on the left and the high ground to the north, the Umurbrogel. Intelligence is very sketchy. We'll have to learn as we go. The 5th Marines will land in the center and take the airfield. The 7th Marines will land to their right and clear the southern part of the island. The 1st Marines have beaches White 1 and White 2. Colonel Sabol, 3/1 will go in on the left. Your job is to knock out The Point and push inland. Colonel Honsowetz, 2/1 will go in on the right. You will tie in with the 5th Marines on your right and push inland. Major Davis, 1/1 will stay in regimental reserve.

"It is extremely important that when you are going in, to stay down and when you hit the beaches get the hell out of those amtracs and fast. They are big targets. Push inland to clear the way for the following waves. We don't want everyone jammed up on the beaches.

"General Rupertus thinks the invasion is going to be rough but fast. I don't feel that way. The Japs have been fortifying this island for years and it could take a long time to clear them out. Be ready for a very hard fight.

"I will be going in on the third wave with half my headquarters in our amtrac. Also in the third wave will be our communications equipment. Colonel Ross will take the other half of my headquarters and come in on the eighth wave.

"The first wave leaves at 0800, the second at 0805, the third at 0810 and so on. The goal is to have 4500 Marines ashore in twenty minutes. From the line of departure it is a thirty minute trip to the beach.

"One other thing, I think it is pretty clear that we have drawn the toughest job: seizing The Point and taking the high ground beyond the beaches. As long as the Japanese hold the high ground the Marines below will be vulnerable to artillery and mortar fire. We have to take those objectives."

Puller slowly looked around the room at each man. Then he said, "Gentlemen, good luck."

We went down below; Pop finished a letter home and hit the sack. Some of the men were cleaning weapons and others finished loading up their packs. A few were talking. Slowly, it got quiet. As I laid in my bunk, I prayed that I would make it. I'm sure that every man prayed that night. I tried not to think about tomorrow. I didn't sleep very well.

DAY 1 – SEPTEMBER 15TH

It was still dark when a sergeant woke us up.

"Wake up. Hit the deck."

We got up, got dressed and ate the typical pre-invasion breakfast of steak and eggs. I would have enjoyed the breakfast much better if I could have eaten it back home in Chicago. After breakfast I went out on the deck to have a look. Around 6:00 AM the sun came up into a cloudless sky. The sea appeared calm and there was a light breeze. I could see the island. The Navy was shelling it with their big guns and tearing it apart. Our planes also hit the island and I wondered how anyone could survive such a pounding. I was leaning on the railing and watching the island wishing I was somewhere else.

I didn't want to look at it anymore and I walked down the deck and went below.

Pop was sitting on his bunk, closing his pack and I was standing when a bell rang, signaling every Marine to put on his gear if it wasn't already on. I tightened the chinstrap on my helmet, put on my pack and slung my rifle over my shoulder. I was scared and my stomach didn't feel right. I felt like a boxer who was about to get into the ring. The bell rang again and we went below to board the amtracs.

When Puller arrived, we climbed aboard and the engines started. The roar of the amtracs was deafening and the fumes were terrible. The LST bow doors opened, the bow ramp dropped and our amtrac moved down into the sea. The air was foul with the smell of fuel exhaust mixed with burnt powder from the naval guns. The amtrac started rolling up and down in the sea and after a few minutes some Marines started vomiting. It was not a good way to start the day.

By 8:10 AM the amtracs in our wave were on line and we started in toward the beach. I could not see the island. It was behind a big wall of smoke. We were crammed in the amtrac and Colonel Puller was in the front, and next to him were his radio operator and Pop. Lieutenant Frank Sheppard and I were close by.

Once we crossed the reef, it took ten minutes to get to shore. All the Japanese guns were registered inside the reef, and once we crossed, all hell broke loose. I was on the side of the amtrac and wanted to take a look but kept my head down. I could hear bullets hitting the side and there were explosions nearby that rained down buckets of seawater on us. As we were nearing the shore, Puller roared out the final orders, "Get ready. When we hit the beach, get the hell off of here. We are all sitting ducks." When the amtrac grinded to a halt in the sand, he screamed, "Go, go, go!"

We went over the side as fast as we could. I followed Puller as he ran up the beach and dove into the sand. I landed right beside him. I turned back to look at the amtrac as a shell hit it. The Marines who didn't move fast enough never made it out and I assumed were killed instantly. As I looked down the beach it seemed that almost every amtrac in our wave had been hit. The five LTUs carrying the command group were shot up as they crossed the reef and lost most of their communications gear and expert operators.

When we landed, the beach was already covered with the wreckage of battle: broken weapons, helmets, gas masks, burning amtracs and way too many wounded and dead Marines.

I saw Puller slowly look from one end of the beach to the other. He then jumped up to his feet. There was a major near him who had a .45 drawn and his hand was shaking like a leaf. Puller tore the weapon out of his hand, shoved it into the major's shoulder holster and snapped, "Keep that goddamn thing there. We've got all these men to do our fighting. Your job is to lead them. Now get 'em moving!"

Puller then sat back on his haunches oriental-style with that pipe in his mouth and as Marines ran by he would yell out, "Go get 'em, Marine!"

Most of the deadly fire had come from The Point to the left of the 3rd Battalion. Puller quickly set up a line of defense and then got everyone to push inland. Since he had lost most of the communications equipment, Puller could not talk to Division Headquarters and had limited ability to talk with his battalion commanders. In addition, the wiremen were just starting to lay wire so there was no communication over the landlines. Puller wanted to know how his battalions were doing. It was total chaos on the beach and it was very obvious by all the dead and dying Marines, that something had gone terribly wrong.

We moved inland about 100 yards and Puller set up his CP between the 3rd and 2nd Battalions in a largely destroyed coconut grove. Puller's command group had followed him there and some of the men were moving logs to provide protection for the CP. It was a madhouse and with no communication Puller wanted to know how the 3rd Battalion was dealing with the Point.

Puller yelled out, "Pop you stay here and wait for Colonel Ross," then he turned to me and barked out, "Abbo!"

I moved over to him and said, "Yes, sir," trying to disguise my fear.

The firing wasn't letting up and it was hard to hear anything. His voice carried, "Let's get over to the 3rd Battalion."

We ran down to the edge of the beach and dove into the coral sand. The Japanese mortars and artillery were whistling over our heads and exploding close to us. Every shell that passed over my head sounded like a freight train screaming by and made my entire body tighten up. When the rounds exploded in a deafening roar the ground trembled and shook, with shrapnel and coral raining down on top of us. Puller looked up and down the beach then he jumped up and ran about twenty-five yards and dove into the sand. Then it happened. I froze. I tried to get up but I couldn't move. I was paralyzed by fear. It was like being afraid of heights and suddenly finding yourself on the outside ledge of a fifty-story building. My whole body had turned to jelly. I saw Puller look for me and he saw me lying on the beach, not moving.

He yelled out, "Abbo!"

I couldn't move.

He yelled again, "Let's go!"

Still, I couldn't move.

This time he roared, "God damnit, get up!"

I don't know if his voice scared me, or I didn't want to fail him, or maybe I didn't want to let myself down. My heart was beating so fast I thought it was going to explode. I was just terrified. Slowly I got up on my knees and elbows and moved my feet under me, then sprung up and ran down the beach and hit the ground beside Puller. I expected him to raise hell with me but he didn't.

All he said was, "Ready?"

"Yes, sir," I replied breathlessly.

We took off running, and a lot of Marines were taking cover in holes in the sand that resulted from the blasts of the naval gunfire. On the beach, wounded men were calling out for corpsmen, but there weren't enough to handle them all. Their cries would haunt me forever. There was a huge tank trap that ran parallel to the beach. It was about ten feet deep and as I was about to jump into it for cover Puller yelled out, "No, the Japs have it zeroed in."

We ran further along the edge of the beach where it met the splintered woods and jungle scrub. At least we now had a little cover. We were still taking fire from the Point. Fire poured down the entire beach, hurting the landing. The Point rose up thirty feet above the water and was honeycombed with caves and crevices. Puller had insisted that the Point be blanketed with fire prior to the invasion but obviously the bombardment had no effect on the Japanese defenders.

We stopped and asked men where Colonel Sabol's command post was. The Marines would say they didn't know or point us further down the beach. The going was slow and we were careful to shield ourselves from the fire from the Point, and we would take cover behind the broken and twisted trees. We came upon more men and Puller yelled out, "Where is Colonel Sabol?"

One man replied, "Sir, down the beach about fifty yards and then go inland."

We followed his directions and in a couple minutes we came to the command post. It was only a big hole in the ground with logs around it. Colonel Sabol was on the radio when we got there.

When he hung up, he saw Puller and said, "Sir, Captain Hunt has taken the Point but he has lost a lot of men. Then we lost radio contact with him. Hunt said there is a gap between him and the rest of the battalion. I'm going to use L Company to close the gap."

Puller thought for a second and said, "We have to find out what's going on. I want you to send someone to the Point. Abbo, you go with him."

I nodded grimly.

Sabol turned around and there was a lieutenant standing there.

"Lieutenant Meyer, you go up there with Colonel Puller's runner," he said.

Puller looked at both me and the Lieutenant and said, "Find out what's happening. How many men do they have? Casualties? What do they need? Lieutenant, can they hold the Point? You report back to Colonel Sabol and Abbo you report to me. And for Christ's sake, be careful."

Reluctantly, the Lieutenant and I took off. I followed Meyer back to the edge of the beach and we slowly worked our way toward the Point. The fire from the Point had stopped since Hunt had secured it.

We reached the end of the 3rd Battalion's line and a Marine said, "I wouldn't go any further – there's a gap in our lines between here and the Point. The place is lousy with Japs."

Lieutenant Meyer and I kneeled down on the coral.

Meyer said, "It looks like it's about 200 yards to the base of the Point. Let's work our way through the trees. We'll use them for cover."

"What about the Japs?" I asked.

"We'll just have to stay alert. Ready?"

"I'll follow you," I said.

Again, my heart started beating hard and I could feel the adrenaline racing through me. Meyer stood up and ran about twenty yards and dove behind a fallen tree, and I landed right beside him.

I followed Meyer. He carefully went from tree to tree. When he moved to another position, I took his old one. This was working pretty well. Some places had no standing trees so we would crawl behind the downed ones.

We made it about halfway, only about a hundred yards to go, racing from tree to tree through the shell-blasted coconut grove. I was breathing heavily and sweating. It was starting to get hot. The beach was fifty yards to our left and the Japs were still throwing mortar rounds on it, so that was not a safe place to be. I didn't exactly feel secure hiding behind logs in the bombed-out coconut grove, either.

We tried to stay low as we went from tree to tree. About fifty yards from the base of the Point a bullet hit a downed tree beside us. We dove behind the long trunk. My face was in Meyer's boots.

The Jap had us. If we raised our heads to find him, he would've shot them off. We were in big trouble.

"Can you see him?" Meyer asked me.

"Hell no, I can't see him," I yelled.

Three more shots hit the log and bits of wood flew all over us. This Jap was going to get us and there was nothing we could do about it. I have never felt so helpless.

A second later two shots rang out behind us and I rolled over on my side, staying down, but looking at the Point. At first I didn't see anyone then a voice said, "Up here."

I looked up and there was a Marine about half way up the hill.

He said, "The Jap that was shooting at you is dead. When I give you the word, run towards me. I'll cover you."

Meyer yelled out, "Okay!"

The Marine then yelled, "Go!"

We both jumped up and sprinted to the base of the Point where we dove into the ground. The Marine was crouched halfway up the hill and he said, "What in the hell are you doing here? They're Japs all over the place."

"Colonel Puller sent us over," said Meyer.

"Follow me," said the Marine.

The Point was a mass of big boulders and we climbed hand over hand to the top. It was only about thirty feet high so we were there in less than a minute. There, we were greeted by Captain Hunt. He was sitting on a rock, smoking a cigarette.

"You men lost?" Hunt asked.

"No sir," said Meyer, "Colonel Puller sent us up here. He wants to know what's going on."

Captain Hunt took a long drag on his cigarette and said, "It took us a little over an hour to take the Point. We destroyed five pillboxes and killed 110 Japanese. Of the 100 men in the 1st and 3rd Platoons, only 33 made it. I don't know what happened to the 2nd Platoon. The entire Point and its defenses were untouched by naval gunfire."

He pointed to his remaining men. They were getting ready for a counter-attack; piling up rocks and fallen logs for cover.

"We need water, grenades, ammo, batteries, and barbed wire, and as many reinforcements as you can scrape together. Only way in is by tractor along the reef. We are isolated up here and the Japs have us surrounded."

Meyer said, "Colonel Sabol is going to send L Company to fill the gap."

"We'll be ready for them," said Hunt.

"Good luck, sir," Meyer said, and we started to leave the Point the same way we had come.

Hunt said, "Lieutenant, if I were you I wouldn't go back that way. Go down the nose of the Point and into the ocean. It'll be a lot safer."

I thought this was the smartest thing I had heard all morning.

We said goodbye to Hunt and walked downhill and into the ocean. We waded out as far as we could, and kept our rifles above our heads. It was slow going for those two hundred yards back to where the Marine line started. When we saw the Marines on the beach we walked into shore.

Meyer said, "I'll report back to Colonel Sabol and you report to Colonel Puller."

"Yes sir," I said.

Now I had to find Puller. I ran back to the command post. When I got there I found out that it had taken a direct hit that killed three men and wounded several others. Puller was not there when it happened. He then moved his command group inland and closer to the gap in the 3rd Battalion.

A Marine came up to me and said, "Abbo, one of those men killed was Pop."

I couldn't believe what I had heard. "Are you sure?" I asked.

"Yes, they took all three men down to the beach," he replied.

I was shocked and felt like someone had punched me in the stomach. I felt sick and as I turned away from the Marine I started crying.

How could this have happened? He was my best friend in the Marine Corps. We had been friends since we first met in February of 1942 and we had shared so much together: the hardships, the laughs, and two years of savage fighting. His tragic death made me take a close look at my own life. We had just invaded this damn island a few hours ago and I wondered if I would get out of here alive. Somehow I had always felt secure around Pop in this insane world of combat. Now he was gone, and with him a part of my life.

I suddenly realized I had a job to do and moved inland to find Puller.

When I found him he was on the radio in his new CP. When he got off the radio he said, "I guess you heard about Pop."

"Yes, sir," I answered with my head down.

"I'm sorry, Pop was a good Marine, Mike."

Puller hesitated a few seconds as he too stared at the ground. Then he looked up and asked, "How is Captain Hunt holding on?"

I gave Puller the full report.

He then said, "We'll try and get him re-supplied."

The battle was not going well so Puller threw his regimental reserve into the fight: Major Davis' 1/1.

A runner from the Second Battalion came charging up and reported to Puller that his battalion had moved inland 350 yards and was on the edge of the air field and tied in the with the 5th Marines.

The Colonel asked him, "How many casualties?"

He replied, "Sir, several dozen."

Puller said, "Tell Colonel Honsowetz to keep moving, and that the Point has been taken."

In the late afternoon we got a call from Lieutenant Colonel Honsowetz that the Japs were pouring out of the Umurbrogol near the airfield with tanks and a company of infantry. They came across the airfield where the lines of 2/1 and the 5th Marines met. Our Sherman tanks and 37mm guns destroyed most of the Japanese tanks and infantry in a few minutes. It was not a reckless banzai charge but rather a well-planned attack, and this was maybe our first clue that the Japanese had changed their tactics.

By late in the day I had run out of water. The temperature had climbed to over a hundred degrees and there was no shade. I had gone through two canteens. Marines had brought water forward in five-gallon cans so we could refill, but the water was bad. The water had come ashore in 55 gallons oil drums that were supposed to be clean. The water was smelly and oily. I drank some to quench my thirst and almost threw up. Puller was furious. He called the ship and raised hell.

"Goddamn it, what the hell is wrong with you people? All this water you are sending is foul. Now get us some clean water fast or we are going to start losing Marines to the heat."

Later, the wiremen had laid the lines and Puller was able to talk to the ADC or the Assistant Division Commander, General O.P. Smith. The Colonel got on the phone and was calm and steady.

"Sir, we have repulsed an enemy counter attack on our right front and we knocked out several enemy tanks. We're holding."

Smith said, "Lewie, how are you making out?"

"All right," replied Puller.

"Do you need any help?" asked Smith.

"No."

"It will be getting dark soon, so hold up," said Smith.

"Aye, aye, sir," replied Puller.

I was surprised that Puller did not mention the gap in his front. He got back on the phone and put C Company, his last reserve, into the gap. He also reinforced C Company with 100 Marines he borrowed from the First Engineer Battalion.

Puller then phoned his battalion commanders.

"Get ready for tonight. Be ready for a counter attack. We will resume the attack tomorrow at 0800. How many casualties?"

We had lost 500 men. I was stunned. Later that night Puller reported to the command ship, "The enemy is well dug in. Opposition strong. Little damage done by our preliminary fire. A hard fight is ahead. Casualties over 20%. I've ordered no man to be evacuated unless from bullet or shell wounds."

Captain Hunt and his men on the Point were still cut off and outnumbered.

When night came, I found cover behind some logs near the CP. I was totally exhausted but my mind wasn't ready for sleep. I couldn't help but think this was not like the jungles of Guadalcanal or Cape Gloucester. We had descended into a hell of indescribable horrors. I didn't sleep at all that night because the incoming shells from the ships were whistling overhead, the Japs kept throwing mortar rounds at us and I couldn't stop thinking about Pop.

DAY 2 – SEPTEMBER 16TH

At 8:00 AM the 1st Marines resumed the attack on the airfield with the 5th Marines. Honowetz's battalion moved forward on the right but when they turned north they ran into heavy fighting in and around the destroyed buildings between the airstrip and the ridges beyond. The attack stalled, and the casualties climbed.

General Rupertus came ashore and, moving slowly because of an injured ankle, made his way to General Smith's advance command post and took control of the operation. I don't think he had a feel for what was happening and because of his prediction for a quick resolution he became very impatient with the progress of the 1st Marines.

He called Puller on the phone and snapped at him, "Can't they move any faster? Goddamnit, Lewie, you've got to kick ass to get results. You know that, goddamnit."

Puller didn't like those comments from Rupertus and all he said was, "Yes, sir, we'll get them moving." Puller was not one to give excuses or explanations.

3/1, under Colonel Sabol was making slow progress, attacking the low ridge to his front along with Major Davis' 1/1.

The gap was still open, however. Later that afternoon, tanks arrived to support Sabol and one by one the Marines began to destroy the caves and pillboxes. Eventually, A and B Companies hooked up with Captain Hunt and closed the gap.

Towards the end of the day Puller got the casualty reports from his battalions. We had lost another 500 men. An infantry regiment has only 3,000 riflemen and in two days we had lost one third of our regiment. I wondered if it could get much worse.

Puller was on the radio or phone a good part of the night. He got a call from Colonel Sabol that Hunt's company on the Point was under a frontal assault from a lot of Japanese. Puller said, "Can we get him any help?"

Sabol answered, "Hunt has B Company and the mortar platoons are registered on the ground to his front. We can't spare any more men."

"Keep me informed," Puller said and hung up.

After midnight Sabol called back. "I've just talked to Hunt. The attack is over. They have beaten them back and we'll see what it looks like in the morning."

Puller replied, "Stay on the alert, they may be coming back."

It stayed relatively quiet the rest of the night.

DAY 3 – SEPTEMBER 17TH

When the sun came up Colonel Sabol called Puller once again. "Sir, I just spoke with Captain Hunt. They counted over 400 Japanese bodies to their front. They just blew them away. The Point is now totally under our control."

Puller shook his head and said, "Tell Captain Hunt and his men that they have done one hell of a job. I want you to put Captain Hunt's company in reserve. Those men need a rest. C Company will take over their position at 0800, and continue the advance."

Sabol replied, "Yes, sir."

When K Company came down from the Point, Hunt could only find 78 of his men. They had landed on D-Day with 235 men. The other 157 were either dead or wounded. Captain Hunt was awarded the Navy Cross for taking and holding the Point.

Early that morning Puller reorganized the lines of the 1st Marines. He kept 3/1 on the left flank, gave Major Davis total control over 1/1 in the middle and 2/1 remained on the right flank tied into the 5th Marines. Puller gave the order to his battalion commanders to start the attack. Davis' battalion ran into a large block house, sixty feet square and twenty feet high. Naval gunfire blew it away and 1/1 continued the attack. At mid morning they were at the foot of the Umurbrogol and it took them until sunset to seize the forward slope. 1/1 had taken heavy casualties.

3/1 on the left had it a little easier than the other battalions. They had advanced 700 yards and had taken the nose of the Umurbrogol.

Late in the day, Puller called Colonel Selden, the Division Chief of Staff, "Johnny, I've lost a lot of men. I need some help!"

"We don't have any men to give you, Lewie."

"Hell, I've lost 1,200 men."

"What do you want me to do?" asked Selden.

"Give me those men on the beach," said Puller.

"I can't do that. They are not trained infantry."

Puller said, "Send them up here and by tonight, they will be trained infantry."

Selden said, "You know we can't do that, Lewie."

When it got dark Puller told me to come with him. We visited every battalion commander. We had no flashlight because it was too dangerous and when he talked to each commander he told them the same thing, "We continue the attack at 0800. We'll use every man."

When we got to Colonel Honsowetz's battalion (2/1) Puller asked him how things were going.

"Not too good," answered Honsowetz, "I've lost a lot of men."

"How many?" asked Puller.

Honsowetz said he wasn't sure, but maybe a couple hundred.

"How many Japs did you kill?" Puller asked.

Honsowetz again said that he didn't know, but there were lots of dead Japs around, maybe fifty, he guessed.

"Jesus Christ, Honsowetz, what are the American people going to think?" yelled Puller. "You lose 200 Marines and you kill only fifty Japs? I'm putting you down for 500."

On the way back to the command post I noticed that Puller was limping badly. He stumbled a few times, moving slower than he normally did. When we returned, he slowly climbed into his hole and I took up my position behind a few logs.

Fear, fatigue, and filth became our constant companions. We couldn't wash. There was barely enough water to drink. And the air was foul with the smell of death, human waste, and rotting food. When the wind blew it was the worst. The Japanese bodies lay where they were killed and within hours the stench filled the air. Because of the coral ground, the human waste could not be covered up and ration cans were discarded and could not be buried. And the flies gorged themselves on all of this and quickly multiplied. When you opened a can of rations, the flies covered it in seconds. It was a dirty, disgusting way to live.

As I dozed off into a fitful sleep I wondered how long this nightmare was going to last. We were losing men at an alarming rate and no one was doing anything about it. Three days of heavy fighting and temperatures above one hundred degrees were taking a deadly toll. If it continued like this, soon there would be no one left.

DAY 4 – SEPTEMBER 18TH

Major Davis' 1/1 was so badly shot up taking the blockhouse area that Puller pulled them off the line and they were replaced by the Second Battalion, 7th Marines. At dawn, the new line, going left to right was 3/1, 2/7, 2/1.

Puller's Marines attacked early after a thirty-minute barrage by air, artillery and naval gunfire, and they soon found themselves in the middle of a meat grinder.

As the attack started Puller moved his CP to a small stone quarry 150 yards from the front lines. The fighting soon turned savage and the Marines again started taking casualties.

In the early afternoon Colonel Honsowetz of 2/1 called Puller, "Sir, the situation has become desperate. There's no possible way I can take that hill without reinforcements."

"Come into the flank and take the ridge," barked Puller.

"We can't do it, Colonel. The casualties are too high. We've been fighting all day and all night," Honsowetz said, desperately.

Puller didn't miss a beat, "You sound alright, you're there," he responded. "Goddamnit, you, get those troops in there and you take that goddamn hill."

I could not give orders like that but maybe that is why I was a corporal and Puller was a colonel. Puller gave Honsowetz B Company and he took the hill and fortunately there were light casualties.

Later in the afternoon Marine guides brought up General O.P. Smith, and a few admirals who wanted to visit Puller's command post, which was nothing more than a hole in the ground that was covered by an old piece of tin and a poncho set up to keep out the sun. As I watched Puller and the group of brass, I couldn't help but notice that the admirals were all in clean khakis; they were shaved and wore helmets. The contrast between them and Puller was almost comical. Puller was stripped to the waist with that stubby pipe in his mouth. He hadn't washed or shaved since we landed. His trousers were covered with coral dust and sweat. He was wearing no helmet and his hair was sticking up in the air. He was as filthy as the rest of us.

In the late afternoon Colonel Honsowetz attacked a steep coral ridge. The Japanese opened up with machine guns, mortars and artillery. This piece of ground was soon nicknamed "Bloody Nose Ridge". Someone described the Umurbrogal with its jumble of ridges, ravines and caves as a mouth full of bad, black, broken teeth. Bloody Nose Ridge was just the beginning. As the day ended, Puller had found the heart of the enemy resistance. He had gained little ground, his casualties continued to mount and he had now lost fifteen hundred men or one-half of his regiment.

DAY 5 – SEPTEMBER 19TH

The day started off with the usual heavy shelling by artillery and naval fire. I noticed that Puller's limp had worsened. Lieutenant Sheppard, when Puller was out of earshot, said that the piece of shrapnel that he left in his thigh from Guadalcanal was giving him a lot of trouble. Puller was sitting down and not walking around like he always did.

Honsowetz's battalion was making progress on the right flank and to keep up the momentum Puller put A and C Companies of 1/1 back into action. At the end of the day, A Company was down to sixty-seven men. C Company was progressing under the leadership of Captain Everett Pope. He had landed with 230 men but now his company, reduced to just 90 men was as typical as any of the depleted rifle companies. His objective was Hill 100 and he took the hill after a full day of fighting only to find that it wasn't the top of a hill but the nose of a higher ridge and that the Japanese held the high ground all around. As night fell the Marines took cover wherever they could. Puller heard the call from Pope over the radio, "The line is flimsy as hell and its getting dark. We have no wire and need grenades badly."

Puller then called Major Davis, "Is there anything we can do?"

Davis answered, "We can't get to them and they are too closely engaged for artillery support."

Pope's Marines managed to hold on, but when dawn came they were almost out of ammunition. At daylight Pope received orders to withdraw. Of the ninety who had started the attack the day before, only nine returned without serious wounds. Seven of the eight junior officers were dead and Lieutenant Burke, the sole survivor, had a serious bayonet gash in his leg. When Captain Pope left Peleliu he was the only company commander or platoon commander in the First Battalion, 1st Marines to retain his post throughout the entire operation. For his actions, Captain Pope would receive the Medal of Honor. These five days had seen some of the most vicious fighting in the Pacific. Puller's men were spent and did not have much left to give.

DAY 6 – SEPTEMBER 20TH

Hill 100 remained a key objective for the 1st Marines. Pope's costly, bloody stand of the previous night didn't deter the perceived need to break the Japanese resistance by taking Bloody Nose Ridge. The shattered Marine forces prepared for another try.

Puller gave it everything he had. He called on the 11th Marines' artillery to fire every five minutes on selected targets. Naval guns fired twenty-seven missions. Every able-bodied man left in the regiment was thrown into the line.

2/1 was so shot up by this time that when 1/1 was attached to it, they still did not add up to a full battalion. The line of assault was from left to right: 3/1, 2/7 and the combination of 2/1 and 1/1. As hard as they tried, the shot-up rifle companies could not make any gains.

Late in the morning a Marine staggered into Puller's command post.

"Sir, we've had such heavy losses that we have nothing better than sergeants to lead our platoons."

Puller stood up slowly and painfully, and tore into the young Marine, "Let me tell you something, son. In the Marine Corps, there is nothing better than a sergeant. Now get the hell back to your unit."

That afternoon, the remnants of the First and Second Battalions, 1st Marines were relieved by 1/7. 2/1, now down to sixty men, was relieved by 3/7 and straggled back to be fed the first hot meal since the landing.

Puller's leg was getting worse and he limped outside to watch his battalions file down out of the hills; the immensity of the disaster became all too apparent.

At the end of the day Puller called Division Headquarters. He told them his casualties now exceeded 1600. The few men who were left were physically exhausted and emotionally drained.

DAY 7 – SEPTEMBER 21ST

Early that morning Sabol's 3/1 went on the attack but Puller pulled 1/1 and 2/1 out of the fight and sent them to White Beach for a hard-earned rest.

Later that day, the Colonel was lying on his cot because he was having a difficult time standing; his leg was very swollen. Someone yelled out that there was company approaching and Puller growled, "Who is it?"

"It looks like some brass," I replied.

"All right," he said, "help me up."

I pulled him up and into the CP came Marine General Roy Geiger, the Corps Commander. Puller said, "Good to see you, sir."

"Lewie, how's it going?" asked Geiger.

When I glanced from the Colonel to Geiger, I could tell that Puller was drained.

Geiger said, "What can I do to help?"

Puller's reply was, "We are doing all right with what we got."

That comment never made any sense to me because half our regiment was gone and Puller was not thinking clearly – we needed all the help we could get.

Geiger looked around at the few of us who were with Puller, and then he barked at us "I want to talk with Colonel Puller in private!"

We quickly moved away and what was said between the two Marines will never be known. The conversation lasted for fifteen minutes, and then General Geiger left. Puller went back to his cot.

When night began to fall I realized that the 1st Marines were done. Our casualties were approaching 1,700. It was appalling. When was someone going to stop this useless slaughter?

DAY 8 – SEPTEMBER 22ND

We started the day off with 3/1 attacking on the western slope of the Umurbrogol and by later in the day we had made some progress, cleaning out a lot of the caves. Unknown to us at the time, some decisions were being made that I'm sure saved our lives. When General Geiger visited us the day before he thought Puller looked exhausted. This and the fact that the 1st Marines had lost so many men convinced Geiger that we were finished. Although Geiger wanted to use a Marine unit, there weren't any. He told Rupertus that an Army unit would have to relieve the 1st Marines. General Rupertus protested but was overruled. Geiger ordered that preparations begin to evacuate the 1st Marines and attach a regiment of the 81st Army Division to the 1st Marine Division immediately.

Late in the day, General Rupertus called Puller.

"Lewie, tomorrow we are replacing the 1st Marines with the 321st Regimental Combat Team. They will start moving into place at noon tomorrow. Your men need a break."

Puller didn't put up an argument. He knew it was all over. All he said was, "Aye, aye, sir."

The Colonel then called his battalion commanders and told them that the 321st RCT would be replacing them at noon tomorrow. The news was received with muted acceptance. There was no joy, only great sorrow over the men who had been killed or wounded.

DAY 9 – SEPTEMBER 23RD

We rested in the lines waiting for the Army to relieve us. The regimental CO of the 321st RCT came into Puller's CP. He introduced himself and thinking he must be in a forward observation post he said, "Colonel Puller, where is your command post?"

Puller gruffly replied, "Right here!"

Thinking that Puller did not understand him, he said, "No, I mean your command post."

Puller harshly replied, "Goddamnit, you're standing in it!"

We left and started moving to the beach. Later we heard the Army commander moved the CP one thousand yards to the rear.

Puller was having a very tough time walking and when we got to a road that was to his rear, there was a jeep waiting for him. As we came down the hill, a newsman stopped the Marine in front of me and said, "Are you with the 1st Marines?"

The Marine hesitated a second and said, "There aren't any more 1st Marines," and kept walking. What was left of the 1st Marines was sent to Purple Beach to recoup. We had lost so many officers and NCO's that it was apparent that we were no longer effective as a fighting force. We would remain on

Purple Beach for the next few days. Some patrols were sent out to search for bypassed Japanese but most of the time we ate, slept and just thanked God we were still alive.

THE CEMETERY

A few days later, Puller approached and said, "I'm going down to Orange Beach 2. They are dedicating the new cemetery there. I'll be back in an hour."

I quickly said, "Sir, could I ride down there with you? I'd like to say good-bye to Pop."

Puller nodded and said, "Hop in."

I climbed into the back of the jeep, the driver took off and we drove over to Orange Beach. When we arrived, Puller slowly eased his way out of the jeep and limped over to where the other senior officers of the division were standing. I stood to the side and watched as the division chaplains dedicated the cemetery. It was a sad sight.

Puller, standing next to Major General Rupertus, was still dressed in his filthy combat gear, holding his helmet with both hands. He looked like hell: dirty, disheveled, fatigued with sunken, bloodshot eyes staring out of his un-shaven face. A great grief seemed to surround his body as he faced the tragic reality that many of the men in this cemetery were his.

I spotted a Marine from Graves Registration and asked him where Pop's grave was. He looked it up in his record book and pointed toward the loca-tion. When the ceremony was finished, I walked over to bid farewell to Pop. His body, like the others, was underneath a mound of fresh dirt, with a white wooden cross at one end.

I said aloud, "Pop, I am going to miss you, but I'll see you in the next world." Then looking up, I prayed, "Dear God, take good care of Pop. He was the best."

As I squatted down to touch the grave and wipe the tears from my face, I saw Puller walking toward his jeep, so I hurried over and climbed into the rear. On the ride back to the 1st Marines' CP, Puller didn't say a word.

OCTOBER 2

The survivors of Chesty Puller's 1st Marines left Peleliu and sailed for Pa-vuvu. It was raining and there were heavy seas. DUKW's took us out to the transport ships that would take us to Pavuvu. Many of the Marines were so worn out they could barely climb the cargo nets. When I was up on deck a sailor asked a Marine if he had brought any souvenirs.

He said, "Yeah, I got the best."

The sailor asked, "What's that?"

"I brought my ass out of there," he replied.

Puller and other wounded Marines sailed aboard the hospital ship, the USS Pinckney. He was operated on for more than an hour and they took an inch-long piece of shell fragment out of his leg.

By the time we reached Pavuvu on October 10th, Puller was well on his way to healing. Because of the high casualties the 7th Marines were relieved on October 5 and the 5th Marines on October 15. The Army would not secure the island until November 27, 1944.

The 1st Marine Division had paid a terrible price for Peleliu: 1,121 killed in action, 5,142 wounded in action and 73 missing in action. The 1st Marines had 56% casualties, 43% for the 5th Marines and 46% for the 7th Marines. Of the estimated 10,900 Japanese who defended the island, all but 202 were killed.

Later, Peleliu would be often referred to as "The Forgotten Battle". The press chose to focus more on both MacArthur's return to the Philippines and the Allied advance across the Siegfried Line in Europe rather than on the horrible slaughter that took place on this tiny coral island. For those of us that fought there, and the families of those that fell there, Peleliu would never be forgotten.

BACK TO PAVUVU

I didn't think it was possible but I was actually glad to be aboard a ship again. There was little merriment onboard ship as we sailed toward Pavuvu. But we had somehow survived the slaughter. There was much discussion as to why we had invaded Peleliu in the first place. Why hadn't we just bypassed the island and left the Japs there?

One of the old sergeants piped in and put things in perspective. "Hell, if we didn't invade that damn island we would have invaded another one and who knows? It could have been worse."

Later we learned that the invasion of Peleliu may have been unnecessary. Prior to the invasion, Navy carriers attacking the Philippines reported surprisingly weak Japanese resistance. Admiral Halsey sent a message on September 13 recommending that MacArthur skip his November 15 invasion of Mindanao and go directly to his eventual objective of Leyte as early as October 15. Nimitz, MacArthur and the Joint Chiefs approved it. Suddenly, the original rationale for invading Peleliu no longer made much sense, but Nimitz was unwilling to cancel the assault just days before its scheduled execution. It was a terrible, costly decision.

We arrived off Pavuvu on October 10 and entered Macquitti Bay and dropped anchor off Pavuvu's steel pier. We picked up our gear and slowly walked off the boat and onto the pier. From there we walked to the beach where trucks picked us up and to take us to the tented areas. We entered our tent and there our sea bags, cots and other gear had been stacked around the center pole while we were gone. The land crabs had moved in and when we started unstacking it, they came swarming out, and we tried stepping on them, or hitting them with our rifle butts, anyway we could kill them. After we got our sea bags and set up our cots, there was still gear stacked in the middle, a sad reminder that these men weren't going home. As I found Pop's sea bag, I began to cry. I soon realized that I was suddenly sobbing like a baby and that the other Marines had left the tent to allow me to grieve alone. As I thought about Pop, I wondered how many more Marines would die before this war was over.

Pavuvu was a better place when we returned than when we had left it. Maybe that was because Peleliu was such a hellhole that, after that, anything would look good. We got the word that the Guadalcanal vets who had fought in three campaigns would be rotated home. That was the best news I had ever heard.

When we arrived in Pavuvu, the island was humming with activity. More replacements were landing on the island. By the end of October the 7th Marines had arrived on Pavuvu and the 5th Marines were just leaving Peleliu.

In the beginning of November, Puller left Pavuvu to fly home. He was to report to Camp Lejeune, North Carolina, where he took over the Infantry Training Regiment or ITR. Their mission was to teach advanced infantry skills to boot camp graduates. Puller was obviously selected for the job because of his extensive combat experience as well as his keen interest in tough training. He would be the perfect man for the job.

Before he left he called me into his tent.

"Mike, it has been a long war for all of us, and the closer we get to Japan, the worse it is going to get. I probably won't see you again so I wanted to thank you for doing a fine job. Good luck, Corporal."

As I looked at Puller it was obvious that he was worn out after two years of hard fighting, terrible living conditions, and his leg wounds. I guess I was as burnt out as he was.

He shook hands with me and I said, "Thank you, sir."

As I walked out of his tent I thought I'd never see him again. I was going to Camp Elliot in California and was assigned to the ITR, which had the same mission as Puller's at Camp Lejeune.

HEADED HOME

The next day I boarded the *Billy Mitchell*, a converted passenger liner, manned by the U.S. Coast Guard. The Commanding Officer of Troops was Puller's Battalion Commander of 1/1 at Peleliu, the newly promoted Lieutenant Colonel Ray Davis.

Later that evening when we were waiting in line for chow I saw Davis and an Army colonel and they were having a heated discussion on how to supervise the mess line.

The Army colonel said, "Every meal in the mess I want a major or above to be in charge of each mess line."

"That is just ridiculous and it's not going to happen. That is what Marine sergeants are for. It would be an embarrassment to my Marines to have a field grade officer standing around watching them eat," replied Davis.

"Alright, then let's go to the captain of the ship, we'll let him decide."

Davis said, "That's fine with me."

They walked out and ten minutes later a Marine sergeant came in and took over the mess line. Davis was a great Marine and he wasn't about to take any guff from an Army officer, regardless of rank. And I would soon see him again.

We arrived in California at the end of November and I reported in to Camp Elliot. I was granted three weeks leave and wasted no time in going home. Because of the travel time, I could only spend two weeks in Chicago. It was a wonderful, happy time at home. My mother and father asked me little about my experiences in the war and as yet I was not ready to talk about it. I had to be back at Camp Elliot before Christmas and so this was the fourth Christmas in a row that I had to spend away from home and my family. But after all, there was a war going on and as far as I was concerned I was the luckiest man alive because I had survived some of the worst fighting in the Pacific.

Once back at Camp Elliot I was assigned to a unit to help train new Marine infantrymen. It was very serious and intense training because these young Marines would be leaving to go fight the Japanese as soon as the training was over. By now the Marine Corps had six Marine Divisions fighting in the Pacific. Because of the high casualty rates, the divisions were being depleted at an alarming rate. As a result, men were pulled out of ITR after only a few weeks training to get ready for the attacks on Iwo Jima and Okinawa.

In August 1945 the atomic bombing of Hiroshima and Nagasaki and the subsequent surrender of Japan brought about an end to the advanced infantry training and all training was scaled back to peacetime levels. The First

Marine Division had started the war on Guadalcanal and had then taken Cape Gloucester on New Britain, and then Peleliu. They finished off the war at Okinawa. These were all costly fights: the Division's losses for the entire war totaled more than 20,000 killed and wounded.

In January 1946 I was discharged from active duty and went home.

Chapter Five

The Korean War

Tomorrow we leave for Korea. Watching these young, naïve Marines, eager to fight, I often think I am too old for this. And how's this for luck? Colonel Puller asked me to be his runner. – Here we go again . . .

M. Abbo, letter to parents, 14 Aug 1950

THE BENDED KNEE

When World War II ended the Marine Corps was downsized from a wartime peak of 485,000 men and women to 156,000 – and by February 1948, it was down to an actual strength of 92,000. One year after the war, the Marine Corps faced one of their toughest battles and not a shot was fired. If they lost this battle they would cease to exist.

At the end of World War II the pressure was on to unify the armed services. The leadership of the Army wanted unification; the Navy was against it.

President Truman, a former Army Captain had no love for the Marine Corps. Army wartime leaders like Eisenhower and Bradley pushed hard to downsize the Corps to regimental size. Eisenhower didn't want two "land armies" and Bradley foolishly announced that the atomic bomb had made amphibious landings obsolete. It was also no secret that the Army wanted the Marines' weapons and manpower and the Air Force wanted their planes.

The Marine Corps of course opposed unification and the former commanding General of the 1st Marine Division on Guadalcanal, and now the Commandant of the Marine Corps, General Vandegrift, led the charge against unification.

In May of 1946, appearing before a Senate Naval Officers Committee, Vandegrift delivered a very articulate and emotional statement:

We have pride in ourselves and in our past but we do not rest our case on any presumed ground of gratitude owing us from the nation. The bended knee is not a tradition of our Corps. If the Marine as a fighting man has not made a case for himself after 170 years of service, he must go. But I think you will agree with me that he has earned the right to depart with dignity and honor, not by subjugation to the status of uselessness and servility planned for him by the War Department.

On July 26, 1947 President Truman signed the National Security Act, organizing the military under a single Secretary of Defense and establishing the Air Force as a separate service. The Act formalized in law for the first time the Corps' special amphibious function.

NORTH KOREA

After the war, I went back to Chicago. I applied and was accepted back at Notre Dame. At the same time I decided to stay in the Marine Corps Reserve. Even with the G.I. bill's assistance, I needed the money. I was assigned to the 9th Marine Corps Reserve Infantry Battalion in Chicago. I graduated from Notre Dame in June of 1949. After graduation, I got a job with the *Chicago Tribune* as a reporter in the city section. I was finally starting my career.

Later that year I was promoted to sergeant. Early in the fall of 1949 the Chicago Reserve received a new commanding officer, Lieutenant Colonel Ray Davis, Puller's Battalion Commander on Peleliu.

When I reported in for my monthly training, early on a Saturday morning, I was told to report to Lieutenant Colonel Davis. When I walked into his office he told me to stand at ease.

He looked at me and said, "It's nice to see you again, Sergeant Abbo. I think the last time we were together was on the *Billy Mitchell*, coming home from Pavuvu. In looking through your service records, I noticed that Colonel Puller rated you outstanding in his reports. Sergeant, you've had a lot of experience and you're going to be a great asset to this duty station."

"Thank you, sir," I replied, "Welcome to Chicago."

Davis smiled and said, "I'm glad to be here, Sergeant."

On June 25, 1950, the North Korean People's Army (NKPA) stormed across the 38th Parallel into South Korea with three tank regiments followed by 90,000 infantry troops. The Republic of Korea (ROK) Army could not hold them back. On June 27th, with United Nations approval, President Truman ordered U.S. Forces, under the command of General MacArthur into the fight. The following day, Seoul, the capital of South Korea, fell.

Army units began arriving in Korea on July 1st and they were fed piecemeal into the turmoil. MacArthur then requested a Marine regiment supported by an

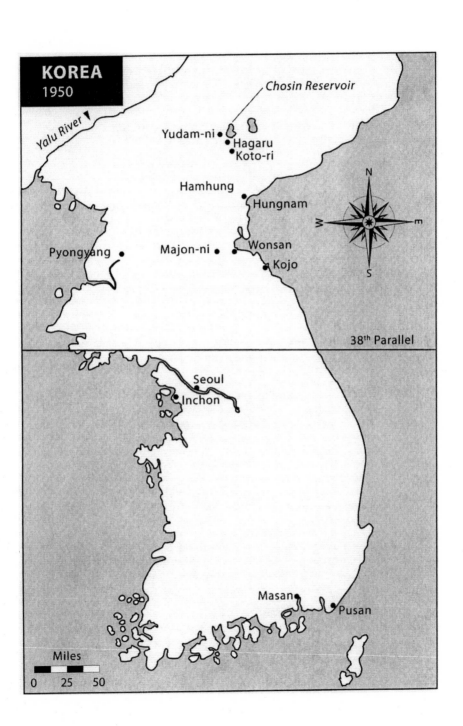

KOREA
1950

Yalu River

Chosin Reservoir

Yudam-ni
Hagaru
Koto-ri

Hamhung
Hungnam

Pyongyang   Majon-ni   Wonsan
                                 Kojo

N
W   E
S

38th Parallel

Seoul
Inchon

Masan
Pusan

Miles
0   25   50

air group. The 1st Provisional Brigade (the 5th Marine Regiment and Marine Aircraft Group 33) sailed on July 12th. The Marines would be the first combat troops to ship out from the United States.

MacArthur then asked for a whole Marine Division. On July 19th, President Truman authorized the activation of the Marine Corps Reserve. The Commandant ordered all units of the 2nd Marine Division in Camp Lejeune, NC to report immediately to Camp Pendleton in California. By the end of July, Marines were flowing into Camp Pendleton.

Colonel Puller flew out of Hawaii on July 20th and a few days later arrived at Camp Pendleton and took over his old regiment, the 1st Marines.

On July 25th the Commandant ordered the 1st Marine Division to expand to full strength and get ready to deploy to the Far East by August 10th.

By July 26th the Army had three divisions and a regiment in Korea and they were pushed back to an area in the Southeastern corner of Korea known as the "Pusan Perimeter."

The Fifth Marines landed at Pusan on August 2nd and went into action five days later. They would soon be named the "Fire Brigade" and would help stop the North Koreans and save the Pusan Perimeter.

At the beginning of the Korean War less than ten percent of the diminished United States Marine Corps had combat experience. The officer and NCO ranks, however, were comprised of battle tested veterans. These men knew how to fight.

THE RUSH TO WAR

When the North Koreans invaded South Korea, I knew there was a good chance that the Marine Reserves would be called up. Over the next few weeks, I hoped that I was wrong but when President Truman activated the Marine Corps Reserves on July 19th, I knew I was heading west. My whole reserve unit in Chicago was ordered to Camp Pendleton immediately.

The train station was crowded with Marines, but quiet as they said goodbye to their families. My mother began to cry when I turned toward the train, and my father remained ever stoic as he told me to be careful and wished me good luck. I had said my farewells to my sister, Annie, the day before. She had recently graduated from college and was busy starting her career in retail at a department store in Chicago. Seven hundred of us boarded the train. Many of the older Marines sat silently and gazed out the windows at the passing landscape. We had been to war before and knew it was no lark. The younger Marines, however, were excited and for many of them it was their first trip across the country. It took a long three days for us to get there. We arrived on

July 26th, got off the train and formed into platoons and were marched off to Tent Camp Two. Before we got there a Marine Captain stopped us and took the first nine men and me. He told us we were going to the 1st Marine Regiment, we were to grab our gear and get into the truck.

After a short drive we were taken to a big field full of tents. It was apparent that this "tent city" was recently put up because weeds were easily discernible amid the stakes and canvas. We pulled up to a tent where there were about fifty Marines waiting in line. A staff sergeant told us, "Get your gear, get off the truck, get in line and hurry the hell up." I felt like saying, "Yeah, hurry the hell up and wait," but I kept my mouth shut.

I got in line and waited there for about thirty minutes and when I finally got inside the big tent, it was a mad house. Everyone was yelling and screaming. A sergeant yelled at me, "Sergeant, over here." I walked over quickly and he said, "Give me your orders." I handed them over to him and he said, "You are being assigned to the 1st Marines. When you leave the tent, turn left, they are down on the left. Report to the first sergeant."

After being shuffled around for an hour, I ended up in my old unit, the 1st Battalion, 1st Marines. It didn't take me long to find out that the regimental commander was Colonel Puller. It surprised me because the last I had heard was that he was in command of the Marine Barracks at Pearl Harbor. I certainly didn't expect to be serving under Puller again. Events were really moving fast. We were getting beat badly in Korea. This war had caught the entire country by surprise. About all I knew for sure was that I did not want to be a runner for Colonel Puller. I had previously had too many close calls and I knew too much about the dangers of being Chesty's runner. No one really knew what was going to happen in this war. I finally fell asleep after I convinced myself that Puller wouldn't even know I was in the 1st Marines and even if he did, the chances were slim that he would request me for a runner.

The next day we spent on the rifle range. The rifles we received were left over from World War II and were in terrible condition. Obviously, the people who put these weapons away in storage thought there were not going to be any more wars. Over half the weapons in our platoon were bad and needed to be turned in, including mine.

When we were on the firing range I saw an individual from a distance, walking back and forth, observing the Marines on the range. He had a pipe stuck in his mouth, an old crumpled utility cap on his head and sun-bleached utilities that were almost white. The casual observer would think it was an old gunnery sergeant, but he would be mistaken; it was Chesty Puller. We were off to war and his Marines were going to have weapons that worked and would fire accurately.

The following day I was issued a new rifle and was back on the range and this time my weapon worked fine, and Chesty Puller was there watching us.

The next day we worked hard getting the supplies ready and that night went to the enlisted man's club for a beer. The word had spread quickly that the night before, Puller had chewed out the lieutenant who was in charge of the enlisted man's club because he had run out of beer and he was serving warm beer. That night the beer was cold and they didn't run out. When I left the club, there were beer cans all over the company streets. I guess the lieutenant got the message.

The following morning the first sergeant told me to "Report to Colonel Puller's office at 0900."

I was dreading this meeting and reported to his office, which was just a tent. As I walked in he was standing and reading something. When he saw me he threw the papers on his desk, shook my hand and said "Welcome aboard, Mike."

Puller sat down, pulled out his pipe, lit it, leaned back in his chair and said, "I was reviewing the roster of the regiment and came across a Sergeant Michael Abbo. I thought, I wonder if it's the same Michael Abbo. I'm glad it is, Mike, I need a runner."

I had a feeling this was coming. "Yes sir," I said.

"Good, Mike. What did you do when the last war was over?" he inquired.

"Sir, I joined the reserves, got my degree and started working for the *Chicago Tribune*," I answered.

Puller smiled, "Oh God, not a newspaper man!" He paused a moment, then said, "You should be proud of yourself for getting an education. How's your family?"

"Mom and Dad are in good health, but it was hard on them, having to worry about me fighting in another war." Then I asked, "How is your family, sir?"

Puller looked at me and smiled, "Growing. We had twins in August of '45: Lewis Jr. and Martha Leigh, and everyone is doing fine. Thanks for asking."

He then told me to get my gear and report into regimental headquarters and to tell 1/1 to transfer my records. As I walked out of his tent, I thought what a damn fool I was to stay in the reserves. I knew Puller would be right in the middle of the action and now I would be right there with him. I hoped to God I would make it.

The next few days flew by and I spent most of the time waiting in line or loading trucks. We were issued summer utilities and 782 gear. We were given shots and filled out forms for insurance. When a division goes to war, especially on short notice, the work never ends.

The 1st Marine Division would be commanded by Major General O.P. Smith, the 5th Marines by Lieutenant Colonel Ray Murray and the 7th

Marines by Colonel Homer Litzenberg. The 1st Marine Division would be well led.

The 1st Marines had a lot of experience in its senior commanders. They had all served in World War II but were new to Puller: Lieutenant Colonels Robert Rickert, Puller's executive officer and the battalion commanders Jack Hawkins (1/1), Allan Sutter (2/1), and Thomas Ridge (3/1).

The Colonel was looking for a driver and wanted someone who was aggressive, could read maps and judge distances, as well as have mechanical ability. He found a WWII veteran, Sergeant Orville W. Jones. He also wanted a bodyguard. He was looking for someone who was an expert shot and had a reputation as a fighter. Another veteran surfaced and his name was Sergeant Jan Bodey. Most people called Bodey "Bo" and Jones preferred to be called "O.W." His father had named him after Orville Wright. These two men and I would be with Puller all the way through Korea.

The 1st Marine Regiment was a combination of Marine units: many were from the Second Division at Camp Lejeune, some were from Navy bases, and a few, like me, were from the Marine Reserves. We had no time to train, other than test-firing our weapons. There was no time to work in the field or get to know the men in your unit. Although the Colonel did not know many members of his 1st Marines, almost all of them were familiar with the Puller legend. His Marines had heard all the stories. There was just no time to mold these men into a cohesive fighting unit, but Puller and his reputation quickly gave the members of his regiment a special pride and esprit de corps. It was pride by association.

After hours when we returned to the enlisted man's club for a beer, a lot of Marines would ask each other, "What unit are you with?" The typical answer would be a number like "1/1" or 1st Battalion, 1st Marines or "2/5," etc., but Puller's men always answered, "I'm in Chesty's outfit."

One night shortly before we left for Korea the Colonel had a meeting with all of his officers.

"Gentlemen, I'd like to welcome all of you to the 1st Marines. As I'm sure you all know this is one helluva regiment. They fought on Guadalcanal, New Britain, Peleliu and Okinawa. This regiment has an outstanding combat reputation and by God we are going to keep it that way. Most of you have had combat experience in World War II and you know what you have to do. I don't know where we are going in Korea, but I do know that we are going there. I want you to keep two things in mind: number one is that you are Marine officers and I expect you to lead from the front. And number two is that you better take damned good care of your men because they are going to be the ones that get the job done. We've had five years of peace and now it's time to earn our pay. Thank you, gentlemen."

When everyone left, Bodey, Jones and I remained behind. He told us to grab a seat. He asked a few questions and wanted to know if we were ready to go to Korea. We all answered, "Yes, sir." He told us that this would be his fourth war.

"Colonel, when did you enlist in the Corps?" I asked.

"In 1918," he said, "I dropped out of VMI after my freshman year. World War I was going on and I wanted to join in the fight, but by the time I was an officer, the war had ended. The Marine Corps didn't need all those officers, so I could either go on inactive status or resign my commission, start over as a private and go to Haiti to fight with the Gendarmerie d'Haiti. So, I went to Haiti."

"Sir, what was Haiti like?" Jones asked.

"It was tough. I served two tours there. Most of the people were poor, uneducated, and unhealthy. They lived in squalor. The Cacos were lawless, native tribesmen. They ruthlessly attacked the villages and cities."

"Even though I was a private in the Marine Corps, I served as a lieutenant in the Gendarmerie. Our job was to train this new force and then patrol the countryside to maintain stability."

"Did you see much fighting?" I asked.

"There were lots of small fights but no major battles. The Cacos were poorly organized and poorly armed, but they were vicious bandits."

Bodey then asked, "What were your men like?"

"Once the Haitians were trained, they were good fighters. I had a sergeant major named Napoleon Lyautey. He was tall, tough and had the respect of all the men. His brutal discipline sometimes shocked me. Once we were hiking along a trail and one of Lyautey's men near the back of the line dropped out and sat down. He was a fat man and looked exhausted. The sergeant major spotted him, yelled out orders and the man was then tied to a pack mule and dragged along the trail for a few hundred yards. Lyautey then untied him and I was surprised to see the man fall back in line."

"I learned a valuable lesson from the sergeant major that day, when he said, 'the patrol must not fail, and if one soldier falls out, others will follow. This can not happen. If the Cacos had found this man alone they would have butchered him.'"

"Sometimes training has to be brutal to be effective."

"Sir, when did you become an officer again?" I asked.

"I returned in June, 1923 after my second tour in Haiti," Puller answered, "I went to officer candidates school and became a second lieutenant in March of 1924. I had been an enlisted man for six years."

When I left Puller's tent, I thought about what I had just heard. It gave me more insight into Chesty's harsh training methods as well as his affinity for the enlisted man.

In mid August, the Marines started boarding ships in San Diego. The Colonel and his headquarters group were the last to board a few days later. We sailed aboard the attack transport U.S.S. *Noble*.

Before we boarded the ship the Colonel gave me a box of books.

"Mike, make sure this gets to my cabin. These are all books on Korea and Manchuria. This has been such a rush job – we don't know a damn thing about Korea: the people, the weather, the topography, we know nothing. I guess I got a lot of homework to do."

The trip to Kobe, Japan took almost two weeks. The deck was packed with gear so that there was limited room for training, but the officers and NCOs got the men together in small groups for exercise, cleaning their weapons and other things that would be important in Korea, such as first aid, map reading and night patrols.

We finally pulled into Kobe, Japan on September 2nd. It was rumored that we were going to land at Inchon, Korea, but it was not official. We spent the next few days combat-loading the USS *Noble* and all the LSTs that would carry the rest of the regiment.

We were surprised to hear that on September 5th, in response to a congressman who had written suggesting the Marine Commandant be accorded a voice on the Joint Chiefs, President Truman unleashed his fury and replied, "For your information, the Marine Corps is the Navy's police force and as long as I am President, that is what it will remain. They have a propaganda machine that is almost equal to Stalin's."

There was great backlash of public opinion and the next day the President apologized to Commandant Cates. Truman was an Army artillery officer in World War I and I couldn't figure out why he didn't like the Marine Corps, but we had other things to worry about.

The 1st Marine Division would be part of X Corps which would be commanded by Major General Ned Almond, MacArthur's chief of staff. Also part of X Corps would be the Army's 7th Infantry Division.

On August 22nd, General O. P. Smith, the commanding officer of the 1st Marine Division, met with General Almond, for the first time. Generals Smith and Almond were the same rank: Major General. When Smith met Almond, Almond kept him waiting an hour and a half. Then to add insult to injury, Almond called Smith "son." Smith was 57 years old and Almond 58. If that wasn't bad enough, when Smith tried to explain the difficulties of an amphibious landing, Almond discounted the problems by saying that they were "purely mechanical." Smith had more combat experience than Almond and this meeting would be the start of the legendary feud between the two generals.

Very little was known about the Inchon operation. Colonel Puller flew up to Tokyo for a briefing from the Division Staff and then quickly returned with the plan. That night he called his senior commanders together and laid out the plans for the operation.

"Gentlemen, I've just returned from division headquarters and it's official: we are back in the amphibious assault business. We will be landing on the west coast of Korea at Inchon on September 15th. The 1st Marine Division will lead the assault and we will be part of X Corps, which will be commanded by Major General Almond. The name of the operation is 'Chromite'. Don't anyone ask me where MacArthur came up with that name because I sure as hell don't know. On the table is a set of aerial photos. I want the battalion and company commanders to study these very carefully.

"Colonel Sutter, your 2nd Battalion will land on the left of the regimental zone. Colonel Ridge, your 3rd Battalion will land on the right and Colonel Hawkins' 1st Battalion will land in reserve. The 5th Marines have been pulled from the Pusan Perimeter and are on their way. They will land to our left. The 7th Marines will not get here in time to make the landing, so we will be a regiment short.

"Because of the tides, this will be a very tricky landing. The first problem is the island of Wolmi-Do, which guards the harbor. 3/5 will have to seize this on the morning tide. The tidal range is over thirty feet, maybe the highest in the world. Therefore, 3/5 will have to hang on for twelve hours-we can not land until the tide returns in the evening. This is going to be tough because it only gives us two hours of daylight after we land. There are no beaches, just seawalls along an industrial waterfront. We will take ladders to get us over the walls.

"Our objective will be to come in southeast of the city of Inchon, seize the high ground, cut off the enemy and stop any reinforcements from helping them out. The 5th Marines will land at the same time as we do and pick up 3/5 on the way and then attack through Inchon.

"Another big problem is that we are going to end up fighting in the city of Seoul. We never did this type of fighting in World War II. It could be a very tough fight. Good night, gentlemen."

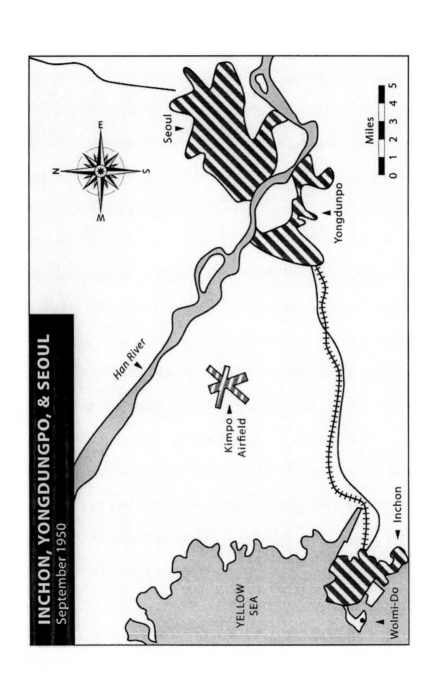

INCHON, YONGDUNGPO, & SEOUL
September 1950

Seoul

Yongdunpo

Han River

Kimpo
Airfield

Inchon

Wolmi-Do

YELLOW
SEA

Miles

0 1 2 3 4 5

Chapter Six

Inchon and Seoul

*Our landing at Inchon changed the whole course of this war. We com-
pletely surprised the North Koreans. We've cut their supply lines and it
appears that we have many of them trapped. If all goes well, I could be
home by Christmas.*

M. Abbo, letter to parents, 6 Oct 1950

INCHON

We left Kobe on September 12th and headed toward Inchon. As we approached our goal the convoy grew larger. On the night before the landing
there were endless briefing sessions and when his staff had finished, Chesty
took over.

"Gentlemen, you don't know how lucky you are. I had to wait twenty
years between wars. You only had to wait five. We live by the sword and if
necessary we will be ready to die by the sword. Good luck, gentlemen. I'll
see you ashore."

At dusk on September 15th, the Marines started landing. Puller, Bodey,
myself and part of Puller's staff went in on the third wave. In the fading light
we climbed a high seawall on a ladder. Puller briefly sat on the wall with
his pipe in his mouth and looked back at the ships in the harbor and all the
Marines on the beach climbing the ladders. He then looked ahead to where
the enemy was.

"It looks like we caught 'em off guard," he yelled.

He jumped down from the wall and we followed him inland. In the early
darkness a light rain started and the Colonel set up his command post in a

ditch between the 2nd and 3rd battalions using a poncho as cover. For a while there was a lot of confusion, but the officers and sergeants soon had their men moving inland.

Reports from the battalions began to come in. Sutter's 2/1 on the left and Ridge's 3/1 on the right had seized most of their objectives and Puller ordered Hawkins' 1/1 to land.

Late in the evening, Sergeant Jones brought in the Colonel's jeep on an amphibious tractor, parked it near the seawall and somehow found the CP sometime after midnight.

At about the same time, Division called and General Smith gave the order to continue the attack in the morning. The two regiments would drive east with the Inchon-Seoul highway separating them. The 5th Marines were to the left of the highway and the 1st Marines to the right. Puller called his battalion commanders and gave them the order for the next day, and received the casualty reports: 2/1 and 3/1 had five killed and thirty-four wounded.

Later that night when things had slowed down, I said, "Bo, what in the hell is that smell?"

"These people fertilize their fields with human shit," he replied, "That's what you're smellin' Abbo."

The fields, the rice paddies, the whole country smelled somewhat like a neglected outhouse. I would never get used to the smell.

THE STARS AND THE SILVER STAR

We moved out early the next morning. Because the 1st Marines had such a wide front to cover, Puller put all three battalions on line, which left no reserve. Jones retrieved the jeep and we followed the battalions. The terrain became increasingly hilly and at the end of the second day the casualties were similar to those of the first. The assault phase of the landing was over and in the morning the drive for Seoul would start. The capital was seventeen miles away.

The following morning the three battalions moved forward. The 2nd Battalion was held up by the North Korean counter attack.

Around noon, the Colonel got a call on the radio from MacArthur's headquarters, "General MacArthur has come ashore and would like to award Colonel Puller the Silver Star. Can the Colonel come to the rear?"

Puller got on the radio, "We are fully engaged and fighting every foot of the way. I can't leave here. If he wants to decorate, he'll have to come up here."

Puller put his binoculars up to his eyes to follow the battle from the top of the hill. About a half hour later I noticed a large convoy coming up the road behind us. Major Reeves, Puller's adjutant was also on top of the hill and I said, "Major, we've got company."

He turned to look and shouted to Puller, "General MacArthur's coming."

"How do you know?" Puller asked.

"It looks like a parade coming down the road with all those jeeps; it must be MacArthur."

The vehicles stopped at the bottom of the hill and MacArthur got out and climbed up the hill with Marine Generals Smith and Shepherd, Vice Admiral Struble and General Almond. They were followed by reporters and some of MacArthur's senior staff. I have never seen so many stars in all my life.

Puller took the pipe out of his mouth, saluted and asked "How are you General?"

"I'm doing fine." Then MacArthur said "Colonel Puller, the 1st Marines have done an outstanding job and it is my pleasure to present you with the Silver Star."

MacArthur then looked at one of his aids, expecting to be handed a medal to present to Puller. The aid said, "Sir, we have no Silver Stars at the moment."

"Well then, make sure the Colonel gets his Star."

"Thank you, General" replied Puller as he put the pipe back in his mouth and then pointed straight ahead. "Those bastards are right over the next hill."

I was standing next to Jones and said, "O.W., take a look at Chesty and the General. In a way, they are pretty similar: the General in his crushed hat, sunglasses and corncob pipe, and Chesty maybe a bit disheveled after two days of fighting, in his wrinkled, sweat-stained utilities, his utility cap at a rakish angle, and his pipe stuck in his mouth."

"Yes, they are' Jones replied, 'You know what, Mike? MacArthur's plan of landing at Inchon and the Marines' execution of it was a pretty good combination."

"It sure was," I agreed.

The two men talked while the reporters gathered around them. The Marines and soldiers on top of the hill gave them a little more space. MacArthur, of course, asked all the questions.

"How long until you to get into Seoul, Colonel?"

"Maybe three or four days, General."

"You sound pretty sure, Puller."

"Resistance is increasing as we approach Seoul, but we'll get there. We got more firepower than they do and these Marines are better fighters. We'll drive em back."

MacArthur then said "Colonel, I expected you to be back in your CP."

Puller smiled and patted his hip pocket containing his field map and said, "Sir, this is my CP."

"Keep up the splendid work, Colonel," and MacArthur, the generals and the admiral, his staff and the reporters walked back down the hill to the jeeps and drove off.

Puller kept pushing his battalions for the rest of the day and they made good progress, meeting light resistance. The 5th Marines late in the day took Kimpo Airfield. This was key because now American air support could fly from land bases.

MILITARY JUSTICE

The next day we awoke early, ate quickly and the attack jumped off. Ridge's 3/1 attacked down the road to Seoul; Sutter's 2/1 was north of the highway and Hawkins' 1/1 moved ahead south of the highway. Puller's jeep followed Ridge down the highway.

In the middle of the morning Puller tried unsuccessfully to contact Colonel Sutter by radio. Because of the steep hills, Sutter's radioman was probably beyond the crest of the hill and out of radio contact. I was sitting in the back of the jeep with Bodey and the Colonel was in front, with Jones driving.

Puller yelled out, "Stop the jeep! Sergeant Abbo, get up on top of that ridge and tell Colonel Sutter to stay in contact. I want to know what the hell's going on up there."

"Yes, sir."

I jumped out of the jeep and quickly walked about one hundred yards north to the base of the hill and started to climb up. I looked at my watch. It was 10:10 AM. The hill was steep, it was hot and when I reached the top I was soaking wet, completely drained and it was 10:45 AM. I looked down into a little valley and could see Sutter's battalion moving east. After about ten minutes I caught up with some of the Marines and asked them where Colonel Sutter was. They pointed out his CP and I headed in that direction. The hills were killing me and I thought I was in good shape. A few minutes later I reported to Colonel Sutter. He turned toward me and said, "What's up?"

I said, "Colonel Puller can't reach you on his radio. He thought the signal wouldn't go over these high ridges."

Sutter looked at his radio operator and said, "Pull up Colonel Puller on the radio."

After a minute of fussing around the operator looked at Sutter, "Sir, I can't reach him."

Sutter then said, "Let's move this CP up to the ridge."

We all moved up to the top of the ridge and you could see Sutter's men on the left and Ridge's men attacking down the road and Puller was down there somewhere.

Sutter got hold of the Colonel, who asked, "What's going on up there?"

Sutter replied, "The hills are slowing us down and we've taken some casualties but we are advancing."

"Alright, keep pressing ahead, stay in radio contact and send Abbo back."

I climbed down to the road and my rear end was dragging. There was a little more traffic on the road, most of it heading down to the front. I hitched a ride in a truck and in about five minutes spotted Puller's jeep.

I called out, "You can let me out here."

The driver stopped and said, "See ya, Sergeant," turned around and headed to the rear.

When I walked up to the jeep Puller was in the middle of an intense conversation with a couple of officers. Apparently, a Marine jeep driver was ordered to take a load of North Korean prisoners to the 1st Marines' CP but instead they were gunned down. There were no witnesses. The driver's CO and some of the regimental staff were talking to Puller about what disciplinary action should be taken.

The Colonel dished out a little military justice, "There will be no court martial in this regiment. What unit was it that had all those casualties last night?"

"Captain Barrow's company, sir."

"All right, send him up there. He can kill all the Commies he wants."

THE GENERALS RETURN

We started out in the morning of September 19th. Hawkins' 1st Battalion was moved north of the highway so that going from left to right it would be 1/1, 3/1 in the middle and 2/1 next to the highway on the right flank. The 32nd Infantry would take the position right of the highway previously held by 1/1. The 32nd Infantry Regiment instead of continuing the attack spent the afternoon setting up. As 2/1 fought down the road, a gap opened on its right flank. Puller was furious and immediately called General Smith on the radio.

"Sir, we are taking fire on our right flank. Where the hell is the Army?"

"Lewie, I don't know what is holding them up. I'll call the 7th Division and tell them to get moving. Be careful."

When the day ended, Puller's CP was on the top of a hill where you could see all the way to Seoul.

Puller had part of his staff in the CP and he was in a somber mood.

"The Corps has fought few battles in cities. Casualties are always high, and it takes a long time to go from house to house. I hope this is not another Peleliu."

Early the next morning, we didn't start the attack, the North Koreans did. They counterattacked along the highway with five tanks followed by a battalion of infantry. It was still dark but 2/1 was ready for them.

When the battle was over, Sutter's Marines had killed over three hundred North Koreans.

That day the 5th Marines had crossed the Han River, the 1st Marines were preparing to attack Yongdungpo and the 7th Marines were to land the next day.

Sometime after noon we were on the side of the road and Puller was talking on the radio to one of his battalion commanders when we saw a line of jeeps coming down the road. The lead jeep stopped next to us. General Almond was driving and General MacArthur was riding shotgun. Sitting in the back were the Marine Generals Smith and Sheperd. Puller walked over, put his right hand up on top of the windshield and started talking to MacArthur. They were all paying close attention to Puller as he briefed them on the battle. I thought the Colonel must rate pretty high with MacArthur because this was the second time in four days that he had sought out Puller. They talked for about five minutes and then the generals left.

After they drove away, O. W. said to me, "I don't think those generals all riding around together in that one jeep is such a good idea."

"That's for sure," I said.

"If a round came in and hit that jeep that would be the end of those guys. The Army would never forgive the Marines if MacArthur was killed on our watch", O.W. replied.

Later that day, Puller had moved his CP to the rear slope of a ridge overlooking Yongdungpo. Early that evening, the XO, Lieutenant Colonel Rickert, a tank commander and Puller were standing on the forward crest of the ridge looking towards the city. The North Koreans saw them and started firing. Rickert and the tank commander dove on the ground but Puller didn't move and kept talking until he was finished and then calmly walked back to his CP. We had all witnessed this incident, including Jimmy Cannon, a reporter from the *New York Post*. As a fellow newsman in civilian life, I had been talking with Cannon earlier in the day.

Cannon looked at me and said, "My God, Puller walks along the battlefield like he is killing time on a hunting trip. It's like he has contempt for the marksmanship of the enemy."

"That's the Colonel," I replied.

YONGDUNGPO

The attack kicked off at 6:30 AM on September 21st.

The Colonel was watching the battle when General Smith came up to his CP. They both watched the fighting and Smith said, "Lewie, it looks like the whole city is on fire."

"General, there is a lot of fighting going on down there and we got the momentum. We're going to drive 'em right out of town."

Smith stayed for about five minutes and then got in his jeep and drove off. All day Puller paced back and forth watching the progress of the attack and talking to his commanders on the radio.

As night came Hawkins called and said, "We got a problem, Colonel. A Company is isolated. They made good progress today, and punched through the North Koreans, now they are on the far side of town, dug in on top of a dike. Captain Barrow called in and said they're holding their own and then the radio went dead. I am not exactly sure where they are. Is there anything we can do?"

The Colonel replied, "The whole regiment is dug in for the night. A night attack could be costly. We'll wait till morning. It's too risky to do anything tonight. If you hear anything, let me know."

When the sun came up the next morning, Puller ordered the 1st and 3rd Battalions to go to the aid of A Company. Much to everyone's surprise, Captain Barrow's A Company was in good shape and the enemy had fled, leaving behind 275 of their dead and four tanks. A Company's dramatic stand had broken the North Korean hold on Yongdungpo. After two days, the 1st Marines had cleared a fairly large city and much of it was destroyed.

By the evening of the following day, Puller was prepared to cross the Han River and join up with Murray's 5th Marines. Lieutenant Colonel Rickert went to Division Headquarters to iron out the plans for the 1st Marines to cross the Han River in the morning.

Before sunrise Puller called his battalion commanders on the radio and gave them the plan for the day, "The 2nd Battalion will cross first, followed by the 1st. The 3rd Battalion will remain by the Han bridges until ordered to move out.

There was a lot of pressure from MacArthur and Almond to retake Seoul by September 25th, the three month anniversary of the start of the Korean War, and Almond channeled the pressure to General Smith's 1st Marine Division. Unfortunately, no one told the North Korean Army.

THE HAN RIVER

Early on September 24th, Sutter's 2/1 began crossing the Han. Their orders were to cross and head east to take Hill 79. When they were across, Hawkins'

1/1 started crossing and it was slow going because they were ferried over on LVTs. When Hawkins made it to the other side Puller, Bodey and I crossed over with Jones and his jeep.

Hawkins came up to Puller and asked what his orders were.

"Take Hill 79," the Colonel said.

Hawkins replied with the obvious, "Colonel, the 2nd is already attacking in that zone. You need to stop them so I can get out front."

Puller retorted, "Hell no, I'm not stopping them. I had trouble enough getting them started."

"They should halt and let us pass through them," Hawkins said.

"Hawkins, I'll give them the word to cease fire and you'll just have to move a little faster."

Puller looked at Jones and asked him for a folded flag from the jeep. The Colonel gave it to Hawkins and said, "When you take the hill, raise it up."

The plan for the next day was for Puller's 1st Marines to establish contact with Murray's 5th Marines and drive north through the heart of the city. Both the 1st and 5th Marines would each have to cover a front one and a half miles wide. Lieutenant Colonel Raymond Murray flew over to Puller's CP in a helicopter to coordinate the attack. The two regimental commanders had never met. It was unusual to have a lieutenant colonel commanding a regiment but then again Murray was no ordinary Marine: he had earned a Silver Star on both Guadalcanal and Tarawa, a Navy Cross on Saipan, and in command of the 1st Provisional Marine Brigade in the defense of the Pusan Perimeter he earned his third and fourth Silver Stars.

When Murray got out of the helicopter, the two men shook hands and talked for a few minutes. Puller had a unique way of evaluating an officer's combat effectiveness. He asked Murray how many men his regiment had lost. He replied, "Since we landed at Pusan, the 5th Marines has had 17 platoon leaders, and five company commanders killed or wounded." I never understood or liked that about Puller. Judging a leader's worth by how many casualties his unit suffered was just wrong. Casualties had nothing to do with a commander's ability or his combat effectiveness – what Puller really valued in a leader was aggressiveness. Satisfied that Murray passed muster, they made their plans for the next day and then Murray left.

At about 5:00 PM Captain Robert Barrow's A Company took Hill 79 and raised the flag on a bamboo pole over an old school house.

When Puller saw the flag he got on the radio and called Division. "C.O. 1st Marines reports American flag now flying on Hill 79, city of Seoul."

Later that evening General Smith and an X Corps staff officer visited the CP. The staff officer made the mistake of saying that the Marines had a habit of flying the flag over everything they captured.

Puller growled at the officer, "A man with a flag in his pack and the courage to put it on an enemy strong point is the best fighter there is."

The staff officer didn't open his mouth again.

SEOUL

In defending Seoul, the North Korean People's Army, or NKPA made a big
mistake. Instead of defending buildings, they fought in the streets. At major
intersections in the city they set up barricades of rubble filled rice bags that
were piled eight feet high. They were defended by anti-tank guns, machine
guns and mines. Puller could have bypassed these roadblocks but instead he
chose to break right through them.

Puller told his commanders, "We'll send the engineers in to clear the
mines. Then we'll bring in the tanks and blow those barricades apart."

On September 25th, the 1st Marine Division launched its attack on Seoul.
The city, with over a million people, was the fifth largest city in the orient.
The 1st Marines would drive to the north, through the heart of the city on a
mile-and-a-half front. Korean Marines would follow Puller's regiment and
then mop up any North Koreans that were left behind.

Puller had two platoons of tanks that we were waiting on for help, but they
hadn't shown up yet. We pulled the jeep off to the side of the avenue and
Puller kept saying, "Where the hell are they?"

Around noon the tanks showed up and the tank commander reported to
Puller, "Sir, I am sorry I'm late, but we ran into a fight crossing the river. We
killed fifteen and captured 131."

Puller cut him off, "I don't have time to listen to your sea stories, young
man. You're late. Now get your men moving. We've got fish to fry."

Progress was painfully slow. The city was being torn apart. Everywhere
you looked you saw downed power wires, rubble filled streets and burning
buildings with blown out windows. It took about 45 minutes to an hour to
blast our way through each barricade and when we did there was debris, dead
bodies and weapons all around. Then it was on to the next one. And caught in
the middle of this utter chaos were thousands of Korean civilians.

Puller was standing by his jeep watching as our artillery came crashing
down on top of the homes and buildings and he said to me, "The way the
North Koreans are defending this damn city, they are forcing us to destroy
it. They'll remember us for a thousand years for this, and they'll hate our
guts!"

Puller was up front most of the day and he was usually positioned behind
the lead platoons. Instead of a helmet he wore his battered utility cap, and the

pipe, of course, was always in his mouth. There was a lot of sniper fire in the area, but he didn't pay any attention to it.

By the end of the day we had only advanced 2000 yards. When it got dark we were going to hold up for the night, but we received a call from Division and Puller got on the phone. General Almond had reports of the enemy fleeing Seoul and he wanted the Marines to push the attack. It was agreed that the 1st and 5th Marines would hook up with each other and would start the attack at 1:30 AM.

When Puller got off the phone he said, "How stupid is this? Launch an attack in the middle of the night? These men are exhausted. How would X Corps know who's fleeing the city? Are they soldiers or civilians?" He called division back and ordered a fifteen-minute artillery preparation to soften up the area. The attack was delayed until 2:00 AM.

A few minutes before the attack was to begin, Lt. Colonel Ridge called Puller to report that the North Koreans, supported by tanks and self-propelled guns, were moving down Mapo Boulevard towards the 1st Marines. General Smith postponed the attack.

From midnight until dawn, Ridge's battalion held back the North Koreans. With an amazing display of firepower, the machine guns, riflemen and artillery tore the NKPA apart.

Major Simmons, the commanding office of Ridge's Weapons Company called for artillery concentrations out to his front. For the next hour and a half the 11th Marines kept firing their 105's until the tubes became so hot they had to stop to allow the guns to cool down. Then Simmons called for 155mm howitzer fire from the Army. They fired 360 rounds along the battalion's front.

All night long we could hear the battle raging and Puller was next to the radio following the flow of the fight. At dawn, Chesty picked up the handset of the radio and called the 155 howitzer unit. He wanted to thank them for a job well done.

"This is blade", (Chesty's call sign) "I don't know who in the hell you are, but thank God you're out there."

When daylight arrived on the 26th, we drove over to Lt. Colonel Ridge's position. He showed Puller the shattered remains of the battle; seven tanks, two self-propelled guns, eight 45 mm anti-tank guns and over 250 dead North Koreans lying in the street.

Chesty said to Ridge, "It's a damn good thing General Smith cancelled that attack last night or it would be our Marines dead out there instead of those North Koreans. Colonel, your men fought one hell of a fight last night."

Ridge smiled and said "Thank you, sir. I'll pass it along."

Fifteen minutes later we left and when we arrived at the CP there were some reporters waiting for Colonel Puller. They gravitated to Puller because they knew he was always good for a great quote. One of them wanted to know about the fleeing enemy. Puller gave them an unexpected answer, "All I know about a fleeing enemy is that there's two or three hundred lying out there, that won't be fleeing anywhere. They're all dead."

The Colonel, Jones, Bodey and I jumped into the jeep and followed 2/1 as they pushed through the city. Jones skillfully weaved the jeep between the debris that covered the avenue.

At one point Puller yelled, "Hold it." Jones stopped the jeep and the Colonel said, "Bo, Mike, let's walk ahead. Jones, follow us in the jeep."

Snipers were firing and bullets were kicking up dust but the Colonel seemed oblivious to it. It wasn't a place a regimental commander belonged.

Puller glanced over at us and said, "Those damned snipers are a pain in the ass. If we send patrols after them we'd stop the advance. Better to let the Korean Marines take care of them. They'll do it better anyway. They know how to tell the cowboys from the Indians."

As we moved further down the avenue the shooting picked up. Puller saw some Marines behind a barricade taking cover from the fire down the street. He walked up behind them and quickly ended their hesitation: "Get in the goddamned fight!"

The Marines jumped up and moved on. When the sun went down the regiment took up defensive positions after gaining almost a mile.

Before it got dark, Puller told Jones to pull over.

"We're going to set up our CP here," Puller said.

We were outside a small three-story building on Mapo Boulevard. Most of the windows had been blown out.

Puller roared, "Sergeant Abbo, get some men and secure the building."

I ran across the street where I saw a group of six Marines smoking cigarettes.

"You men follow me, let's go," I ordered.

We ran back across the street to where the front door had once been. It was now lying in pieces just inside the building.

I turned to the men, "Alright, we're going to secure this building, one floor at a time."

I looked at them, and then the building.

"Ready?" I asked.

They all nodded.

"Let's go."

We charged into the building. The first floor had once been a café but was now filled with debris. The tables and chairs were scattered all over the floor. I pointed for two Marines to check the kitchen. The others searched the first floor. In less than a minute the two men came back.

The first said, "Sergeant, the kitchen's clear, but there's a back door."

"Okay," I said, "go back and guard that door."

I looked at the other Marines.

"Is there a basement in this place?" I asked.

"No, Sergeant, I checked," one of them answered.

I had no idea what the hell I was doing; I had never secured a building before.

The straight staircase ran up the right side of the building towards the rear.

"Get your rifles up, we're going up the stairway."

I led the way and the five Marines followed. When we got to the top, I saw two doors to what I presumed were bedrooms. I told three of the Marines to take the door on the left while the other two and I checked the one on the right.

"Check the knob," I said in a low voice, "if it's locked, kick the door in, if it's unlocked, stand back and swing the door wide open so we can see into the room."

The others nodded at me and I said, "Do it with me, we'll go at the same time."

I put my hand to the knob and turned.

It was unlocked. I pushed the door open an inch. The Marine down the hall did the same. He looked up at me and nodded. I used my left hand and counted down: 3, 2, 1. We stepped back and pushed the doors wide. We waited a moment and charged inside the room. There were thin mattresses stacked in a corner, and various pieces of furniture throughout the room. There were torn curtains on the broken windows.

I motioned for the two other Marines to cover me as I checked the bathroom and closet. The rooms were empty. We exited to the narrow hallway and soon met the other three, who also found the rooms empty.

"Okay," I said, "follow me to the third floor. This time I'll take the room on the left."

"Yes Sergeant," they said.

The staircase leading to the third floor was also straight and led back to the rear of the building. We ascended slowly and quietly and took our places in front of our respective doors. Once again, the other Marine and I were in sync and put our hands to the knobs. I didn't notice if the other door opened because as soon as I turned my knob, gunfire shattered the silence and splintered the door. I jumped back to the left side of the door and slammed up against the frame of the window that faced the front of the building.

I took a deep breath, realized my lungs were still working and quickly grabbed a grenade from my belt. I pulled the pin. While keeping my back to the window and my body to the left of the door, I pushed it open and tossed the grenade in. I dropped to the ground. I hadn't realized it, but the other five Marines had hit the deck a few moments before. Now they covered their heads, waiting for the blast of the grenade. It was a long three seconds.

The explosion was deafening. It shook the walls, floor and blew the flimsy door apart.

I jumped up immediately with my rifle at the ready. I spotted a man lying on the floor in the corner to my right. When he reached for his rifle, I fired three times and his body went limp.

I looked to my left and there was another North Korean sprawled on the floor. The grenade had obviously killed him.

I motioned for the five Marines to get up and get moving. I sent three into the room on the right and the other two followed me.

The room smelled like burnt powder and I immediately went over to the dead man and kicked the gun away from his body. I sent the two Marines to check the bathroom and closet.

I looked at the face of the man I killed and was drawn to his staring eyes. I stood there for what seemed like a long time, but the two Marines came back to me in what must have been just a few seconds. They both stood next to me. Neither one said a thing. Just then the other three appeared in the doorway.

"All clear, Sergeant," one of them said.

"Alright, Marines," I said "get these bastards out of here. Colonel Puller won't want any dead bodies in his CP."

"Yes, Sergeant," they said in unison.

I walked down the stairs and out to the sidewalk. I watched as they dragged the bodies out into the street. I wiped my sweaty hands on my trousers.

Puller walked up to me and said, "Mike, after all that racquet, I assume this building is secure."

"Yes, sir. All secure," I said.

"Good work, Mike," he said, while he puffed on his pipe.

The next morning, 2/1 continued its push through the city knocking out one barricade after another. Using tanks and air power they punched their way through the city. Throughout the day Puller was always at the front where the action was. Puller saw Lieutenant Lew Devine's rifle platoon destroy a barricade and then they moved out down the street. The Colonel caught up with him. Devine had been wounded two days earlier and a corpsman had replaced his bloody jacket with that of a dead sergeant. Puller congratulated him, saying, "Great work, Sergeant."

Lieutenant Colonel Rickert, his XO, had recognized Devine and pointed out the mistake to Puller. His expression changed, and he said, "Lieutenant," and walked off. It was obvious that Puller preferred sergeants to lieutenants but I don't think that bothered Devine too much. It was well known among the junior officers that Puller had a great affection for his sergeants.

By the end of the day, enemy resistance had crumbled and the regiment had reached the eastern end of the city. Except for the mopping up operations of the Korean Marines, the battle for Seoul was largely over.

A BATH

In the morning, the regiment resumed the attack but found very little opposition. The Colonel set up his CP on the grounds of the Duksoo Palace. The place was a mess but still usable. As we were clearing out a few rooms, Jones pulled up in the jeep.

Puller walked outside and said, "We all need a bath so find a bath house, and make sure they've got plenty of hot water and soap."

Jones came back an hour later and said he found a swell place for a bath and the Colonel, Bodey and I piled in the jeep with Jones for the drive to the bath house.

Many of the surrounding buildings had been damaged by the battle, but from the outside it looked like it was in pretty good shape. When we walked inside, we were met by a Korean man who apparently owned the place. There were a couple holes in the roof, yet the interior was fairly clean. We undressed and entered the water very slowly because it was hot. This felt fantastic because it was the first bath we had had since landing at Inchon. When we finished we dried off and got back into our dirty clothes, but we were clean. Puller opened his wallet and had only ten-dollar bills.

He looked at us and said, "Does anyone have any money?"

Jones took some Korean money out of his pocket and paid the man who was overjoyed at our generosity.

When we walked outside Puller said to Jones "Is that money any good?" Jones replied, "I don't know. I found it in a blown up building."

THE PALACE

The next day, September 29th, MacArthur and President Rhee entered Seoul for a ceremony restoring the city to the Republic of South Korea. There would be only six Marines attending the ceremony in the damaged government palace: Generals Smith and Craig, Puller and Murray, and two aides.

Puller told Jones to drive him over and told Bodey and me to get in. Bodey sat behind the Colonel and I sat behind Jones.

We were halted at the gate of the Government House compound by a smartly dressed Army MP Major.

"Colonel," the MP said, "only staff cars are allowed in the compound."

Puller pulled the pipe out of his mouth, "Major, I don't have a goddamn staff car. There is a war going on here."

"Sir, staff cars only."

"Listen Major," Puller said, "my men took this damn place."

"Sorry, sir. I can't let you pass," said the MP.

Puller stood up, holding onto the windshield, "I don't give a damn what your orders are. My orders are to go in there and I'm going. Now get the hell out of my way."

The MP stood firm, "Sorry sir. Only staff cars."

Puller roared, "Run him over, Jones!"

Jones jammed his foot on the accelerator and the jeep lunged forward so quickly that Puller flew backward and was caught by Bodey. The MP dove out of the way and Puller settled back in his seat. His face was noticeably red and he looked over at Jones and said, "The son of a bitch probably doesn't even know how to shine his own boots."

We drove up to the front of the palace and Puller got out, walked up the steps, and into the front door. The place was surrounded by Army people who of course were all spit and polish. We got out of the jeep and waited.

Forty-five minutes later people started pouring out of the palace. It was easy to spot the Marines and two aides. They were the only ones in combat utilities. Puller, Murray, Smith and Craig, the Assistant Division Commander, talked for a while and then Puller walked over to the jeep, jumped in and said, "Let's go."

It was obvious by the look on his face that he wasn't happy. As we drove off he said, "The Marines capture the damn place and the Army gets all the honor. MacArthur brings in all these spit-shined Army Military Police from Tokyo and he lines the hall with these guys. Hell, they never fired a shot. MacArthur never said a damn word about the Marine Corps. Who in the hell do they think did all the fighting?"

The battle for Inchon and Seoul had ended. Seoul was taken in less than two weeks. Total casualties for the 1st Marine Division were 421 dead and 2,029 wounded in action.

FLOYD GIBBONS AND DAN DALY

On October 5th we received orders to return to Inchon where we rested for a few days. Puller spent most of that afternoon and the next morning preparing reports. Jones and Bodey were away doing something for the Colonel and I was sitting in a chair outside the Colonel's tent when he walked out and sat down next to me. It was a beautiful fall afternoon and there wasn't much going on. Puller seemed very relaxed, now that the battle was over and his reports were finished. He was in a talkative mood. He asked about my family and he spoke about his wife and their children.

When he was finished I said, "Colonel, can I ask you a question?"

"Sure, Mike, what's up?"

"Why do the Marines and Army dislike each other so much?"

A smile flashed across Puller's face, "Did you ever hear of the Battle of Belleau Wood?"

"Yes, sir," I said, "World War I. Belleau Wood is near Paris."

"That's correct. There was a war correspondent from the *Chicago Tribune* named Floyd Gibbons. That's your newspaper isn't it?"

"Yes, sir" I replied.

"Did you ever hear of Gibbons?"

"No, sir."

"Well, I guess he was way before your time. Anyway, Gibbons was with the 4th Marine Brigade and was probably with them for one reason. One of their men, Gunnery Sergeant Dan Daly had won the Medal of Honor twice, once in the Boxer Rebellion and once in Haiti, and Gibbons figured there would be a lot of action wherever Daly was. He would not be disappointed. It was the afternoon of June 6th, 1918. The Marines were on the edge of a wheat field which was being raked by German machine gun fire. No one was moving. All of a sudden Daly leaped up, turns around, looks at his men and yells, 'Come on you sons-of-bitches, do you want to live forever?'

"The men jumped up and charged across the field with many of them being killed or wounded. A few minutes later Gibbons gets up to follow and is hit by three bullets: one in the left eye and two in the chest. The word races to the rear that Gibbons is dead. Earlier in the day Gibbons had filed a report about the bravery of the Marines at Belleau Wood. The Marine Brigade became the first American unit mentioned by name, when a sympathetic censor, believing Gibbons had been killed, let his dispatch go out unedited.

"June 6, 1918 had become the bloodiest day in the history of the Corps. The 4th Brigade had suffered over 1,000 casualties, losing more men in that one day than the Marine Corps had in all preceding years combined. Gibbons' story appeared on the front page of every American newspaper in the country, and it made it look as if the Marine Corps had done all the fighting and saved Paris all by themselves. Well, this brought the Corps some much needed publicity, but it was a double-edged sword. Hell, the Army was fighting and dying too. Why should the Marines get all the glory? General Pershing and the Army were furious. To make matters worse, the French, convinced that the Marines had saved Paris, renamed Belleau Wood, Bois de la Brigade de Marine.

"Well Mike, that's about it. It was all a fluke. This incident really screwed up Marine Corps – Army relations. That is why the Marines didn't fight in Europe in World War II. There was no way in hell the Marines were going to grab any more glory in Europe. We did all our fighting in the Pacific. MacArthur, Eisenhower and Truman never forgave the Marines."

"Did Gibbons live?" I asked.

"Yes, but the damage was done, and for once, the Marine Corps had nothing to do with it."

"Sir, what happened to Daly?"

"Well, I'll tell you. Daly was seriously wounded in a later battle, but he recovered. He was awarded the Navy Cross."

We talked about the Corps a little longer and then Jones and Bodey returned. The Colonel stood and said, "We've got some work to do. I just got the word from Division: we will start loading ships on the 8th and will set sail on the 15th."

Jones asked hopefully, "We going home, Colonel?"

"Hardly. We are on our way to Wonsan, on the east coast of North Korea." The Colonel walked back to his tent.

The next week was spent loading equipment, weapons, supplies and Marines aboard the ships in the harbor. On the evening of October 15th we were aboard and Puller called a meeting with his officers and senior enlisted men.

"Here's what's going on. Tomorrow at noon we leave for Wonsan on the east coast. General MacArthur's plan is for the Eighth Army to drive north to Pyongyang, the capital of North Korea, and X Corps, which is the 1st Marine Division with attached Army units, will land at Wonsan. We will cut westward to trap any North Korean forces retreating from the south. Both commands will then advance north. That is all I know right now."

An hour later I was up on deck looking for the Colonel. It was dark and there was an individual in an undershirt leaning on the railing, smoking a pipe. He was looking out into the harbor. It was Puller.

"Good evening, Colonel," I said.

Puller turned around, "Evening Sergeant. We've got a big day tomorrow. Go get some sleep."

I went down below and as I lay in my bunk I had to admit that things had worked out very well. We had pushed the NKPA out of Seoul and South Korea and we were going into North Korea. MacArthur had said we'd be home by Christmas. With this thought lingering in my mind, I slept very well.

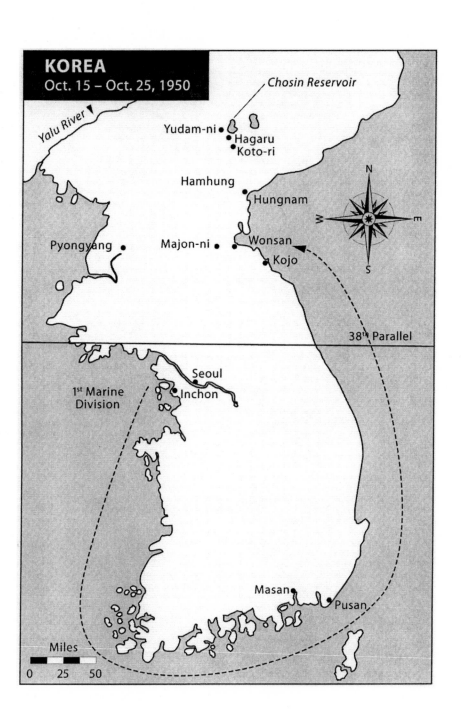

KOREA
Oct. 15 – Oct. 25, 1950

Yalu River

Chosin Reservoir

Yudam-ni
Hagaru
Koto-ri

Hamhung
Hungnam

Pyongyang
Majon-ni
Wonsan
Kojo

38th Parallel

Seoul
1st Marine
Division
Inchon

Masan
Pusan

Miles
0   25   50

Chapter Seven

Chosin Reservoir

I suppose by the time you get this letter, you will have read about us being surrounded at Chosin Reservoir. I am optimistic that we will be able to fight our way out of this trap – after all, we're Marines. It's so cold we're calling this place "Frozen Chosin." . . .

M. Abbo, letter to parents, 2 Dec 1950

A DISASTROUS PLAN

As brilliant and as bold as the Inchon landing was the push to the Yalu was equally as reckless and irresponsible, especially for a man with MacArthur's experience. He was quite simply out of touch with the realities of North Korea: the rugged terrain, the bitter cold winters and most especially the presence of the Chinese Communist Army.

The Marines and soldiers heading into North Korea would pay dearly for MacArthur's arrogance and over confidence. And so would the thousands of Marines and soldiers who would fight in Korea during the next two and one-half years.

On October 15th President Truman met with General MacArthur on Wake Island. Truman asked MacArthur his opinion on the likelihood of the Chinese coming into the war. The General told the President it was unlikely, and added that North Korean resistance would end by Thanksgiving.

On the night of October 19th, that prediction was proven faulty as hundreds of thousands of Chinese Communist soldiers crossed the Yalu River and hid themselves in the mountains of North Korea.

MacArthur's plan called for dividing his Army; the Eighth Army in the northwest and the X Corps (made of the 1st Marine Division and elements of the U.S. Army's 7th Infantry Division) in the northeast, would drive north toward the Yalu. There would be no direct communication between the two armies, which would be separated by the rugged Taebek Mountains. It was a disastrous plan. If these two armies got into trouble they would be unable to help or support each other.

We left Inchon on October 15th. After fighting our way through Seoul, it was nice to be onboard ship again. The weather and food were good and it was wonderful to do absolutely nothing.

Four days later, as we approached Wonsan, the transports turned around and headed south. The ships spent the next five days cruising up and down the coast, changing direction in the morning and in the evening. The Marines called it 'Operation Yo-Yo'. The harbor at Wonsan was heavily mined and we would have to cruise back and forth until the harbor was cleared by mine sweepers. During this time fresh food was running low and dysentery had broken out. On October 24th Bob Hope, Marilyn Maxwell and a group of entertainers flew into Wonsan and put on a great show for the 1st Marine Aircraft Wing. Since we were still onboard ship, we missed the performance. I was very disappointed because I had really enjoyed his show on Pavuvu in August of 1944.

We came ashore early the next day. Puller, Bodey and I rode in on a landing craft. Jones stayed behind to wait for the jeep to be unloaded from the ship. Wonsan was 110 miles north of the 38th parallel. The North Koreans had blown up some of the docks and burned down some houses but the port was still operating.

One of the first people we met was General O.P. Smith. He had a big grin on his face and said, "Lewie, I've got some good news for you. You've been selected for Brigadier General. Congratulations."

Puller smiled, "Thank you, General. It's been a long time getting here." But there was no time to celebrate. The 1st Marines set up camp by the airfield in Wosan.

KOJO

On October 26th the 1st Marine Division was split up by General Almond. General Smith was not pleased. He did not think much of the 'drive to the Yalu' or the 'home by Christmas' talk. His protests, however, were in vain: Litzenberg's 7th Marines were sent north to Chosin Reservoir; Murray's 5th Marines would follow; Puller's 1st Marines would stay behind and be divided into isolated battalions.

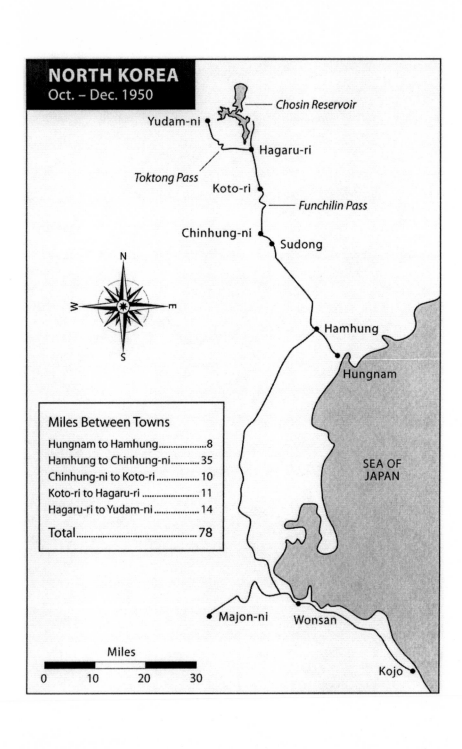

NORTH KOREA
Oct. – Dec. 1950

Chosin Reservoir

Yudam-ni

Hagaru-ri

Toktong Pass

Koto-ri

Funchilin Pass

Chinhung-ni

Sudong

Hamhung

Hungnam

N
W   E
S

SEA OF
JAPAN

Miles Between Towns

Hungnam to Hamhung....................8
Hamhung to Chinhung-ni............ 35
Chinhung-ni to Koto-ri 10
Koto-ri to Hagaru-ri 11
Hagaru-ri to Yudam-ni 14

Total...78

Majon-ni   Wonsan

Miles

0   10   20   30

Kojo

Puller came up to me and said, "Abbo, get the battalion commanders."

I returned in about five minutes with the colonels. Puller was in his tent pacing back and forth when they walked in.

"Good morning, gentlemen, we've got new orders. Colonel Ridge, you take the 3rd Battalion to Majon-Ni, twenty-nine miles away. It's hilly country with a road that winds its way up there. Majon-ni sits at a key road junction. Set up a perimeter defense and you are there to stop the North Koreans from going north. They'll truck you up there.

"Colonel Sutter, the 2nd Battalion will stay here with me. You have responsibility for the area around Wonsan.

"Colonel Hawkins, I'm sending your 1st Battalion by train to the town of Kojo, forty miles to the south of here. You are to relieve a ROK (Republic of Korea) unit guarding a supply dump. The only intelligence we have is that there are North Korean guerillas that are active in the area. I don't know what's down there, but if the Commies do hit you, you can beat the hell out of them."

Hawkins looked at the Colonel and said, "How do we get there?"

"There is some old junky train that will run you down there. Make sure you load up with plenty of ammo and rations."

"Yes, sir."

Puller said, "I am not happy with this. I'm a big believer in concentration. I don't like my battalions spread out all over the goddamned place."

Hawkins' battalion arrived at Kojo in the middle of the afternoon. Hawkins set up his command post on a large hill about 1,500 yards northwest of the village. Captain Wes Noren's B Company was to the south. To the west was A Company under Captain Bob Barrow. The relieved ROK unit left on the old train.

There was a fifty percent watch with half the men in their fighting holes and the others in their sleeping bags. Before midnight, B Company began taking heavy fire, followed by a charge. Several Marines were killed in their sleeping bags. All the companies except H&S, headquarters and supply, were hit hard. Due to transmission difficulties the message did not reach Puller's headquarters until the next morning. By dawn most of the North Koreans had fled into the hills. Hawkins reported nine killed, thirty-nine wounded and thirty-four missing. He felt things were serious after his heavy losses. He sent another radio message at 10:00 AM: "Received determined attack from south, north and west from large enemy force estimated at 1,000 to 1,200. Civilian reports indicate possibility of 3,000 enemy in this immediate area. Shall we hold or withdraw north? ROK supply dump removed. Request immediate instructions."

General Smith came over to Puller's headquarters and the two of them talked. Smith was very concerned about the attack and said, "Hawkins needs some help. He sounds like he is in a funk."

Puller asked, "What do you want me to do?"

The General answered, "Go down there and straighten things out," then he left.

Puller came charging out of his tent, "Abbo, find Colonel Sutter."

I returned a few minutes later with Colonel Sutter. Puller wasted no time.

"Allan, I guess by now you've heard that Hawkins got hit. We're going down there to help him out. Get your battalion ready. We'll take that old train."

Colonel Sutter left and Puller said that Jones, Bodey, a radioman and I would accompany him to Kojo. We left late that afternoon with 2/1 and arrived in Kojo late that night. The 2nd Battalion went into position next to 1/1 while Puller checked the perimeter. When the Marines heard that Puller was here, the mood changed. Bodey, Jones and I followed Puller as he walked the line, talking to the men.

He started with the mortar platoon, "You boys know how to shoot those things?"

"Colonel, you bet we do."

"How's your ammo?"

"Got plenty sir."

"Well by God, tonight we're going to kick some Communist asses. You be ready," Puller grinned.

The Colonel walked along the line chatting and asking questions of the riflemen and machine gunners. Again, he asked if they had enough ammunition. When they answered "Yes" he cautioned, "Now don't waste it. Wait until you're getting Commies with it. Let them get in close. Remember, you can't hurt 'em if you don't hit 'em."

As we walked along, I could see a visible change in the men. No longer were they isolated and on the defensive. Now they were ready. If the North Koreans came back, they were prepared to 'mow 'em down'.

We climbed up the hill to the command post and were met by Lieutenant Colonel Hawkins and Captain Hopkins, the C.O. of H&S Company.

Puller said to Hawkins, "The men seem ready. If the North Koreans come back, we'll give it to 'em."

Captain Hopkins was from Roanoke, Virginia and apparently Chesty knew him because he said, "Roanoke, how's it going?"

"Doing all right sir."

Chesty sat on a log next to Hopkins, opened a can of beef stew and began to eat. The Colonel and the Captain talked for a while, about home as Puller ate his dinner. They were both from Virginia.

Hopkins mentioned that he had served with Puller's brother, Sam, in both Basic School at the Philadelphia Naval Yard at the beginning of World War II, and then again in the Pacific with the 3rd Marine Division.

Puller nodded.

"Did you know he was killed in Guam?" asked Chesty.

"Yes, sir," Hopkins replied.

"I miss him, I sure do," Puller said, as his voice trailed off.

Hopkins changed the subject, "Colonel, does this operation make any sense to you? Why was the 1st Marine Division sent to Wonsan after we took Seoul? Don't you think we should have been sent north to capture the enemy capital, Pyongyang?"

As usual, Chesty quickly put things into perspective, "Who's in charge of this whole show?"

"General MacArthur, sir," Hopkins answered.

"Okay. The Marines captured Seoul, didn't they?" Puller asked, without giving time for an answer, "If you were MacArthur would you let the Marines capture both capitals?"

"No sir, I suppose I wouldn't," Hopkins answered, with a tinge of realization.

We spent three days in Kojo and the North Koreans never returned. Of the thirty-four missing Marines, all but four turned up. Puller concluded that a northbound enemy unit had found Hawkins' battalion in its path and had hit it while retreating.

The two battalions returned to Wonsan by sea and camped around the airfield for a few days. Hawkins was ordered back to the States and was succeeded by Lieutenant Colonel Donald M. "Buck" Schmuck. The 1st Marines got ready to join the movement to the Yalu.

ARMY INTELLIGENCE

Brigadier General Charles Willoughby was MacArthur's intelligence chief and his responsibility, as he saw it, was to support his boss. And if MacArthur said that the Chinese were not coming into the war than it was his job to produce intelligence to show that MacArthur was right.

On November 1st a regiment of the Eighth Army, moving up the West coast of Korea after they captured the North Korean capital, was badly mauled by the Chinese Communists at a town called Unsan. The Eighth Cavalry Regiment suffered some 800 casualties – one-third of its regiment.

On the east coast of Korea, on November 2nd – 4th, the 7th Marines fought the Chinese at Sudong. The Marines lost 44 men killed and 162 wounded. After these two battles it was apparent to the Marines that the Chinese had entered the war in mass. It was the last time to stop the insane drive north. MacArthur's headquarters ignored the obvious. Willoughby chose to believe that the Chinese forces were volunteers. It was a massive intelligence failure that bordered on the criminal and lost thousands of lives. Then, the Chinese just disappeared into the snow covered mountains.

MAJON-NI

Puller had his hands full. When we returned to Wonsan he got a call on the radio that a patrol of 3/1 had been ambushed along with a convoy bringing supplies to Majon-Ni. Lieutenant Colonel Ridge reported that twenty-five of his men had been killed and forty-one wounded. For now, Ridge's battalion was isolated and would have to depend on airdrops.

Division told Puller to open the road. Puller then told Captain Barrow, the C.O. of A Company 1/1 to get going. Barrow received his orders late in the day. Halfway to Majon-Ni they were stopped by a North Korean roadblock and received heavy fire. It was getting dark and there were too many vehicles for Barrow's men to protect so he went back to Wonsan.

When Barrow returned he reported to Puller, whose CP was now in an abandoned schoolhouse. I think Barrow was a little discouraged because he didn't get the road open and wasn't sure what the Colonel would say. He found Puller in a classroom sitting at a teacher's desk.

Puller got right to the point, "That was my fault. I started you off too late in the afternoon. Captain, what do you need to get this convoy through to-morrow?"

Barrow answered, "Sir, I need a team to control close air support and I want to leave early."

Puller nodded reassuringly and said, "You've got it."

He then pulled a bottle of bourbon out of a field desk that was set up behind him.

He pointed to a chair and said, "Sit down and have a drink, Captain."

"I think I will, sir," replied Barrow.

Puller did not drink often, but he believed there were occasions when a drink might settle the nerves. Obviously, this was one of those times. Captain Barrow had a drink with Chesty and then left.

Barrow took off early in the morning, and he came up with a better plan: the North Koreans would be waiting for the sound of trucks, so his infantry platoons led the column on foot, keeping a thousand yards in front of the vehicles.

Near the scene of the previous roadblock his men surprised a large group of North Koreans who were eating breakfast. Quickly the Marines fired on the Communist soldiers, killing fifty-one and capturing three. The convoy had no further trouble and arrived at Majon-Ni in the early afternoon.

The next day Puller ordered E Company 2/1 to occupy positions along the road to Majon-Ni. The move along the road started another fight, which lasted all afternoon. Eight men from E Company were killed and thirty-eight wounded. Helicopters evacuated the critical casualties and Barrow brought back the lightly wounded and some prisoners to Wonsan without further fighting.

COLD WEATHER GEAR

On November 10th Puller's 1st Marines were in a very festive mood. It was the 175th birthday of the Marine Corps. Puller stood up on a small table and read the traditional birthday message from the Commandant then tore into a short stirring speech to fire up the troops "to get ready to fight." He ended by saying, "We can pound the hell out of anything that gets in our way – that's why we are the best division in the world."

The Colonel then jumped to the ground and began cutting a huge 100 pound cake with a captured North Korean sword, and, in true Marine Corps tradition, the first piece was given to the oldest Marine present and the second to the youngest Marine.

It was during this time that Puller handed out awards for the battles for In-chon and Seoul. Captain Barrow was awarded a Silver Star for his defensive stand in Yongdungpo. Others were also awarded medals.

Chesty told the group of Marines after the ceremony, "There is nothing I like better than decorating people. Now go out and earn some more."

On November 15th the 7th Marines arrived in Hagaru.

The following day we boarded trains to ride north to Chigyong, a town about eight miles west of Hungnam. We rode up on open flatbed cars. It was a cold ride. The 3rd Army Division took our place in Wonsan.

We were issued cold weather gear from the beach dumps at Hungnam. We were given three sets of 'long Johns,' or wool underwear. Wool trousers and a flannel shirt were worn over the underwear. A high-necked sweater, buttoned to the chin and a second pair of waterproof trousers formed a third layer. The second set of trousers required suspenders and were tucked into our boots to keep out the cold air. On top of this we put on a field jacket. Another layer was added by a pile-lined parka with hood. The parka was a long Navy type, more suitable for standing watch aboard ship than long marches in the mountains. We were also issued three pairs of heavy socks, two pairs of felt inner-soles and boots or "shoe packs" – they were more like duck-hunting boots. As we were to find out later, when we hiked in these boots, our feet would sweat and when we stopped, the moisture would freeze and greatly increase the risk of frostbite. You had to change your socks and innersoles frequently and put the wet ones inside your shirt next to your skin so your body heat would dry them for the next change.

Our heads were covered by a cap, which keeps the head warm without restricting the helmet. The parka hood went under the helmet and buttoned around the chin so that most of the face was protected. Mittens with a trigger finger opening were supplemented by wool inserts, and finally we were issued mountain sleeping bags. As I was issued my gear two thoughts immediately came to mind: how was I going to walk in all this stuff, and how would I go to the bathroom?

For the first time since sailing from Inchon, Puller had his entire regiment in one place. General Smith then gave Puller his new orders.

HEADING NORTH

On November 22nd Puller called in his battalion commanders and his regimental staff and laid out the marching orders:

"Gentlemen, we leave tomorrow for points north. The 7th Marines are on their way to Yudam-ni on the west side of the Chosin Reservoir, and the 5th Marines are right behind them, heading to the east side of the reservoir. Our mission is to guard the MSR, the Main Supply Route, between Chinhung-ni and Yudam-ni. Because of the tactical situation, Division is going to spread out our battalions again," Puller said, as he pointed to a big map of the area.

"Take a look at this map: the distance from Hungnam to Chinhung-ni is forty-three miles. The road is a narrow, two-lane dirt and gravel one and it moves across rolling ground. Colonel Schmuck, your 1st Battalion will occupy Chinhung-ni.

"Alright, at Chinhung-ni the terrain changes. From here it is a single lane road, more like a goddamn goat track, mountains on one side and a drop off on the other. The road rises up 2500 hundred feet into cold thin mountain air. The road goes over Funchlin Pass and then down to the village of Koto-ri. This village ain't much. From Chinhung-ni to Koto-ri it's about ten miles. Koto-ri is in the center of a big bowl ringed by hills. Colonel Sutter, your 2nd Battalion and the regimental headquarters will take over this town.

"From Koto-ri to Hagaru it's another eleven miles. Hagaru was once an important town but we bombed the hell out of it – not much left. It is at the southern end of the Chosin Reservoir. This is another bleak bowl of frozen earth, three miles across. Here the road forks. The right fork passes north and east into equally miserable terrain. The left fork goes north and west and climbs 4000 feet to Toktong Pass and then down again to the village of Yudam-ni.

The village is surrounded by hills on all sides except the east, where it meets the shoreline of Chosin Reservoir. Yudam-ni is fourteen miles from Hagaru. Colonel Ridge, your 3rd Battalion will occupy Hagaru and this town will also be the forward headquarters of the 1st Marine Division.

"General Smith has deliberately slowed down Colonel Litzenberg's 7th Marines. He does not want the whole division spread out. At the same time, General Smith is building up our levels of ammo, rations and fuel at selected dumps along the road. He has also directed his engineers to build emergency airstrips at Koto-ri and Hagaru. If we get into trouble it's the only way we could evacuate our wounded and bring in fresh troops.

"There is something strange going on here. MacArthur and Almond say there are only a few Chinese in North Korea and that they are 'volunteers'. I'll tell you this – there is no such thing as a Chinese 'volunteer'."

"Questions?" he asked bluntly.

The regimental supply officer said, "Sir, there aren't enough trucks to haul up all the ammo, tents, and stoves. What do you want to do?"

Without hesitation Puller answered, "The tents and stoves have priority. Then the ammo. We'll take care of the men first. Frozen troops can't fight. If we run out of ammunition, we will go to the bayonet."

KOTO-RI

On November 23rd Puller's 1st Battalion took over Chinhung-ni.

The 7th Marines arrived in Yudam-ni on Saturday, the 25th. That morning, the temperature at Chinhung-ni at the base of the mountain was below zero. We left Chinhung-ni later that day on our way to Koto-ri. The road was a single-lane dirt road. It was frozen and slippery. We slowly drove up into the mountains and the road got narrower and steeper and the weather turned colder. Around noon we crossed a one lane bridge. When we crossed to the other side Puller told Jones to pull over. Puller hopped out and looked down over the side and then across the bridge, and then he jumped back into the jeep.

He said, "It's a hell of a long way to the bottom, maybe a thousand feet. If something happens to that bridge, we're in trouble. Boys, this is Funchilin Pass."

We drove over the pass and down into a big bowl of a valley that was maybe three miles long by three miles wide. This was Koto-ri. The road ran through the center of town. To the west was a stream and a berm where the North Koreans were going to build a railroad. The town was largely destroyed. The buildings were made of concrete block and rough sawn lumber.

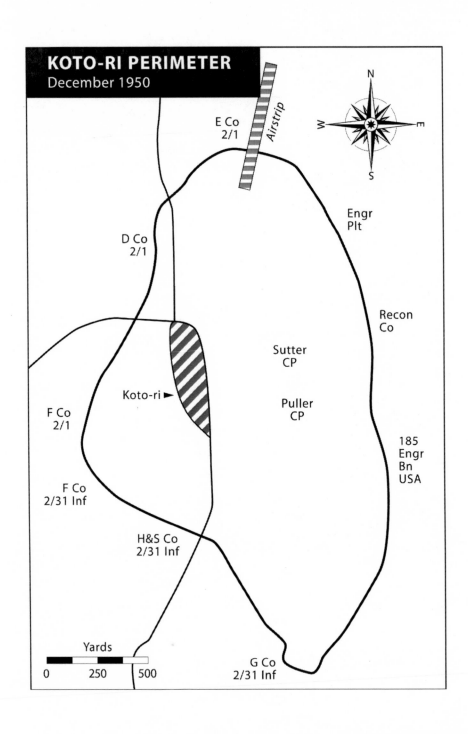

KOTO-RI PERIMETER
December 1950

Airstrip

E Co
2/1

Engr
Plt

D Co
2/1

Recon
Co

Sutter
CP

Koto-ri ►

Puller
CP

F Co
2/1

185
Engr
Bn
USA

F Co
2/31 Inf

H&S Co
2/31 Inf

Yards

0   250   500

G Co
2/31 Inf

It was a dingy, depressing looking place. Koto-ri was surrounded by mountains and dark, hostile clouds hung over them, and it began to snow.

The trucks and jeeps pulled off the road and the Marines started unloading the tents and supplies. Someone had already picked the spot for the regimental CP and so we were guided there. We unloaded Puller's tent and Jones, Bodey and I worked fast to put it up. Puller would share this with his XO, Lieutenant Colonel Rickert. We installed a potbellied oil-burning stove which quickly warmed up the tent. It was very cold.

An hour before dark Puller came out of his tent and yelled, "O.W. Mike."

"Yes, sir," we replied.

"Let's go find Colonel Sutter."

We found him nearby and Puller said to Sutter, "Let's take a look – to defend this place properly we gotta take all the high ground but we don't have the people to do it. I don't like this at all. So, set up a tight perimeter. We also want to control the fires of all supporting weapons. We have your whole battalion plus an artillery battery and about three hundred engineers. We also have medical personnel, military police, communications and transport troops. Am I missing anyone?"

"No, sir."

"Also send out patrols. I don't want any surprises," Puller said, "Get the tents set up – we have to keep these troops warm. Fifty percent alert."

Puller looked at Sutter, "Alan, how cold is it?"

Sutter answered, "Sir, it's about ten below, but when it gets dark, it'll get colder."

Puller said, "That goddamned wind is coming straight out of Manchuria. I believe ol' Genghis Khan was right – no one's going to win a winter campaign in the land of the Mongols."

"You know Alan, Koto-ri might be about the coldest and most disagreeable spot in this whole damned country."

"I can't imagine what could be worse," replied Sutter.

The four of us drove around what would be the perimeter – men were coming into position. Colonel Sutter made a few changes. It was almost impossible to dig fighting holes, the ground was frozen solid. The cold had become a vicious enemy. We had to live with great care; the penalty was frostbite; frozen feet, hands and faces. We had to carry our canteens on the inside of our parkas. Men on guard duty were allowed to put their feet and legs inside their sleeping bags if it didn't interfere with their ability to fight. Rations froze in the cans and if eaten that way, would cause dysentery. Oil froze the weapons and all the oil was wiped off and replaced by hair oil, which contained alcohol and wouldn't freeze. Many automatic weapons would only fire one shot at a time. Artillery fire was slowed and ranges shortened. The batteries in the radios didn't last long, the cold drained them fast. Plasma froze and when the fighting started syrettes of morphine were carried around in the mouths of the corpsmen so they wouldn't freeze.

After we finished driving around the perimeter it started getting dark. Puller returned to his CP as did Sutter. It was brutally cold. Fortunately it was a quiet night, although the temperature dropped to twenty below zero.

Bodey, Jones and I set up our tent ten feet away from Puller's. Because of the bitter cold one of us would get up every few hours to warm up the jeep. There was a lot of noise all night because all vehicles had to be run to stop them from freezing.

On the western side of the Taebek Mountains the Eighth Army, under the command of General Walker, had advanced without opposition. They had walked into a trap. At sundown on the 25th the Chinese attacked and the grand offensive was shut down. They started to retreat.

NOVEMBER 26

Early the next morning before day break, Bodey, Jones, and I walked over to the cook tent for breakfast. There was no mess tent. You ate outside in the cold. We stood in line waiting to be served. We had our backs to the wind. It was awkward trying to eat with gloved hands and the pancakes and eggs got cold before I could fork them into my mouth. By the time I sipped the coffee from my canteen cup, it was ice cold.

"Christ, this is like eating in a meat locker," I said.

Bodey looked at me and said, "There aint a meat locker this cold."

When we returned to Puller's CP, he was there waiting for us.

He said, "I want to check the perimeter. Get the jeep."

We drove north toward the unfinished airstrip. Then we got out of the jeep and walked while Jones followed us in the jeep.

Every breath was painful. If I breathed through my mouth, the cold burned my throat. If I breathed through my nose, you could feel the mucus begin to freeze. I was twenty-seven years old and found this bitter cold almost unbearable. As we walked along, I noticed that Chesty was breathing hard and sometimes he would put his scarf over his nose and mouth. I wondered how a man almost twice my age could cope with this weather, especially since he had spent most of his years in Marine Corps, in the tropics and his blood had been thinned by heat and humidity. It had to be hard on the old Marine.

Men who had manned the fighting holes during the latter part of the night were leaving and were being replaced by those who had slept. Puller would stop and banter with the men. "How did it go out there last night?"

"Colder than hell, Colonel, but it was quiet."

"All right, you boys stay on your toes. There's Chinese up in those hills. They're up to something." Then Puller walked along and talked to the next group of men. After an hour of this, we got in the jeep and drove back to the CP.

I had seen pictures of the gold rush in the Yukon in 1898 and Koto-ri, if you got rid of the trucks and jeeps, looked a lot like one of those mining camps: snow covered tents, lots of activity, and cold miserable men. As I looked around at this dismal scene, I thought to myself, what in the hell are we doing here?

The 5th Marines turned the east side of Chosin Reservoir over to three battalions of the Army infantry, and were then trucked to Yudam-ni, where they hooked up with the 7th Marines. Puller's 3rd Battalion, 1st Marines arrived at Hagaru that night minus G Company, which had been held up in Koto-ri due to a lack of transportation.

It wasn't until Sunday evening, the 26th that General Almond received the shocking news that the Eighth Army had been shattered and that their retreat was threatening to turn into a rout. Neither Almond nor any member of the X Corps staff bothered to warn the 1st Marine Division.

NOVEMBER 27

That afternoon the Division ordered F Company 2nd Battalion, 7th Marines under the command of Captain Barber to guard Toktong Pass. This was the high ground between Yudam-ni and Hagaru and was a good location for guarding the MSR.

Puller had great doubts about the quality of intelligence coming from Almond and X Corps, so he ordered Sutter to mount several deep patrols. E Company was sent out and was fired upon by about 200 Chinese, who occupied the high ground just west of Koto-ri. After taking a few prisoners, the Marines withdrew. The captives stated that they were members of a Chinese division that was assembling west of Koto-ri.

Puller became very concerned and told Sutter, "Pass the word to all your men, goddamnit, stay alert!"

Shortly after 9:00 PM tens of thousands of hardened, highly disciplined Chinese Communist soldiers came screaming out of the cold, dark night to the sound of bugles and burp guns and attacked the Marines. Wave after wave of Chinese crashed into the Americans. The assaults were vicious and continuous, and they didn't stop until the sun came up.

Especially hard hit were the 5th and 7th Marine regiments at Yudam-ni, F Company at Toktong Pass and those Army battalions on the east shore of the reservoir. Eight Chinese divisions with sixty thousand troops had surrounded the Marines at Yudam-ni, Hagaru, Koto-ri, and everywhere along the MSR, the road was now cut. Red China had entered the Korean War with a vengeance.

That night we had very little activity at Koto-ri. Due to the high mountains, radio communication between General Smith and his regimental commanders was not very good. As a result, Smith and Puller did not know about the extent of the attacks around the reservoir until the next morning.

NOVEMBER 28

In the morning we could see the Chinese troops en masse. They were plainly visible in the mountains north, south, and west of Koto-ri. Puller ordered the artillery to fire on them and they broke up one concentration after another, but they kept coming back. There seemed to be a never ending supply of Chinese soldiers.

General Smith arrived at Hagaru by helicopter early in the morning and opened his forward command post. He was shocked to learn that the total division casualties had approached seven hundred and that the 5th and 7th Marines were surrounded at Yudam-ni. The drive to Yalu was over.

Puller received his orders from General Smith to mount a clearing operation up the MSR. D Company, 2nd Battalion was sent out on trucks at 1:30 PM to clear the road. After going less than a mile they were fired on by Chinese and the fighting was heavy. Late in the day, F Company 2nd Battalion was sent out to reinforce D Company but they too ran into trouble. With the help of air cover, both companies pulled back to Koto-ri. They had four dead and thirty-four wounded. By the time both companies returned, Koto-ri was jammed with men and vehicles. Many units coming from the south to join their units in Hagaru had to be stopped: G Company, 3rd Battalion, under the command of Captain Sitter, B Company, 31st Army Infantry, commanded by Captain Peckham and the 41 Royal Marine British Commando, commanded by Lieutenant Colonel Drysdale. There were scores of trucks full of Army personnel and a unit of ROK troops. Puller tried to put as many of the transients as possible in tents that night.

As night came on, Puller was worried about his overcrowded perimeter. Every warming tent was packed to capacity. A single mortar round or a series of coordinated barrages could inflict great damage.

The MSR was closed to both the north and south. A spotter plane had called in that there were Chinese roadblocks between Koto-ri and Hagaru to the north and that there were at least three roadblocks along the road to Funchilin Pass to the south. Communication between Puller and General Smith was poorly maintained by radio.

Hagaru had to hold. It was the only escape route leading south. Lieutenant Colonel Ridge did not have many troops: two-thirds of an infantry battalion, with some artillery plus some rear echelon troops, a total of 3,300 Marines and 500 soldiers. Ridge spread his men around the perimeter and waited.

That night, as expected, the Chinese attacked Hagaru in force. When morning came, Lieutenant Colonel Ridge had suffered 500 casualties. The need for reinforcements from Koto-ri was urgent.

NOVEMBER 29

In the morning General Smith radioed Puller to get through at all costs. Hagaru could not withstand another night without more troops. After Puller spoke to General Smith, he told me to find Captain Sitter, Captain Peckham and Lieutenant Colonel Drysdale. I got two other men and it took us a while to find them because Koto-ri was jammed up with many units that had arrived the day before, which were spread out all over the place.

When the commanders arrived at Puller's tent he was inside smoking his pipe. As usual, he was very calm when he spoke to the men.

"I've been ordered by General Smith to open up the MSR. They got hit bad last night at Hagaru and need help. I'll give it to you straight: Between Chinhung-ni and Yudam-ni the road is cut and the Marines are surrounded. Intelligence reports that we are surrounded by eight Chinese divisions. Colonel Drysdale will be the commander of the breakthrough force. Colonel, you will be accompanied by Captain Sitter's G Company and by Captain Peckham's B Company. All told, you should have roughly nine hundred men. Hagaru needs you. They've got us surrounded. The bastards won't get away this time."

I was stunned to hear that the whole division was surrounded.

Everyone had left Puller's tent except Colonel Rickert and me. "I guess we can thank the three wise men for this fuckin' mess," Chesty said in disgust.

By this time in the war, Puller had a very poor regard for the Army and based on his comment, his professional opinion of MacArthur, Willoughby and Almond had sunk to an all time low.

Task Force Drysdale left Koto-ri at 9:45 AM. The fighting started right away and it would never stop. The Royal Marines and Sitter's company would work the hills in leap-frogging style, while the Army company kept to the road. In three hours the task force had only moved two miles, with nine more to go. They fought their way through roadblocks and by late in the afternoon the column was halfway between Hagaru and Koto-ri, but stalled in the road. By radio, Puller, General Smith and Drysdale agreed that the task force must push on to Hagaru "at all costs."

When it got dark and the task force had lost their air cover, the Chinese attacked in force and cut up the long thin line of trucks into tiny separated pieces. The front of the column made it to Hagaru after midnight, including Lieutenant Colonel Drysdale and Captain Sitter. The tanks in the back of the column made it back to Koto-ri the following morning. The troops in the middle weren't so lucky. After a long night of brutal fighting, finding themselves cut off and out of ammunition, they had no choice but to surrender. Of the 900 men who had started out, 150 had been killed, 150 had been wounded and over 300 Americans had been captured, including Captain Peckham. Of the 141 vehicles in the convoy at least 75 were destroyed. It would be one of the worst defeats in Marine Corps history. Added to the slim garrison at Hagaru were a tank company and some 300 seasoned Marine and British infantrymen.

Now it was Koto-ri's turn. As the darkness came on, the Chinese unleashed their first attack against Puller's packed perimeter, charging down from the higher ground near Captain Jack Smith's E Company and penetrating his defenses. In the fighting that followed, seventeen Chinese were killed behind the Marine lines, but the Chinese were pushed back. In the morning, Captain Smith's men counted 175 enemy bodies in the snow.

The long night was not without a little bit of Puller humor. A ROK commander in a nearby unit called Puller to report that the Chinese had launched an attack in his sector.

"How many Chinese?" Puller asked.

"Many, many!" replied the excited Korean.

"How many?" yelled Puller.

"Many, many!" the Korean replied again.

"Goddamnit," swore Puller, "get my Marine liaison officer on the radio."

Eventually, an American voice was heard, "Yes, sir?"

"Lieutenant," roared Puller, "exactly how many Chinese you got up there?"

"Colonel, we've got a whole shitpot of 'em up here."

Puller looked around at us in the CP and said, "Thank God we got someone up there who knows how to count."

He followed by saying, "Alright Lieutenant, you buck up that commander and hold the line."

"Yes, sir," replied the Lieutenant.

After midnight elements of the Army's 2/31 began straggling into Koto-ri from the south. The commanding officer reported to Colonel Puller.

"Your battalion is now attached to the Marines and will be assigned a section of the perimeter," Puller informed him.

He asked Puller, "What is the line of retreat?"

Puller quickly picked up his field phone and called his artillery people, gave them the firm order, "If they start to pull back from their position, open fire on them."

Puller then turned to the Army officer, "Is that clear? Our orders are to defend this place. There will be no retreat."

The Marines would hold at Koto-ri.

NOVEMBER 30

When dawn came, the 5th and 7th Marines were cut off and surrounded at Yudam-ni on the west side of Chosin Reservoir. In Hagaru, at the foot of the reservoir a lone Marine battalion was surrounded and holding on by its fingernails. Puller's perimeter at Koto-ri was under siege. Captain Barber's F Company at Toktong Pass was barely hanging on. He could not withdraw because over half of his Marines had been killed or wounded. On the east side of the reservoir, Task Force Faith's three Army battalions were in big trouble. They had been badly chewed up the nights of November 29-30 and if they survived the night, they would try to break out for Hagaru on the morning of December 1st.

A major problem was the large amount of casualties: there were 600 wounded men at Hagaru. Assuming the Marines at Yudam-ni could fight their way south, they would bring at least another 500 casualties with them. The Army troops on the east side of the reservoir, assuming they could reach Hagaru, would also bring about 500. Casualties would keep building up and Hagaru would not be able to handle them.

Even though the runway was half finished, General Smith said to give it a try. At 2:30 PM the first plane landed and half an hour later it took off with seriously wounded Marines. Not only could they fly out the wounded but they could also fly in replacements. The airstrip became the lifeline to the outside world.

I was standing outside Puller's tent when a clerk from Headquarters Company approached me. He looked worried.

"Sergeant," he said, "Is it true that we are surrounded?"

"Yeah," I answered.

The young Marine suddenly looked more frightened.

"Sergeant, are we going to make it out of here?" he asked.

I looked at the kid sternly and said, "It seems that you've forgotten your Marine Corps history. Don't forget that we were surrounded on Guadalcanal.

The Japs had control of the air and sea and a large part of the island, but they didn't get us, did they?"

"No, Sergeant," he replied.

"We're Marines, Private," I said, "this division is the best fighting force in the world. I don't know when or how, but we are breaking the hell out of here, you got that?" I was almost yelling now.

"Yes, Sergeant," he said.

When he walked away, I said, "Private!"

He turned and said "Yes, Sergeant?"

"Remember something. You're in good company."

I knew exactly how the Marine felt, because I felt the same way.

Towards the end of the day General Smith told Colonel Litzenberg and Lieutenant Colonel Murray to fight their way from Yudam-ni to Hagaru. But General Smith had another large problem to deal with: the Chinese had destroyed the bridge at Funchilin Pass, south of Koto-ri. Now the Marines were completely trapped.

Throughout the day heavy troop movements were detected in the hills surrounding Koto-ri. That night the Chinese struck again. Puller and Sutter kept the Chinese at bay, hitting them with artillery and mortars. The Chinese threw an occasional shell into Koto-ri but the heavy Marine fire held off a ground attack. At midnight the temperature was reported to be twenty-five degrees below zero.

DECEMBER 1

The three Army battalions east of the reservoir loaded its 500 wounded on trucks and tried to fight its way south to Hagaru. The Chinese set up roadblocks that the Army units could not break through. Then the Chinese attacked along the length of the stalled convoy. Lieutenant Colonel Faith, who assumed command, was killed, as were many of the officers and senior enlisted men. Without leadership the taskforce fell apart. Small bands of wounded and frozen men tried to cross the ice of the reservoir.

The Marines started their breakout at 8:00 AM. It was only fourteen miles from Yudam-ni to Hagaru, but it would take three days to get there. The vehicles in the column were packed solid with wounded and dead Marines as well as critical supplies. Litzenberg and Murray had made a tough decision: the rest of the dead would be left behind at Yudam-ni. Bulldozers gouged out a long pit about six feet deep. A total of eighty-five bodies, wrapped in parachute cloth, were laid out in a mass grave just south of the village. As the Marines slowly moved down the road, Chinese snipers were shooting at the drivers. It was not a good day to be behind the wheel.

As part of the plan, Lieutenant Colonel Ray Davis, the C.O. of 1/7 and my old C.O. from Chicago would march through the mountains at night with his battalion to rescue Captain Barber and F Company. It was a carefully crafted plan to push the Chinese off of Toktong Pass.

The battalion would have to cover about four and a half miles as the crow flies but in actual distance it was twice that because of the steep hills. It would be a night attack to catch the Chinese off guard. The Marines would take only the most essential gear. Each man carried an extra bandolier of ammo and a sleeping bag. They took only six heavy machine guns and two 81 mortars. Mortar and machine gun ammo was carried on litters. If the ammo was used up and casualties mounted, the litters would be put to other use. The men could take whatever food they wanted but most chose fruit cocktail, peaches and the like. By carrying this close to the skin, it wouldn't freeze, it could be eaten quickly and the sugar would give them much needed energy.

When Davis left that night it was twenty-four below zero. The battalion had been up since dawn, preparing, fighting and climbing. Before them lay miles of dark, frozen waste and uncounted Chinese. Lieutenant Colonel Davis and his troops were totally on their own. It was a huge, gutsy gamble.

Throughout the day cargo planes began to drop ammunition and other critical supplies by parachute at Koto-ri. The first flight came in too high and the parachutes drifted west into enemy lines. The next mission came in too low and the chutes did not open. The heavy pallets came hurling into the crowded perimeter, killing and injuring several Marines. Puller was standing outside watching this and was furious when he found out that some of his Marines were killed.

The Colonel jumped on the radio and roared with anger at the Air Force pilot who circled above, "Goddamnit, your negligence just killed a few of my Marines. What in the hell is wrong with you?"

Puller looked at Rickert and said, "So those wing wipers think we're on holiday down here?" Puller's harangue worked. The next drop was right on target and thereafter the fliers worked fearlessly to keep the division re-supplied.

DECEMBER 2

It was another day of heroics.

Marine pilots flying over the reservoir reported Army survivors walking out on the ice. This was reported to Lieutenant Colonel Olin Beall, who was the grizzled old salt, commanding the 1st Marine Motor Transport Battalion at Hagaru. Beall quickly organized a task force of trucks, jeeps and sleds to rescue the survivors of Task Force Faith. Beall personally drove two miles onto the ice, and then walked even further to test the surface to see how far he could safely drive his heavy trucks. He and his crews were fired upon but kept going. Beall rescued over 300 soldiers that day, most of them wounded or frostbitten. He then drove over to the east side of the reservoir and walked up to the place where Task Force Faith was attacked. He walked from truck to truck, inspecting them all. When he returned, he reported that they were all dead, estimating there were 300 bodies in the convoy. In all, 1,050 of the original 2,500 soldiers were saved. Beall would be awarded the Distinguished Service Cross.

Lieutenant Colonel Davis and his men were on the move all night. His battalion was strung out for half a mile, as it picked its way over dark slopes, ridges and valleys. The trail became icy, packed down by the Marines in the lead. Men continually would slip and fall, pull themselves up, only to slip and fall again. The downhill slopes were the worst, especially for the machine gunners and mortar men, with their heavy loads.

Davis had been on the move for six straight hours. At 3:00 AM he realized that his troops were in a state of total exhaustion, and it was time to give them a major break. He deployed his men in a tight perimeter as quickly as he could and formed two-man patrols to make certain the men on twenty-five percent watch were awake. Less than a mile away was Captain Barber's company.

Just before dawn the battalion saddled up and moved out. At 11:25 AM they spotted Fox Company. The Marines stopped and stared in awe. F Company was surrounded by a sea of frozen Chinese bodies. It was estimated that 1,000 Chinese had been killed by Barber's Marines. F Company's defense of Toktong Pass is considered one of the greatest holding actions in Marine Corps history. After five days and nights of brutal fighting they had twenty-six killed, three missing, and eighty-nine wounded, fifty percent casualties.

Barber and six of his officers were wounded and most of the unwounded men suffered from severe frostbite and digestive ills. Only 82 of his original 240 men could walk. Both Captain Barber and Lieutenant Colonel Davis were awarded the Medal of Honor. Davis's battalion spent most of the day resting, securing and patrolling the area around Toktong Pass.

In the afternoon Davis met up with the 5th and 7th Marines as they were coming down the road. The wounded from Barber's company were loaded onto vehicles. The dead were buried on the hill, there just wasn't any more room in the trucks and there were hundreds of Marines who walked through that pass that should have been riding in ambulances. Litzenberg and Murray walked; their jeeps were full of wounded.

At Koto-ri Puller got word that the breakout had started and that the Marines were passing through Toktong Pass. His biggest concern was holding onto Koto-ri. He could not let it fall. He had to prepare for the arrival of approximately 10,000 men in his already packed perimeter. Also, the airstrip had to be completed because there would be more wounded.

That afternoon some reporters flew into Koto-ri on a helicopter and Jones picked them up and drove them to Puller's CP. As soon as they walked in Puller said, "How was the flight in?"

"It was cold and it looked like there were lots of destroyed trucks on the road south of here," one of the reporters said.

Puller answered, "Let's take a drive so I can show you fellows what's going on around here."

As we were driving along, one of the reporters asked Puller, "What are you going to do, since you are surrounded?"

Nonchalantly, Puller told them, "This makes our problem of killing these bastards a little easier."

The two reporters looked at each other as if they just realized that perhaps they didn't belong here. I noticed that neither of them was taking off their gloves to write things down as reporters normally did. If they had, their hands would have frozen. It was twenty-four below zero.

The reporters only stayed for half an hour and then got back on the helicopter and left. I know all of us at Koto-ri would have liked to leave on that chopper too, but it was not to be.

DECEMBER 3

At dawn the ground was covered with six inches of new snow. The lead elements of the 5th and 7th Marines were fighting their way to Hagaru and the front of the column wouldn't arrive until 7:00 that night.

Preparations for the arrival of thousands of exhausted Marines at Hagaru had been made as best as they could. Guides were on hand to lead the units to selected areas within the perimeter. Wherever possible the weary Marines were placed in tents and given time to sleep. Hot stew, coffee and pancakes were prepared in vast quantities and replacement clothing was issued. Most of the wounded arrived that night and were given as much care as the overburdened medical staff could handle.

In World War II I heard several people say that Puller's presence alone was worth a whole battalion. He was a great motivator and when he spoke he always did so in bold and positive terms. It was not a false bravado but a great confidence in both himself and his men. It was no different in Korea.

When we walked the line that night it was bitter cold. We knew we were surrounded and we were scared: scared of the dark and the unknown, afraid of being killed or maimed, and terrified of freezing to death or being captured by the Chinese. It was a big burden for us to shoulder, but we were Marines and Puller knew how to pump us up.

"How you men doing?" he asked.

"Alright, Colonel."

"Got enough ammo?"

"Yes, sir."

"Ready to use it?"

"Yes, sir."

"Now remember something. We got the advantage. We're surrounded. If they want us, they gotta come get us. And when they do, we'll mow the bastards down."

"Yes, sir."

"Alright, stay alert."

"Yes, sir."

It was dark but I knew the Marines were smiling.

DECEMBER 4

The tail of the long column pulled into Hagaru early in the afternoon. The head of the column needed fifty-nine hours to cover the fourteen miles to Hagaru, the rear units needed seventy-nine hours. Some 1,500 casualties had been brought out, a third of them suffering from frostbitten hands, feet and faces.

While the Marines rested, regrouped and prepared to fight their way to the sea, the Chinese were strangely absent. The most urgent problem was the evacuation of the wounded.

It was clear to General Smith that his troops at Hagaru could not afford to rest for long; the longer they remained there, the stronger the Chinese would become. The most important priority was the evacuation of the wounded from the air strip.

Lieutenant Commander Chester Lessenden, the regimental surgeon of the 5th Marines would make the final decision on who would fly out of Hagaru and who wouldn't. Despite painfully frostbitten feet, he refused to be evacuated and was working round the clock. The screening process was abrupt, but efficient: "You fly.., You walk.., You ride.., Next."

Late in the afternoon General Almond and his aide flew into Koto-ri. Jones picked him up and drove him to Puller's CP. When he got there, Puller briefed him on what was happening at Koto-ri and how the preparations were coming for the arrival of the 5th and 7th Marines.

After the briefing, Almond looked at Puller and said, "It's my pleasure to present you with the Distinguished Service Cross. The citation reads as follows: 'Colonel Puller has distinguished himself by extraordinary heroism in connection with military operations against an armed enemy during the period 29 November to 4 December 1950. His actions contributed materially to the successful breakthrough of United Nations Forces in the Chosin area.' Congratulations, Puller."

He looked at Almond and said, "Thank you sir, but we are not out of the woods yet."

The General answered, "Colonel, we're going to make it."

Puller then said, "Abbo, you and Jones drive the General and his aide over to the strip."

We walked outside into the bitter air and climbed into the jeep. Jones took off and we made it to the airstrip in five minutes. The General and his aide jumped into the helicopter and it flew away.

It was starting to get dark as we began to pull away and a major from the Marine Air Wing told us to stop.

"There's a downed Navy pilot and a Marine pilot who picked him up," he said, "they're coming in now. Can you wait a minute and take them over to Headquarters & Supply Company? They know they're coming."

A few cold minutes later a helicopter flew in and two pilots hopped out. The helicopter pilot was Marine Lieutenant Charlie Ward and the other pilot was Navy Lieutenant Thomas Hudner.

The major motioned to the pilots and us, "Would you come with me, please? It won't take long. I want you to debrief me on what happened."

We followed him into a warming tent. Both Hudner and Ward walked a little gingerly, and it appeared they had both endured something wretched.

Lieutenant Hudner spoke first; "My wingman, Jesse Brown, and I were looking for targets in and around the Chosin Reservoir when Jesse's plane was hit by ground fire. He was going down fast and had no choice. He found a spot and crash-landed. The impact pushed the fuselage forward and pinned Jesse's legs underneath the hydraulics panel. At first, I thought he might be dead because it was such a violent landing, but I then noticed that he opened the canopy and was waving. He couldn't get out of the cockpit and there was smoke pouring out of the engine."

"One of my other wingmates called for a rescue helicopter, but I knew they had a long distance to travel, and Jesse didn't have a lot of time. I felt I could drop into the field where Jesse landed. I was afraid the fire in the engine might spread and endanger his life, so I jettisoned my fuel and ordinance and crash-landed my plane."

We were all staring at Hudner incredulously. The tent was quiet for a few seconds. The major was writing all this down and frequently looked up at the Navy pilot as he calmly recounted the events.

The major asked, "Did you get permission to crash land your plane?"

"No, sir," Hudner quickly replied.

"Then what happened?"

"I got out of my plane and struggled through the snow to get to Jesse's plane. He was conscious but obviously in a lot of pain. I couldn't get him out. Then I threw handfuls of snow into the openings of fuselage where the smoke was pouring out. I went back to my plane, grabbed a scarf and a wool cap and returned to Jesse to wrap the scarf around his freezing hands and pulled the cap down over his head and ears. It was brutally cold."

Hudner continued, "About forty-five minutes after Jesse went down, Charlie landed his chopper. He brought with him an axe and a small fire extinguisher. Both were useless. We tried, but couldn't get Jesse out of the plane. It was hopeless."

Then Charlie Ward said, "I pulled Tom aside and told him that we had to get out of there before it got dark. The helicopter doesn't have the capabilities for night-flying."

Hudner began again, "I went back to Jesse to say goodbye and he was unconscious at this point. I assumed he was dead. I like to think he was. At least he wasn't alone at the end. I keep thinking about him stuck up there in the mountains." He was silent for a long moment. "Major, I don't know if you knew this, but Jesse was the Navy's first black pilot. He had a lot of friends."

The major nodded. "One more thing," he asked, "why did you crash that plane?"

Hudner looked him in the eye without hesitation, "Sir, he was my friend and he needed help."

We left the tent and dropped the two pilots off at H & S and then returned to Puller's CP.

As we walked in he asked, "What in the hell took you so long?"

Jones told Chesty the whole story.

Puller nodded and said, "Those Marine and Navy pilots are the best. We sure as hell couldn't get out of here without their help."

Then a strange look appeared on his face and he said, "Boys, I don't know if you knew this, but in 1926 I went to flight school at Pensacola, but they didn't think I was aviator material. I was dropped. It was probably a good thing; I wasn't much of a pilot."

Lieutenant Thomas Hudner would become the first American serviceman to receive the Medal of Honor in the Korean War. Unable to recover Jesse

Brown's body from the downed plane, the Navy sent four Corsairs to the crash site the following day and cremated their fallen friend in a blaze of napalm.

DECEMBER 5

A massive air evacuation had been taking place at Hagaru since the airstrip first opened four days earlier. By nightfall more than 4,000 wounded and frostbitten men had been flown out of Hagaru. Many of the dead were flown out as well. The whole evacuation was just an incredible operation. In addition, over 500 Marines had been flown in to build up the badly depleted ranks.

To prepare for the next stage of the breakout, more than 370 tons of supplies were flown in or air dropped on Hagaru; ammunition, hand grenades, fuel, rations, communication wire and medical supplies.

That day the press met with General Smith at Hagaru and a British correspondent asked if this was a "retreat."

"Certainly not," replied Smith. "There can be no retreat when there is no rear. You can't retreat when you are surrounded. We are attacking in another direction."

Within twenty-four hours his reply had appeared on the front pages across America. Only the reporter had added one word: 'Retreat, hell, we are attacking in another direction.'

At Koto-ri Puller brought his regimental staff and Lieutenant Colonel Sutter together and gave them their orders:

"Tomorrow the 5th and 7th Marines will start their breakout from Hagaru. Even though it's only eleven miles, it might take two full days to get here. There will be a lot of fighting and more casualties. It appears that they will be coming with about 10,000 men and 1,000 vehicles. We want to make sure there are enough warming huts and plenty of hot chow. These men are already half frozen and badly beaten up. They are going to have to rest for at least a day and then we will break out from Koto-ri. We have to get the airstrip finished to handle the casualties and the men who are killed. But most important of all we have to hold this damned place. I know the men are exhausted and brutally cold, but we have to keep them alert. There are one hell of a lot of Marines counting on us."

It was twenty-six below zero at Koto-ri. Although the Chinese had eased up on us, the Artic air was as vicious as ever.

DECEMBER 6

At 4:00 AM the 7th Marines led the breakout to Koto-ri. Murray's 5th Marines would hold the perimeter until Litzenberg had moved far enough down the road to allow Murray to follow. The drivers and the wounded would ride, everyone else would walk. This would not only provide close-in protection for the trucks, but it would reduce frostbite casualties by keeping the troops active. Marine Air Wing 1 would provide cover for the column with twenty-four planes while Marine, Navy and Air Force search and attack planes scouted ahead along the ridges on the flanks.

General Smith left Hagaru that morning and flew to Koto-ri. The flight only took ten minutes. Smith set up his new command post and started organizing the next move south. Smith asked Puller to come over and review the plans. Puller told me to come along.

When we walked into Smith's tent, Puller said, "Welcome to Koto-ri, General."

"Thanks, Lewie. Bring me up to speed on what's happening here."

"Well sir," Puller replied, "it appears that Koto-ri is surrounded by two Chinese divisions, however, the perimeter is well-defended and hot food and warming tents will be ready for the Marines fighting their way south.

"The road leading south out of Koto-ri is blocked and as you know the bridge at Funchilin Pass has been blown. Also south of there, the Chinese blew up a train trestle that ran over the road. The whole damn road is blocked – we can't drive around it. The runway should be ready tomorrow. The engineers have been working around the clock."

The General said, "Lewie, the biggest problem we have is the blown bridge at Funchilin Pass. The Army is going to airdrop eight treadway bridge sections. These things weigh about 2,500 pounds apiece, but have never been dropped by parachute before. It's scheduled for 0900 tomorrow."

Smith was taller than Puller and appeared to be more of a gentleman than a general. I never heard him use any profanity. He was steady, rarely got excited, and he seemed to have a lot of common sense. If he wasn't wearing his uniform, you might think he was a college professor. Smith would issue orders to his regimental commanders and then it was up to them to get the job done. He never interfered. He acted on two simple principles: the first was to be prepared for the worst and the second was to be optimistic when it came. This would serve him well at Chosin. Smith was a pipe-smoker like Puller, but never talked with the pipe in his mouth. Puller frequently did. They were different but both perfect for the task at hand. When the meeting was over we left – there was much to do. When the 5th and 7th Marines arrived, Koto-ri would triple in size.

While the 7th Marines were fighting their way south to Koto-ri, the 5th Marines fought the fiercest battle of the entire breakout, pushing the Chinese off of East Hill. The hill dominated the high ground east of Hagaru. The Marines' firepower was so devastating, it was estimated that they killed over

800 Chinese in the all-night battle. Securing East Hill opened the back door out of Hagaru.

DECEMBER 7

Early in the morning Puller got a call on the radio that the 7th Marines were coming down the road. Puller, Jones, Bodey and I climbed into the jeep and drove to the north end of the perimeter to watch the 7th Marines as they entered Koto-ri. It was one of those tragic sights that I will never forget: many of the trucks and jeeps had their windshields shot out and the hoods and sides of the vehicles were full of bullet holes. Wounded men were piled in the backs of trucks and the dead were tied to the hoods or fenders. The Marines who were walking were in bad shape. The convoy had driven through a twenty-five mile shooting gallery from Yudam-ni to Koto-ri and somehow had made it. Puller stood there with gloved hands in pockets and watched the shot-up vehicles and the exhausted Marines move by. He didn't say a word. He just stared. After about five minutes he turned around, we climbed back into the jeep and drove back to the CP.

When the 5th Marines left Hagaru late in the afternoon they provided security for the engineers who blew the town and the remaining supply dump to pieces. In the morning the Air Force dropped eight large bridging sections by parachute over Koto-ri. Six of the sections landed safely; one fell into Chinese hands and the last was damaged.

In the middle of the day an individual showed up at Puller's CP. Jones and I were waiting inside when someone walked in and said, "May I see Colonel Puller please?"

O.W. and I were stunned by the voice. It was a woman. She was dressed in a big hat with earflaps, a Navy parka and shoepacs. When she took the hat off her blonde hair fell almost to her shoulders. She was beautiful and looked like a movie star. I hadn't seen an American woman in over four months and the sight of her made me speechless.

She abruptly asked again, in a louder, annoyed voice, "Well, can I see the Colonel?"

Jones answered before I could, "What's your name, ma'am?"

"Marguerite Higgins of the New York Herald-Tribune," she answered proudly.

"I assume you're a reporter," I said, and immediately regretted it.

She looked me up and down, "Well, Sergeant," she replied curtly, "you are very perceptive."

"Wait here and I'll see if the Colonel is available," I said. I walked to the rear, behind a partition and Chesty was on the radio.

When he hung up I said, "Sir, there is a lady reporter out there who wants to see you. Marguerite Higgins."

"What the hell is a woman doing here?" Puller said. "Send her back."

I walked out front and said, "The Colonel will see you, now, Ms. Higgins."

She stormed past me and I heard her say, "Colonel, I'm Maggie Higgins."

"I know who you are," Puller replied.

Apparently Maggie Higgins was well known among Marines, from the Pusan Perimeter and both the Inchon and Seoul campaigns. Previously, Higgins had won fame as one of the first women war correspondents to cover WWII and the Nuremberg Trials. She also had been in Korea since the beginning of the war, and had intended to march out of Chosin Reservoir with the Marines.

They talked for a while and she asked Puller a lot of questions, which he answered. He finally said, "Miss Higgins, you are going to have to leave Koto-ri. It's just not safe here."

She protested loudly, "Colonel, I should be treated the same as a man. Besides, this is the biggest story of the Korean War and I don't want to miss it."

"I'm sorry, Miss Higgins," Puller said. Then he yelled, "Sergeant Abbo!"

I came back to him and said, "Yes, sir."

"You and Jones drive Miss Higgins to the airstrip. Now."

She continued to protest, but it was a done deal. She was not happy. The runway opened that morning and all day small planes landed and flew out casualties. When we got to the runway, there were wounded men lying all over the place. Most of the senior officers liked Higgins but the enlisted men didn't care much for her. She was going from wounded Marine to wounded Marine asking questions, when she came to a corporal lying on a stretcher who was pretty doped up. I suppose this Marine didn't like her brusque, almost superior New York air.

She bent down on her knees and asked him, "Marine, what was the toughest thing you've had to do since being surrounded?"

A small smile crept to his face, "The toughest thing," he said, "is getting three inches of dick out of six inches of clothing when I have to take a leak."

That was the first time we had laughed in quite awhile, but it didn't phase Higgins one bit. She was already moving on, talking to the next wounded Marine. She flew out on the next plane and Jones and I drove back to the CP.

On the way back O.W. said, "She was sure a good-looking woman, and I'll bet she's close to our age. Maybe early thirties?"

"You know something, O.W.," I said, "When I saw her it sure made me wonder what was hiding under all those clothes."

Jones laughed at me, "Forget it, Abbo. You wouldn't have a chance in hell."

At 9:30 PM the last Marines of the division reached Koto-ri. It had taken almost forty hours for the 10,000 men and 1,000 vehicles to fight their way from Hagaru. The cost: 103 dead, 506 wounded and 7 missing. The tired Marines moved off to the tents and shelters of the Koto-ri garrison. Every stove was fired up and stew and pancakes were served to anyone who cared to eat. There would be no layover in Koto-ri, however. The Chinese were massing in the mountains to the south, and the advance would resume first thing in the morning.

The Division command post was in a cramped tent in the center of the Koto-ri perimeter. Puller and Rickert went over to division and reviewed the plans for the breakout to Chinhung-ni. Over an hour later Puller returned to the regimental command post. He got on the phone and called his two battalion commanders, Ridge and Sutter. He told them both the same thing: "Get your company commanders and report to the CP."

They all arrived ten minutes later. As I looked around the tent, Puller and his officers were exhausted. Our regiment was on the slim side, we had lost a lot of men and there was no fat left. We had to make due with fewer men than we should have. The men who remained were the heartiest or the luckiest. I guess what really mattered is that we were still there.

Puller lit up his pipe and the light from the match illuminated his wrinkled, weather-beaten face and I knew right away that the aging tiger was going to lead us out of these miserable mountains.

He cupped the bowl of the pipe in his hand and said, "We breakout tomorrow morning, 0800. The 7th Marines lead the way, followed by the 5th Marines. The 1st Marines go last. We will hold the perimeter with 2/1 and 3/1. We will be the rear guard. Lieutenant Colonel Schmuck's 1/1 will fight their way north from Chinhung-ni and seize Hill 1081. The Chinese currently have control of this hill, and his job will be to push them off; whoever holds this hill controls the MSR for miles in either direction. Lieutenant Colonel Schmuck has the only fresh battalion in the division and he'll start the attack first thing in the morning. We also have the problem of the blown bridge to deal with as well as the train trestle that is blocking the road. As you all know, the road between Koto-ri and Chinhung-ni is some of the most difficult terrain along the whole MSR. If the weather is good, and that's a big 'if', we will have air cover. If we make it to Chinhung-ni we're in the clear. You know this and the Chinese know it. This is their last chance to get us. I expect the fighting to be savage. It could be the longest ten miles of our lives. You know what you have to do. Good night, Gentlemen."

At two in the morning Lieutenant Colonel Schmuck called into Puller by radio, "The battalion is ready to move out."

Puller replied, "The weather forecast is unfavorable and you should not count on getting air support. Good luck."

DECEMBER 8

A heavy snowfall put an end to air operations, some 400 wounded stranded on the ground for the moment, and the temperature began to drop.

Puller came out of his tent early in the morning and got Bodey and me and told Jones to get the jeep. He said, "We've got to bury the men who were killed on the way down here. There isn't enough space on the planes to fly them out."

In the swirling snow we drove over to a large pit about the size of a basketball court. It was several feet deep with a ramp at one end, so the trucks could back down and unload the bodies of the 117 Marines, Navy Corpsmen, British commandos and U.S. Army soldiers, each wrapped in a sleeping bag or parachute. Along with Puller were General Smith and Colonels Litzenberg and Murray. There was a chaplain of each faith there. It was one of the saddest things I have ever seen. I wondered if these men would ever come home. The Division said goodbye to these courageous men with a short religious service and a rifle volley. When it was over Puller thanked the members of the firing squad and then two bulldozers covered over the mass grave with chunks of frozen dirt.

The 7th Marines pulled out of Koto-ri in a blinding snowstorm. From the start the fighting was fierce. The Marines began clearing the ridges on either side of the road south but the going was slow and the trucks carrying the bridge sections made little progress.

For Lieutenant Colonel Schmuck heading north to attack Hill 1081, the six mile approach was made in almost total silence; a condition enhanced by the blowing snowstorm. It took five hours to climb the steep hill. Captain Barrow's A Company led the way and drove the Chinese off the hill. Nine of his men were killed and eleven wounded. This was the same company that in September had fought the bold battle that opened the door to Yongdungpo. That night the Chinese tried to win back the hill but A Company held with relative ease. The battle was not over, however, they had more ground to take the next day.

The Chinese also mounted several attacks against the shrinking Koto-ri perimeter but Puller's 2nd and 3rd battalions drove them off.

DECEMBER 9

No one was going anywhere until the bridge was fixed; it was a thousand foot drop to the bottom. When the Army bridge company got to the site and measured the gap, they found the bridge sections were seven feet too short. The gap in the roadway was twenty-nine feet long and the steel treadway bridge sections were twenty-two feet long.

They quickly came up with a solution: two officers had found a large stock of pre-cut bridging timbers that could be built up to support either end of the short bridging sections. There was a ledge eight feet below the road on the south side and so there the timbers would be stacked in alternating layers to form an open crib on the ledge. Two steel bridge sections would be placed across the solid roadway on the north, to the crib on the south. Frozen Chinese bodies were used to fill the crib. Four-inch thick plywood sheets were then spread between the sections, resting on steel lips that ran the length of each section. The tanks would be able to cross the deep gorge using the two parallel spans, one track on each section; the rest of the vehicles would cross with one tire on a section, the other on the plywood center section.

The first vehicle to cross, a bulldozer, almost broke through and damaged the plywood. It was quickly repaired. Now the Marines started crossing slowly and carefully, one vehicle at a time.

Next, the railroad overpass had to be dealt with. Part of the overpass had been dropped on ice and so a bulldozer operator just skated the huge object right off the road.

Although Captain Barrow had taken most of Hill 1081, he still had to take the knob of the hill. Barrow captured the knob by noon. In two days of brutal fighting the cost to A Company was 112 dead, wounded and frostbitten out of the original company of 223. Captain Barrow would be awarded the Navy Cross for his actions in capturing the hill.

With most of the division gone from Koto-ri, Puller sent Ridge's 3rd Battalion south first. That night Ridge had to fight off a serious Chinese attack.

I didn't like the idea of being part of the last unit out of Koto-ri. If all went well, we would leave the next day. With everyone gone, Puller had to shrink the perimeter even more.

DECEMBER 10

The lead elements of the division reached Chinhung-ni before dawn.

We spent a good part of the morning preparing to leave Koto-ri. The supplies and equipment that we couldn't put on the trucks were destroyed and extra ammunition was exploded. The last plane flew out in the afternoon through a short-lived gap in the clouds; it carried nineteen casualities. There would be more wounded but they would have to walk or ride.

In the early afternoon we abandoned Koto-ri with the rifle companies leap-frogging down the road to provide cover. The reconnaissance company was the last to leave and Puller talked to the commanding officer for a few minutes. I could see a large cloud of smoke rise up as the ammunition blew up.

Puller came to Bodey, Jones and me and said, "Let's go."

Jones had the jeep warmed up and across the bumper lay a frozen body. Two other bodies were tied to the rear and the top. There were two wounded in the jeep. Jones was still looking for bodies to carry out with them.

Puller barked at Jones, "Just make damn sure they're Marines."

Jones pulled out and Puller, Bodey, and I walked. It was 3:00 PM. As we left, Puller shouted out to a group of men on the side of road, "Don't forget you're United States Marines. All the Communists in the world can't stop you now."

One of the men yelled out, "Damn right, Colonel!"

I can still hear the crunching sound of boots and tires on the frozen hard packed snow as the long column moved slowly down the road. Around 10:00 PM we reached the bridge. It was pitch black and flashlights guided the men and vehicles across the narrow sections of the bridge. I'm glad I couldn't see down, I'm afraid of heights. When I crossed the bridge that night, I never knew about the Chinese bodies supporting the bridge. When I learned about it later, I realized how strange war can be: days before these men had been trying to kill us and now they were literally holding up the bridge so we could escape.

That night was one of the coldest on record and I'm sure the temperature dropped past thirty below zero. We were simply miserable. Hands and feet would freeze if you stopped moving. I was constantly jumping up and down to stay warm. Puller would get in the jeep to warm up and then get back on the road and start walking. It was a long, bitter cold night. I was doing everything I could to stay warm and suddenly started singing.

I then heard Puller yell out, "What in the hell is all that noise?"

"Colonel," I said, "I'm just trying to keep warm."

"Is it working, Abbo?" he asked.

"No, sir."

"Then spare us", ordered the Colonel.

All night long it was stop and go. At some time during the early morning we were held up longer than usual. Puller climbed into the jeep and told Jones to drive ahead so he could find out what was holding up the column. This was no easy task and Jones carefully drove along the cliff side of the one lane road. Bodey and I followed on foot. About fifteen minutes later Puller saw a sergeant stopping each truck. Jones pulled up next to the sergeant and Puller hopped out and barked "Sergeant, what the hell are you stopping all these trucks for?"

It was obvious the sergeant knew who he was talking to and he quickly replied, "Sir our 81mm mortar section is running out of ammo. We are supporting the Marines up on the ridges and one of the trucks has got 81 ammo on it. I've got to find it."

"All right ol' man. I'll give you a hand," replied Puller.

Each truck that drove up, Puller roared out "You carrying any 81 ammo?" The driver would say "No" and Puller would wave him on. After about 10 minutes they found the truck. The sergeant said "Thank you Colonel" and Puller replied "Give 'em hell up there sergeant."

As we continued on down the road, I couldn't help but think that once they unloaded that truck, then some Marines would have to hump the ammo up the hills to where the mortars were.

There was a battle in the rear of the regiment that night and when the last of Puller's Marines crossed the bridge, the engineers blew it up.

As the fighting went on in the rear, the forward units of the 1st Marines had problems of their own. As the trucks passed through the village of Sudong sometime after midnight, the Chinese attacked the front of the column. In a short time they destroyed several trucks which blocked the highway. The Marines quickly got it sorted out, but they lost twenty-nine of their men who were killed or wounded.

DECEMBER 11

When dawn came Puller told Jones to pull over. He wanted to take a look at his men. As they came down the road many were limping because of frozen feet and their eyes all had that blank stare. They were like zombies. They had been fighting day and night for two weeks and having survived the fighting and the cold was nothing short of a miracle. Their parkas and trousers were covered with an assortment of stains: urine, food, oil from cleaning weapons, dysentery, mucus from runny noses and blood. These men had suffered terribly but were still on their feet.

A corpsman behind me said, "Look at those bastards. Look at those magnificent bastards."

Puller was watching his men as they came down the road. All of sudden he tore out into the road and started shouting:

"You're the 1st Marine Division – and don't you ever forget it. We're the greatest military outfit that ever walked the earth. All the Communists in hell can't stop us now. We're going down to the sea and if anything gets in our way we'll blow the hell out of it."

He had a lot of pride in his men so he growled more deeply, "And remember something! We're not retreating! We've about-faced to get at more of those bastards – You're the 1st Marines and be damn proud of it."

When the men saw Puller they started to come alive. They smiled and one of them yelled out, "Hey Colonel, we beat the hell out of them!"

"We sure did, old man!" Puller shouted back.

All the way, Puller would stop often to buck up his men. When we finally reached Chinhung-ni, trucks were supposed to pick us up but X Corps messed up again; there weren't enough trucks so we kept walking.

Puller was furious. "Can't those damn people at X Corps do anything right?" he shouted.

Around noon we entered Majon-Dong. Trucks appeared and we climbed aboard and they carried us down to Hungnam.

That night all the 1st Marines slept in heated tents and the next day we did absolutely nothing but rest. When we sailed on December 14th all the ships were overloaded but the opportunity to eat hot food, sleep and not be shot at was absolute heaven to the men who had suffered through so much.

As Puller was about to board the ship two reporters approached him. Before they could ask him a question he said "Remember, whatever you write, this was no retreat. All that happened was that we found more Chinese behind us than in front of us, so we about-faced and attacked." Then one of the reporters asked him, "Colonel, what is the most important lesson that the Marines have learned in Korea, so far?"

Puller bluntly replied, "Never serve under X Corps!" He had had enough of MacArthur, Almond and the Army.

As we were pulling out of the port of Hungnam I was standing next to Puller. He was in a reflective mood and stared up into the mountains we had just come from.

I said, "Sir that had to be the most horrible weather that any of these Marines have ever been in."

He looked at me and said, "Abbo, I've never been in worse weather and the funny thing is, winter doesn't start for another week."

Marine casualties were heavy. From November 27th to December 11th, the 1st Marine Division had 561 killed, 2,894 wounded, 182 missing and 3,657 injured or sick, (mostly frostbite) out of roughly 15,000 men. The Chinese losses, however, were much greater. It was estimated that they had 25,000 killed in action and 12,500 wounded.

Colonel Litzenberg and Lieutenant Colonel Murray were awarded the Navy Cross. Chesty Puller was also recommended for and received his fifth

Navy Cross for his vital contribution to the defense of Koto-ri and the break-out to Hungnam. Chesty was already in a class by himself with four Navy Crosses – the only Marine ever so honored. The fifth Navy Cross moved him up another rung on the ladder.

And so the battle for Chosin Reservoir was over. It would go down as one of the most savage, dramatic and courageous battles the Marine Corps ever fought. No Americans ever fought in colder weather and in spite of this, the withdrawal was brilliantly planned and superbly executed.

MASAN

We left Hungnam and headed south. Water was to be used only for drink-ing, not for washing. We were filthy, but would have to wait. The ship was packed with people. Even though it was cold, I slept on the deck and had lots of company. It was a lot better than sleeping below. The smell of the unwashed Marines was unbearable. After we were underway, we got word that we were to land at Pusan and from there we would be trucked to a tent camp near Masan.

Along the way it was announced that we would be served only one meal during the thirty-six hour trip. There just wasn't enough food or time to serve all these people. The ship's galley crew did a wonderful job of taking care of us with what little they had. Surprisingly, the trip was relaxing. It was the first time in weeks that any of us could sit around and talk in comfort while not fearing for our lives.

We were worn out physically and mentally. Everyone had lost weight. When I left Chicago in July I weighed 165 pounds. Now, I wondered if I weighed 135. When the ship docked, trucks were waiting to take us to Masan, twenty miles away. Tents were erected on the outskirts of the city in the same bean patch the Marine brigade had used when it first arrived in South Korea. Kitchens were set up and within a few hours we were served a hot meal of stew and coffee. A few days later, fresh food arrived and finally we would have good food at every meal.

On the second day in camp, showers were built, using fifty-gallon oil drums. The water was hot and the showers were always filled to capacity. It felt wonderful to finally be clean again. We were issued new uniforms. I as-sumed they burned the old ones because they were absolutely filthy.

On Christmas Eve, Puller visited all his battalions. Jones and I accompa-nied him. Everywhere we went we sang Christmas carols, and I have to ad-mit, our singing was pretty good. When we returned, Puller invited the senior officers over to share some food and a little whiskey.

The next morning was Christmas Day, and there were a lot of Marines who attended mass and I'm sure we were all thinking the same thing: 'Thank you dear Lord for getting me out of that nightmare at the Reservoir.' We had a lot to be thankful for.

After church we went to the mess tent and had a feast: turkey, cranberry sauce, sweet potatoes, fruitcake, apples and nuts. It was the finest meal I ate in Korea. The next two weeks were spent training, cleaning weapons and getting ready to get back into the war.

Chapter Eight

After Korea

Today is my last day in Korea. I leave here with mixed emotions. They lie somewhere between joy and ecstasy.

M. Abbo, letter to parents, 10 Jan 1951

BACK TO CHICAGO

Late in the afternoon of January 10th I was told to report to Colonel Puller. I went to his CP but he was on the phone so I hesitated to enter. He saw me and waved me in.

When he hung up he said, "Mike, today is your lucky day. You're going home. Your enlistment ends January 15th. Unfortunately, you will have to go by ship but at least you are getting out of here. I wanted to thank you for the fine job you did in Korea, and it will be so noted in your records."

I stood before the Colonel, not sure what to do or say.

He grinned, "One more thing, Mike. If there's another war, I'd be happy to have you along."

I suddenly realized that I probably would never see Puller again, and I felt a little emotional, standing in front of maybe the most famous Marine that ever lived.

The words would not come, and all I could muster was, "Sir, it was a privilege to serve with you."

Puller replied, "Have Jones drive you to Pusan. There is a ship leaving tomorrow for the States."

He offered me his hand and I shook it.

"Good luck, Mike," he said.

"And good luck to you, sir."

And then I left.

I arrived in the States on February 1st and was transferred out of the Marine Corps Reserve. The next day I boarded the train to Chicago for the three-day ride home. The train ride gave me time to put the Chosin Reservoir campaign behind me. It had been absolutely vicious and I realized how lucky I was to get out of there alive. I actually enjoyed the ride home for it gave me plenty of time to think about my future. I decided to get my old job back at the Chicago Tribune.

In March of 1951, I started work again and this time I appreciated my job much more and approached it with a renewed enthusiasm.

Shortly after I left Korea, Puller had been promoted to Brigadier General and became the Assistant Division Commander of the 1st Marine Division. He left Korea on May 20th, 1951.

Chesty Puller arrived back in the United States on May 23rd. When I picked up the newspaper the following morning, Chesty was quoted in bold type. I had to chuckle. It was pure Puller. The headlines read:

PULLER DENIES URGING BOOZE FOR TROOPS
MARINE GENERAL BLASTS AIR FORCE
PULLER SHIFTS HIS FIRE FROM ICE CREAM TO AIR FORCE

Apparently, when he arrived in San Francisco the reporters were waiting for him. I don't know if Chesty was tired, or angry about how the war was being fought, or what, but it was obvious that he was not prepared to face their questions. He gave the writers a very grim, candid picture of the Korean War:

"What the American people want to do is fight a war without getting hurt. You can't do that any more than you can go into a barroom brawl without getting hurt.

"Unless the American people are willing to send their sons out to fight an aggressor, there's just not going to be any United States. A bunch of foreign soldiers will take over.

"Air power can't live up to its billing out there. Somebody – not so much the aviators as the aircraft manufacturers – has sold the American people a bill of goods as to what air power can do. From what I've seen, one bomb will hit a section of railroad track and one hundred bombs will miss, some of them by miles. The enemy puts coolies on the track with picks and shovels and in twenty-four hours they're rolling again. The answer is infantry.

"Our officer corps has had far too much schooling and far too little combat experience. They can't learn war like that.

"Push-button war is as far off as in the days of Julius Caesar. The rifle, hand grenade and bayonet are still the most important weapons. We're going to lose the next war if we don't get back to them.

"We've got to get 'em tougher to survive. Throw all these girls out of camp. Get rid of the ice cream and candy. Get some pride in 'em – that's what we need now most of all, pride."

A reporter asked: "What do you think of the protest of the Women's Christian Temperance Union over sending free beer to the troops?"

"It's news to me. But if a few cans of beer or a snort of whiskey will make them fight better, it might not be a bad idea. At least it's better than ice cream and all this soft training."

After his press conference, General Puller flew to Chicago where he told reporters that there was "too damn much recreation" in military training of men who have only one purpose when they were in uniform – "to fight." He said, "They're not being taught that now."

Then Puller flew to Washington, D.C. where he told the press that the Marines "don't get ice cream." He also said that "the Air Force did not understand close air support, does not believe in it, and has never practiced it."

Chesty also said he saw no need to change Marine Corps training methods. He would follow present methods when, after a thirty day leave with his family in Saluda, Virginia, he would take over the 3rd Marine Brigade at Camp Pendleton, California. "I'm going to train them as Marines have always been trained . . . I want them to be able to march twenty miles, the last five at double time, and then be ready to fight."

He also said he was under strict orders not to criticize other services, and was not doing so. And then he delivered his best line of the day. "I did not get shot in Korea and I hope I don't get hung here."

There were many protest letters against Puller's remarks. Most of these letters were sent to Marine Corps Headquarters. The Marine Corps supported Puller and fortunately, the controversy did not last long and was soon forgotten.

After a few years, I was promoted and moved to the National News department. Life was good, I enjoyed my work and in March of 1954 I got married. I was happy with the way my life was turning out. I kept in touch with some of my old buddies from the Marine Corps Reserve because even though I was out of the Corps, I still held an interest in the Marines, and the career of Chesty Puller.

The Korean War came to an end on July 27th, 1953 and in September of that same year Puller was promoted to Major General. The following July, Puller took over as Commanding General of the 2nd Marine Division at Camp Lejeune, NC. On August 27th Puller suffered a minor stroke; apparently his health was not what it appeared to be. For the next year Puller went through a series of physicals and medical boards. Eventually his case would be decided by the Secretary of the Navy. It was a fight Puller desperately wanted to win but in the end the Secretary informed Puller that he would be forced to retire at the end of October.

RETIREMENT

The Marine Corps announced on October 10th, 1955 that Chesty Puller was retiring. The news sparked a nationwide blitz of stories about Puller's career. I followed these with great interest and much sadness. I couldn't believe that the most famous Marine was being retired from the Corps for heath reasons. I guess the stress of a long combat career had taken its toll. The retirement was scheduled for October 31, 1955.

I went in to see my boss to ask if I could go to Camp Lejeune to cover the retirement ceremony. I think I was more interested in seeing Puller again than writing a story, but if I went to Lejeune I could do both. After my boss gave me the okay I left his office and called Camp Lejeune. A Marine answered the phone and I asked to speak to General Puller.

He said, "Sir, who's calling?"

"This is Mike Abbo with the Chicago Tribune," I replied.

"Sir, just a minute," the voice said.

I was transferred a couple times and finally a voice said, "General Puller's office."

"I'd like to speak to General Puller, please. This is Mike Abbo of the Chicago Tribune."

"Hold on sir, I will see if the General is available," the secretary said.

A minute later a voice growled over the line, "General Puller."

"Sir, this is Mike Abbo. How are you?"

Puller grunted, "Not worth a damn. What's up?"

"Well, sir," I said, trying not to sound nervous, "I was wondering if I could come down and cover your retirement for the Chicago Tribune."

"Mike," he said, "it is just going to be a small ceremony. My family won't even be here. I'm really not looking forward to this day."

"Sir, it would be an honor for me to attend. If you don't want me to write a story I won't, but I'd sure like to be there," I replied.

There was a long pause and Puller finally said, "Alright, 31 October, 1000 hours, General Jordahl's office. I'll see you then."

THE CEREMONY

I drove to Jacksonville, North Carolina the day before the retirement. I stayed in a motel near the base and the next morning I woke up early, ate breakfast and was ready to go.

I arrived at the gate of the base at 9:30 AM and told them I was there for General Puller's retirement ceremony. The corporal at the gate asked for identification and when I showed it to him he told me to pull over and someone would lead me to General Jordahl's office.

"Who is General Jordahl?" I asked.

He replied, "Sir, General Jordahl is the acting commanding officer of the base and General Puller's retirement ceremony will be held there."

A minute later a jeep pulled up and the Marine driving said, "Sir, follow me."

I followed him and a few minutes later we pulled up in front of the base commander's office. I walked in and introduced myself and a sergeant said to take a seat. A few minutes later, Sergeant Jones walked in. I was glad to see him and surprised to learn that he was still Puller's driver, especially since he was now a gunnery sergeant. We shook hands and I said, "How is Chesty doing?"

Jones said, "Let's step outside."

We walked out the door and Jones said, "The old man is very unhappy about this but there isn't a damn thing he can do about it. He's especially disappointed because he didn't think the senior Marine Corps officers stood up for him, and that includes the Commandant. It's a sad day, Abbo."

In changing the subject I said, "What's a gunnery sergeant doing driving a general around?"

Jones laughed and said, "You aren't the first one to ask that. When we got back from Korea the old man asked me if I wanted to continue driving him. I said 'Sure!' Well, when he took over the 2nd Marine Division last year, the Commandant, General Shepherd, came down to Camp Lejeune. I drove him and the old man around for a couple of days. After lunch one day, Shepherd and Chesty are getting in the car and the Commandant says, 'Lewie, what are you doing with a gunny as a driver?' Chesty says, 'Headquarters still owes me a captain as an aide and when the Commandant acknowledged that, the old man said 'Well look – let's make a deal. You keep your captain and I'll keep my gunny.'"

"What did the Commandant say?" I asked.

"He just shook his head and chuckled."

We walked back into the lobby and talked for a few minutes. Then a sergeant major walked in and Jones said "Morning, Sergeant Major, I'd like you to meet Mike Abbo. He was General Puller's runner in World War II and Korea. And Mike, Sergeant Major Norrish was a member of Chesty Puller's 1926 drill team".

We shook hands and I said "Sergeant Major, I've heard a lot of stories about Chesty Puller, but nothing about a drill team".

"Well, Mike", said Norrish, "When Lieutenant Puller arrived at Quantico in 1926 he was soon given the job of preparing a platoon of Marines for the annual interservice drill competition held in Boston. There was a lot of pressure to win the cup because the Army had won it the previous two years and that didn't sit too well with the Marine Corps. When our platoon first met Lieutenant Puller he said, "We're going to win that damn cup or we're going to die trying". He drilled us ruthlessly for the next four weeks. And by God we won it. When we got back to Quantico, the Commandant of the Marine Corps, General Lejeune, sent him a letter congratulating him on winning the cup. I wonder how many lieutenants have ever received a letter from the Commandant".

While I was thinking about this a captain walked in and said, "Will you follow me, please?"

We followed him down the hall to General Jordahl's office. When we entered the room, Generals Puller and Jordahl were talking. Introductions were made and another newspaperman came in.

"Okay," Puller said, "let's get this over with."

Puller was going to retire on his terms and so he broke tradition. It was an unwritten rule that the senior Marine officer on the base would pin Puller's third star (Lieutenant General) on his shoulder as he retired – but Puller had asked Sergeant Major Norrish, the senior enlisted man on the base, to do the honors. Norrish pinned the stars on his shoulders in silence.

Puller stood at attention, looking straight ahead.

When the ceremony was over he said, "I hate like hell to go. In having Sergeant Major Norris attach my third star at my retirement, I wanted to show my great admiration and appreciation to the enlisted men and junior officers of the Marine Corps. I fully realize that without the help of the enlisted men I'd never have risen from a private to a lieutenant general."

Puller, looking around slowly, continued, "I've commanded everything from a squad to a division and without the help of men and junior officers, these units would never have gone forward and achieved their objectives, regardless of almost certain death."

"My only regret is that as things now are, I won't be present for the next war. I'd like to do it all over again, the whole thing. And more than that – more than anything – I'd like to see once again the face of every Marine I've ever served with."

"I also want to express my regret at the deaths of many hundreds of Marines and the crippling and maiming of other hundreds who followed me blindly into battle. Again, I would like to thank all Marines for their feelings toward me."

Someone handed Puller a three-star flag. He shook hands with everyone and when he got to me he shook mine and said, "Go ahead and write the story, and thanks for making the trip, Mike."

Then he left the room and walked down the hall.

Jones and I returned to the lobby. There, we talked for a while.

I said good-bye to Jones and climbed into my car and started to drive back to Chicago. I felt like I had just witnessed something more like a funeral than a retirement ceremony.

Puller had dominated the Marine Corps stage for most of his career, but now the curtain had gone down. But unbeknownst to anyone, the show was not quite over. Chesty Puller would soon be back on center stage.

Chapter Nine

Ribbon Creek

The court martial starts tomorrow. I'm not sure how this is going to turn out. I know that the Marine Corps' training has always been tough and often brutal. No one likes being kicked around by a Marine drill instructor, but is there any other way to get these young men tough enough to face the unimaginable horrors of war?

M. Abbo, letter to parents, 15 Oct 1956

A TRAGIC DECISION

On Sunday, April 8th, 1956 an inexperienced, frustrated and angry drill instructor at Parris Island, Staff Sergeant Matthew McKeon, took his platoon of seventy-five recruits on a night march into a tidal swamp called Ribbon Creek.

McKeon took them on the march in the hope that a little cold water would restore lagging discipline. During the day, fed up with his under performing platoon, McKeon had a few drinks and decided that the best way to give his recruits a wake up call was to march them through the swamp. It was a common, but not officially approved punishment designed to instill great discipline into sub-par platoons. It was a tragic decision. Six men drowned that night. It would take more than twenty-four hours to recover the bodies from the bottom of Ribbon Creek.

McKeon was placed under arrest by Colonel McKean, the officer in charge of the weapons training battalion. The following morning, the Commandant of the Marine Corps, General Pate was notified of the tragedy. At approximately 1:00 PM on Monday, some sixteen hours after the incident, the press was notified. When Commandant Pate arrived at Parris Island later in the day he knew the press would be there. Once he had reviewed the facts, he would hold a press conference and brief the media on what had happened.

General Pate delivered his prepared statement and then offered to answer questions. When asked if Sergeant McKeon was guilty of breaking regulations, Pate responded, "It would appear so."

Another reporter then asked the Commandant if in effect the Marine Corps was going to allow the drill instructor to get away with murder, General Pate replied that McKeon would be punished to the fullest extent of the law. Not knowing the full story, General Pate had prematurely condemned McKeon. I thought this was a foolish thing for the Commandant to say and most Marines were shocked by it.

A court of inquiry was held on Tuesday, April 10th, and its recommendation was that Staff Sergeant McKeon be court-martialed. He was charged with drinking on duty, culpable negligence in six deaths, and oppression. There was a lot of negative press and much of it was not factual. I was very disappointed by all this and it appeared that the tough basic training that molded generations of Marines was now in serious jeopardy.

EMILE ZOLA BERMAN

McKeon would be defended by Emile Zola Berman, a top trial lawyer from New York City. He would be assisted by McKeon's brother-in-law, Thomas P. Costello, who was also from New York City.

As I followed the case very closely, it became apparent that McKeon was going to have a very powerful and competent attorney representing him. Though there was still a lot of negative publicity about the case, in the period between the court of inquiry and the start of the court martial, Berman had masterfully changed the nature of the case. His most important objective was to 'humanize' his client. Although most Marines supported McKeon, the press's vicious portrayal of him had convinced many people that he was a drunken rogue.

Berman did many things to paint McKeon with the underdog brush: he appeared on the nationally televised Today Show and announced he was taking on the case without fee, he convinced many journalists to talk to McKeon and his family and they came away writing positive stories about McKeon, and he did a terrific job of showing the press that McKeon was a good Marine.

Berman then took the offensive. He changed the focus from McKeon to the long established Marine Corps training practices. From then on, the Marine Corps leaders knew that their own future and that of the Corps was in jeopardy if they chose to make an example of McKeon. What Berman was telling the Corps was this: you treat McKeon fairly and I'll treat the Marine Corps fairly.

PARRIS ISLAND RECRUIT DEPOT

The trial was to begin Monday morning, July 16th, 1956. I talked to my boss at the newspaper and told him I would be the best person to cover this story because I had been a Marine. In addition, I had gone through basic training at Parris Island and could write an objective story on the court martial of Staff Sergeant McKeon.

I left Chicago early Saturday morning, arrived in Beaufort, South Carolina late that night, and stayed at the Golden Eagle Hotel. This would be my home, as well as the home of many of the press, for the next three weeks.

Sunday, after going to mass, and then breakfast at the hotel, I drove over to Parris Island. When I arrived at the gate, I told the Marine on guard duty that I was a reporter as well as a former Marine. He told me to check in at the administration building. I was given access to most of the base and because of the court martial they did not want any interviews. I said I wasn't interested in interviewing anyone; all I wanted to do was walk around and see how Parris Island had changed since I had been a recruit fifteen years earlier. Since it was Sunday, there was not much going on. I spent three or four hours walking around the base; I saw the barracks where I lived, the rifle range and the drill field where I had spent a large amount of time.

I walked over to Ribbon Creek where the drownings had taken place. The creek was an ominous looking body of dark, dirty water which snakes its way behind the northwest boundary of the island, less than a hundred yards beyond the rifle range. The bottom of the creek is filled with mud. The marsh banks that bordered the creek were covered with waist to shoulder-high grass. It was not a place I would go during the day let alone on a dark night. Back then I didn't know the creek even had a name. Now, I would never forget it.

It was getting late and I went to my car and drove back to the hotel. After a quick shower to cool off I went down to the bar to have a beer. As expected the place was packed with reporters and the only topics we discussed were McKeon and the start of the trial. It was my impression that many of the reporters had softened their negative opinion of Matthew McKeon, and with the trial set to begin, they appeared to be more open-minded. After a couple of hours, I left the bar, ate dinner and went to bed.

THE TRIAL

The court martial was to begin Monday morning. Usually, a general court martial would have been held in the courtroom located in the administration building at Mainside, but because this trial had turned into one of the most sensational court-martials of the twentieth century, they needed to move the trial to a bigger facility to accommodate the large amount of reporters. The Marine Corps converted the auditorium of the depot school at Mainside into a courtroom.

The Secretary of the Navy, Charles S. Thomas, appointed Marine Colonel Edward L. Hutchinson to serve as president of the seven-member court. The court had six Marine officers and one Navy physician.

Secretary Thomas designated Major Charles B. Sevier as trial counsel. Navy Captain Irving N. Klein was appointed to serve as law officer.

To a great extent Klein was to be the equivalent of a judge in a civilian trial. The seven members of the court were in many respects like a civilian jury, although Colonel Hutchinson as president had broader authority than a jury foreman.

The trial did not begin until Tuesday, July 17th. As expected the courtroom was filled with reporters, spectators, McKeon's family, and the families of the six deceased Marines. It was the middle of the summer and without air conditioning it was brutally hot and humid.

For the first two weeks of the trial, the prosecution presented its case and called its witnesses. They reviewed the relevant events leading up to the march and its immediate aftermath was described by the people who had the most direct knowledge of it. The prosecution concluded with testimony surrounding McKeon's consumption of alcohol and sobriety.

During this time period Berman twice asked for extended weekend recesses, "to undertake a mission which I regard as of the highest importance connected with this case." The court granted both requests, which created a little excitement because everyone wanted to know where he was going.

At the start of the third week, on July 30th, Berman presented his case. Staff Sergeant McKeon testified for a day and a half. Despite the seriousness of the offenses, the members of the Court had a full opportunity to evaluate this combat veteran with an exemplary record, who must have impressed them as a decent and regretful man, as he spoke with honesty and humility.

On August 1st, the Commandant of the Marine Corps, General Pate, testified. He arrived in the courtroom wearing sunglasses, which he never removed during his testimony. In response from questions from Berman, the Commandant completely reversed his earlier public position endorsing McKeon's court martial and calling for the strongest possible punishment. Now he said that McKeon should lose one rank for drinking in front of a recruit. As for the other charges, Pate thought the staff sergeant rated at most, transfer away from his duties "for lack of judgment."

Everyone knew Berman had a star witness and that he would testify the next day. Some said it might even be Chesty Puller, but I didn't think so, since he had retired the year before.

THE LEGEND RETURNS

On August 2nd I arrived at court early to get a seat and see who this "star" witness was. At 10:15 AM Berman stood up and announced, "The defense desires to call to the stand Lieutenant General Puller."

I almost fell out of my chair. His appearance immediately electrified the courtroom. Without hesitation, the president of the court stood and called the large room to attention—a sign of respect not granted Commandant Pate. The standing room only crowd was the largest yet for the trial. Puller quickly showed his skills on this new stage. He boldly walked up the aisle, ramrod straight and took his seat in the witness stand. He crossed his legs and hooked one arm over the back of the chair, his uniform decorated with eight rows of combat ribbons and roared loud enough to be heard at the far end of the island.

"Now if I don't talk loud enough, somebody back there sound off and I'll talk louder!"

The courtroom erupted with laughter.

Sevier asked the General, "Sir, do you know the accused?"

"No, I don't know him except by his pictures in the newspapers and what I've read about him."

Berman then took over and questioned Puller about his career as a Marine.

"How long were you in Korea?" he asked.

Puller answered, "About nine months."

"Were you in combat?"

"Yeah."

"Were you decorated?"

"Yeah."

Berman then asked, "Without going into your other decorations, isn't it true that you have received five Navy Crosses, General?"

"Correct," Puller nodded.

"And for how long have you been in the United States Marine Corps, sir?" Berman asked.

"Thirty-seven years, four months, and two days," Puller answered, without hesitation.

Berman asked, "Where did you, sir, receive your training to become a Marine?"

"Parris Island, South Carolina."

"Can you tell us of the things that you learned here as a recruit, General?"

Puller leaned back slightly in his chair, "Well, the main thing that I learned as a recruit, that I have remembered all my life, is that I was taught the definition of esprit de corps. Now my definition, the definition that I have always believed in is that esprit de corps means love for one's own military legion; in my case the United States Marine Corps. It means more than self-preservation, religion, or patriotism. I've also learned that this loyalty to one's corps travels both ways, up and down."

"What, in your opinion, is the mission of the United States Marine Corps?" asked Berman.

Puller answered, "Well, I would like to say that the definition, my definition, a definition in the drill books from the time that General Von Stuben wrote the regulations for General George Washington, the definition of the object of military training is success in battle . . . It wouldn't make any sense to have a military organization on the backs of the American taxpayers with any other definition. I have believed that ever since I have been a Marine."

"What, in your view, is the most important element of training?"

Puller said, "Well, I'll quote Napoleon. Napoleon stated that the most important thing in military training is discipline. Without discipline, an army becomes a mob."

Berman then asked, "Now, then, in that context, can you tell us whether you have an opinion, based again on your experience, as to whether or not the training in discipline is for all situations, confined to lesson plans, or syllabi or training regulations?"

"No. The training of a basic Marine is conducted almost entirely outside – in the field, on the drill ground, on the rifle range – that kind of work. The Marine gets an idea of how the Marine Corps is run during this training, but his training is outside work."

"Now, General, I want you to assume that what is the evidence in this case is a fact. That on a Sunday evening a drill instructor took a platoon that was undisciplined and lacked spirit and on whom he'd tried other methods of discipline. And that for purposes of teaching discipline and instilling morale, he took that platoon into a marsh or a creek – all the way in front of his troops – would you consider that oppression?" Berman asked.

"In my opinion, it is not," Puller answered confidently.

"General, can you state an opinion as to whether leading troops on a night march for the purpose of instilling discipline was good military practice?"

Puller said, "Any kind of commander or leader is not worth his salt if he does not lead his troops under all conditions. In my opinion, the reason American soldiers made out so poorly in the Korean War was mostly due to the lack of night training, and if we are going to win the next war I say that from now on fifty percent of the training time should be devoted to night training."

"In your opinion, General, is the leading of men into water at night for the purpose of instilling discipline and morale good or bad military practice?"

"Good."

Berman sat down and Sevier took over for cross-examination.

He first asked, "It takes some training for the leader in night work?"

Puller answered, "Well, we take it for granted that when a leader has been made a leader by higher headquarters, the man is qualified."

Sevier then asked, "And if you were taking untrained troops into a hazardous situation, would you make some reconnaissance or take some precautions for their safety?"

"Oh yes. I would take safety precautions," replied Puller.

"Do you believe that night training should be the initial training that any new recruit receives?"

"Well, the trouble is that not enough night training is prescribed . . . and I know that in anything I have ever commanded I got most of the glory and I got all of the blame. I have willingly taken the blame. I would train my troops as I thought – as I knew they should be trained – regardless of a directive."

"If I lead these recruits into waters over their heads and I lose six of these men by drowning, would you say that some action should be taken against me?" Sevier asked.

Puller answered, "I would say that this night march was and is a deplorable accident."

"Would you take any action against me if I were the one who did that if you were my commanding officer, sir?"

"I think what I read in the papers yesterday of the testimony of General Pate before this court, that he agrees and regrets that this man was ever ordered tried by a general court martial."

A dejected Sevier sat down. Chesty Puller walked down the aisle and out of the courtroom. Soon thereafter Berman stood up and declared, "May it please the court and you, Mr. Law Officer, the defense rests."

And then Berman added, "Mr. President and Mr. Law Officer, I have never seen a Marine Corps review. I understand that General Puller will conduct a review tomorrow morning at eight-thirty. Could you start the next day's session at nine-thirty tomorrow? I should hate to have to leave here and not have seen a review."

The court agreed and everyone poured out of the courtroom.

As I drove back to the Inn, I couldn't help but think that out of all the living Marines, both active and retired, Berman had chosen Puller. It was the ultimate compliment.

That night I went to the NCO club because I heard that Puller might stop by. I walked in the door about 8:00 PM, and the place was packed. They were all waiting for Puller. A half hour later, Puller walked in with Berman, two Marine generals and some other officers; the big crowd went silent and the

Marines stood at attention while he was led to a microphone and he roared out an off-the-cuff speech:

"I have talked enough for today. This will be my last request: Do your duty, and the Marine Corps will be as great as it has been for another thousand years."

When Puller stopped talking the Marines started applauding and Puller had a smile on his face. He was then directed over to a table that had been set aside for him. For the next two hours I think every Marine in the club said hello to him. I couldn't get near him. No one was going to leave the club until Chesty did.

Finally, at 10:30 PM, Puller stood up and said goodbye and started walking to the door. Again there was more applause. As he walked out, he waved goodbye. I quickly followed him and before he reached his car I yelled out, "General Puller!"

He turned around and looked at me but because it was dark, didn't recognize me.

"Mike Abbo, sir," I said.

Puller grunted, "I should have known you'd be here."

I said, "Yes, sir, it's a big story. I couldn't miss this one."

"It's a real tragedy," he replied.

"Sir, why did you testify?" I asked.

"Well, I testified because of the Corps. If what I read in the papers is true, it was the Marine Corps that needed help. If we ease up on the way that Marines are trained, the Marine Corps as we know it won't be the same. It's the tough training that won battles in the past. I sure as hell hope my testimony reflected that. Sure, it's a great tragedy that those six men died, but it was a training accident. If McKeon is guilty of anything, it's making a stupid decision. He was a good Marine with a good record."

I decided to ask another question, "Sir, what verdict do you think the court will return?"

"I don't know. I'm too close to it," Puller answered.

He looked at the ground, leaned against his car and said, "Anyway, how are you doing, Mike?"

"Fine, sir," I replied, "and you?"

"I'm doing all right. Are you coming to the review tomorrow?"

"I wouldn't miss it, sir," I answered.

Puller then asked me, "Are you still with the *Tribune*?"

"Yes, sir."

"Do you like being a newspaperman?" Puller asked.

"Yes sir, I do"

"Glad to hear it, Mike. Well, it's getting late," he said.

We shook hands and he left.

The following morning Puller presided over the parade and handed out awards to drill instructors. It was wonderful to see him back in his element. Chesty's career in the Marine Corps had now come full circle. He had arrived at Parris Island in 1918 as a lowly recruit. Now, thirty-eight years and four wars later, Chesty was standing out front, a retired Lieutenant General, reviewing the morning parade. I'm sure that every Leatherneck will never forget the moment they marched past the Marine legend. After the review Chesty returned to his home in Virginia.

Later that morning Berman and Sevier went through the long closing arguments, but it was all over. Puller had made a difference. McKeon was acquitted of the more serious charge of oppression of troops. He was found guilty of culpable negligence in six deaths and drinking on duty. He received nine months of hard labor, reduced to the rank of private, and a $270 fine, and the toughest blow of all, termination from the Marine Corps with the disgrace of a bad-conduct discharge.

Secretary of the Navy Thomas reduced the punishment to a total of three months hard labor and he remitted the bad conduct discharge. McKeon would stay in the Marine Corps.

I drove back to Chicago early on Saturday, August 4th. I couldn't help but think that life is totally unpredictable. Over a year ago Puller had left the Corps a very unhappy man, but now he was back more famous than ever.

He was a man who had given his life to his Corps and his country. Even before World War II started he was a legend and now that legend was even bigger. Would there be anyone who could best what he did? There would be more wars to be sure, but would someone arrive on the scene that would not only fight in four wars but achieve a reputation as an outstanding combat leader in all these wars? Could anyone ever win five Navy Crosses? Would a leader emerge who was as loved by the enlisted men as much as Puller? I didn't think this was possible.

Serving under Puller was a great honor and I will never forget him. He was tough on himself as well as his Marines. He was revered by his men both for his courage and his devotion to them. Unfortunately, that was the last time I saw him.

Epilogue
The Death of a Marine Legend

By
Michael Abbo
October 14, 1971

At noon today in a small cemetery in Saluda, Virginia, the Marine Corps said good bye to one of their legends: Chesty Puller.

Lewis Burwell Puller was the most famous, and most decorated Marine in the history of the Corps. During his thirty-seven years in the Marine Corps, he was awarded an unprecedented five Navy Crosses.

Puller was colorful. That was part of his appeal. It seems like every time he opened his mouth something unforgettable came out. He stood five foot eight inches tall, had a face like a bulldog and a chest that stood out like a pouter pigeon, hence the name "Chesty". He also had a commanding voice. It was part Southern and part Brooklynese. He frequently butchered the English language, and when he raised his voice it thundered. The enlisted men had great respect for him, partly because of his reputation and partly because he took good care of them. At heart, Puller was an enlisted man in officer's clothing.

There was a curious thing about Chesty Puller: everyone always referred to him as Chesty but no one ever called him that. He was always called Lewie or Lewis, and Puller, if he liked you, would call you "old man".

He rose through the ranks from a private to a lieutenant general. He was tough on the junior officers, maybe because it took him six years to become one or maybe because he wanted to impress upon them the tremendous responsibility they carried. But whatever the reason, he gave the impression that his enlisted men were more important to him than his officers. And there was no doubt about it: he loved his sergeants. He knew they ran the Marine Corps and so he gave them the respect and recognition they so deserved. He was a master at his trade.

In combat Puller was frequently criticized for being too close to the front lines. His reply was always the same: "If I'm not up here my men will say,

175

'Where the hell's Puller.'" Puller led from the front. That was his trademark. He led his men against the cacos in Haiti and the bandidos in Nicaragua. During World War II he led his Marines through the jungles and mountains of Guadalcanal and New Britain and into the savage fighting on Peleliu. When the Korean War started he led his 1st Marines ashore at Inchon, through the street fighting in Seoul and when his Marines were surrounded at Chosin Reservoir he led them out, carrying their dead and wounded.

During the battle for Guadalcanal, Puller was wounded but he recovered. His younger brother, Sam, a Marine lieutenant colonel, was killed on Guam. Both of his daughters are married to Marines who have served in Vietnam. His only son, Lewis Jr., a Marine lieutenant, stepped on a land mine and lost both his legs and parts of both hands in that war. The Puller family has given more than their share to our country!

There was the Commandant and more that two dozen generals. There were new recruits who had come down from Quantico. There were the old timers, who had come out of the hills and cities of nearby states, men who had served with Puller. There were more than 1,500 Marines and ex-Marines who paid their last respects to Chesty Puller today. There was a firing party and three volleys to send him on his way. And when the sound of Taps had cleared the air, they buried Chesty Puller, a man who had become a legend in his own time.

About the Authors

Nicholas Ragland graduated from Georgetown University in 1966. He served in Vietnam in 1967-1968 with the Marines as a platoon leader with C Company, 3rd Shore Party Battalion and later as the supply officer of the 1st Battalion 12th Marines. He is chairman of The Gorilla Glue Company. He and his wife, Marty, live in Cincinnati, Ohio. They have five sons and ten grandchildren.

Joseph Rouse graduated from Miami University (Ohio) in 1996, and received an M.A. in English from the University of Cincinnati in 2003. After a stint in the corporate world, he now teaches high school English in Cincinnati, Ohio, where he lives with his wife, Nicole, and two sons.